SACRIFICES

The wind was rising. Spirit tripped over flying books, stagger-ing sideways as much as forward. There was so much dust in the wind she couldn't see where she was going, and its howl was so loud she couldn't hear anything else. One of the Shadow Knight illusions picked up a chunk of debris and threw it; it struck the side of the arch and fell to the ground, sucked into the back room by the inexorable force of the wind. If it got strong enough, it would pin them against the walls, and they'd be battered to death by flying furniture. It was already swirling around the inside of the building like a tornado.

Like a tornado . . .

"Oh god!" Spirit cried.

She heard a ripping sound, saw light where there shouldn't be light as the roof tore away and walls collapsed. The floor shook. She didn't dare look back. She'd gotten to the door. She slammed her body against the crash bar with all her strength.

The door was locked.

Mercedes Lackey and Rosemary Edghill

Shadow Grail 3

SACRIFICES

TOR
TEEN

A Tom Doherty Associates Book

New York

SHADOW GRAIL 3: SACRIFICES

Copyright © 2013 by Mercedes Lackey and Rosemary Edghill

A Tor Teen Book
Published by Tom Doherty Associates, LLC
175 Fifth Avenue
New York, NY 10010

www.tor-forge.com

Tor® is a registered trademark of Tom Doherty Associates, LLC.

Library of Congress Cataloging-in-Publication Data

Lackey, Mercedes.
    Sacrifices / Mercedes Lackey and Rosemary Edghill.
        p. cm.—(Shadow grail ; 3)
    "A Tom Doherty Associates book."
    ISBN 978-0-7653-2825-0 (hardcover)
    ISBN 978-0-7653-1763-6 (trade paperback)
    ISBN 978-1-4299-9719-5 (e-book)
    [1. Magic—Fiction.   2. Supernatural—Fiction.   3. Loyalty—
Fiction.   4. Boarding schools—Fiction.   5. Schools—Fiction.
6. Orphans—Fiction.]   I. Edghill, Rosemary.   II. Title.
PZ7.L13543Sac 2013
[Fic]—dc23

                                                              2012042625

Tor Teen books may be purchased for educational, business, or promotional use. For information on bulk purchases, please contact Macmillan Corporate and Premium Sales Department at 1-800-221-7945 extension 5442 or write specialmarkets@macmillan.com.

First Edition: April 2013

Printed in the United States of America

0 9 8 7 6 5 4 3 2 1

Shadow Grail 3

SACRIFICES

PROLOGUE

The year Spirit White turned fifteen, she'd gone to the fair.

Well, to be accurate, her *family* had gone to the fair: Spirit and Mom and Dad and her baby sister Phoenix, who was just about to turn twelve. And it wasn't a fair like a State Fair, with rides and a midway: it was a Crafts Fair—a *juried* Crafts Fair, Dad had said happily—and Mom had said a jury meant the accused would get a fair trial at least and Fee said Dad was just bringing her and Spirit to have slave labor and he'd laughed and twirled an imaginary moustache.

And they'd stayed at a friend's house, because the show was two days and too far away for them to drive home overnight, and he'd won second prize in the "Decorative Arts" category, and Mom had bought food before they left and they stopped at a rest stop on the way back to have a picnic. It was nice, because it was June.

She couldn't remember the rest of that day. She'd tried and tried until her head hurt and all she wanted to do was lie down and cry, but she couldn't. The doctors had said it was normal. All she could remember was the end of it, almost midnight, when they were almost home and Dad was just making that hairpin turn over the ravine with Keller Creek at the bottom of it.

And then there'd been a flash of dark, all around the car.

That had been the first memory that came back to her after the operations, when she started probing the end of her world as if it were a sore tooth. Darkness darker than midnight. A thing squatting in the middle of the road. (Impossible thing. Monster.)

And it looked at them and Mom shouted and Dad yanked the wheel sideways. . . .

It was somewhere between Operation Number Two and Operation Number Three—when they'd stopped having to remind her that her parents and her little sister were dead in the crash—that a sheriffs' deputy came to her hospital room and told her that there'd been another accident, that her parents' empty house had caught fire and burned to the ground.

(She wondered, later, why Oakhurst had bothered to burn it down, but she'd never figured that one out.)

That was when the lawyer showed up, the lawyer from Oakhurst, the one who'd told her all the lies: that her parents had set up a "trust" for her; that the trust was administered by this "Oakhurst Foundation"; that when she was fully recovered Oakhurst would be sending for her, because she'd be living at

"The Oakhurst Complex" until she was twenty-one. (Oakhurst *did* send for her, but it was still a lie, though it took her a long time—six months—to realize that.)

But she came to Oakhurst by limousine and private plane and private railway car (wondering all the time: *why do they need to try to impress me?* though later she knew), and there she met Doctor Ambrosius for the very first time. His hair was pure silvery white, combed straight back, and long enough to brush his shoulders. His beard was the same color, and his eyes were a pale blue, and he spoke with a faint English accent that Loch said, back in the beginning, was probably put on for the tourist trade.

That was in September, and by the beginning of October Spirit realized that Oakhurst was fanatical about competition: they pitted the kids against each other in the classroom and on the field. Heck, they *turned* them against each other; it had been weeks before Spirit realized how strange it was for her to have friends—Loch and Addie and Muirin and Burke—at Oakhurst.

The five of them were as different from one another as they could possibly be. Addie was wealthy and refined, the sole heir to Prester-Lake BioCo, a major pharmaceutical company worth, literally, billions. Burke was quiet and quietly devout; he'd been orphaned as an infant and grew up in foster care. Loch was the son of a businessman. Muirin's father had owned a construction company—his second wife had sent her to Oakhurst. Cultured, quiet, clever, drop-dead trendy—and *her*—they were the unlikeliest of friends. But their strengths complemented each other.

That was about the time Spirit's life and "normal" parted ways forever. It wasn't bad enough knowing magic was real—or that all your friends had it—or that you were *supposed* to have it and didn't—but then the five of them had to figure out how to battle a bunch of ghosts and elves and demons that someone inside Oakhurst was helping pass through the "protective wards" around the campus. And they'd won, and they'd even survived, and that was the point at which the credits were supposed to roll and the movie was over.

But the Wild Hunt hadn't been the real problem—or not the *only* problem. For the last six months, she and her friends had uncovered enemy after enemy, conspiracy inside conspiracy. They'd destroyed the Wild Hunt that had been preying on the Oakhurst students for decades, only to realize that someone—or some*thing*—had Called it in the first place. And when the Shadow Knights descended on Oakhurst, they'd fought back. They'd *all* fought back.

Before the Shadow Knights could move, Dylan grabbed a piece of burning wood, and charged the nearest Knights with a bellow of fury. The Knights might have been ready to fight, but their horses weren't ready to face a screeching maniac flailing at them with fire. They bolted. At that, almost the entire student body broke out into shouts of defiance and anger. Those who had combat magic used it. Those who didn't picked up anything they could use as a weapon, and charged.

It was like being in the middle of that attack on the endurance riders, except the proverbial shoe was very much on the other foot. Fueled by energy frantic for any sort of outlet, the combat magicians of

Oakhurst filled the air with spells. Spears of ice, gouts of fire, deadly little tornados and fierce blasts of derecho wind pummeled the Shadow Knights who'd been expecting to confront a huddle of terrified youngsters. Illusory copies of Dylan led the ones charging at the lines; kids who were throwing whatever came to hand found themselves with piles of perfectly round ice balls beside them. There were a couple of people who had Animal Telepathy and Animal Control because the mounted Knights found their horses practically turning themselves inside out to be rid of their riders.

The Knights managed to deflect the fireballs, but they did so at the expense of not deflecting ice shards and the objects being hurled like missiles. Spirit had the satisfaction of seeing one of her own ice balls make a direct hit inside the hood of the Knight nearest her, and seeing him go down. Silence from the Shadow Knights turned to cries of fury and pain.

That night they'd danced and partied until dawn, sure they'd won. They'd awakened the next day to find themselves in an armed camp. The attack of the Shadow Knights had been just the excuse that Mark Rider and Breakthrough had needed to *really* take over. Soon after the Shadow Knights had attacked Oakhurst for the first time, Mark Rider, his wife, Madison, and his brother, Teddy, had arrived. Officially, he was here because Mark Rider was moving Breakthrough's HQ to Radial. Unofficially, he was here to protect Oakhurst from the Shadow Knights.

Only he wasn't, because he is a Shadow Knight. They all are. Everyone at Breakthrough.

Almost overnight, Breakthrough had taken over Oakhurst. Classes had gotten harder, the teachers more ruthless. Guards patrolled the campus openly, night and day. But if the regimen had been hard before the February Dance—and the student rebellion—it was brutal now. Academic classes had been slashed. But it didn't matter how many classes had been axed—almost every waking moment was still filled with classes. Magic, folklore, military strategy, wilderness survival, and every kind of combat you could imagine. *We're being brainwashed into becoming good little foot soldiers. Paranoid foot soldiers.* It started almost as soon as you got up, with a "motivational email" you had to read while you were getting dressed—and if you didn't, they'd know, because the Breakthrough staff quizzed everybody on the contents. Every meal now included a "Motivational Lecture" about how they were in a war now—and you'd better show up for meals on the dot, because they closed and locked the doors, and if you weren't there, you didn't eat. Even Muirin didn't dare sleep late any more.

Last year, before she got to Oakhurst, Spirit turned sixteen. The lawyer who came to her at the hospital said she'd be living at "The Oakhurst Complex" until she was twenty-one. That was a lie.

Because Spirit wasn't sure she was going to live to be seventeen.

ONE

Guinevere, High Queen, sat like a statue on the bare back of one of the famous white horses that had been her dowry on the day she had wed Arthur. Only the knights of the Table had ever been permitted to ride them, for they were bred to carry kings.

But there were no more than a handful of Arthur's knights left now.

When Arthur fell at Camlann—and it seemed to all as if the day were lost—it had been Guinevere who had taken command of his army—and they had been eager to have someone, anyone, lead them. That, Mordred had not expected—that she, of all people, would appear on the battlefield in borrowed armor at the head of a vast army. From the moment Arthur had sent her into exile, she had been preparing for this day. But she had come too late to save her husband and lord. Camelot had fallen.

She had given her dying husband into the care of the Lady of the Lake. She had taken his sword from his death-cold fingers.

And she had followed the fleeing Mordred and his army with all her host.

Mordred had broken Arthur's army at Camlann, and the years of fighting that had preceded it had stripped Britain of knights and fighting men. But Guinevere's army did not ride clad in mail and wearing steel. It was made up of Druids and monks, nuns and sorceresses— the Old Ways and the New Faith coming together to oppose an enemy who would destroy all that was. And beside Guinevere rode The Merlin.

Nimue had been the first of Mordred's allies to desert him, and with the breaking of the spell she had put upon him, The Merlin was freed. When he had learned of Arthur's death, his wrath had been terrible to see.

Across all of Britain the two armies rode, one pursuing, one fleeing. And slowly, one by one, Mordred's allies and vassals deserted him. Arthur had died in the springtide. It was autumn when Mordred was brought to bay.

This was the end.

The trees were leafless, now, and the wind was cold. Behind Guinevere stood her husband's army and her own, each man and woman waiting with a deadly implacable patience to witness the end of the man who had destroyed everything they had worked so long to build. Before her stood the ancient oak tree that Mordred had once meant to be The Merlin's eternal tomb.

She would gladly have slain the black snake who destroyed her happiness and her husband's kingdom, but Mordred was so imbued with the powers of Death Itself he could not die. No earthly weapon could slay him—but he could be bound, as he had intended The Merlin to be bound. And since his own magics had prepared the ancient oak, it was all the more fitting that the tree be the vessel to hold him. . . .

Guinevere heard muffled shouting and the clink of chains. She looked to her right. Here came the Bishop of England in his red and white robes, carrying a golden cross atop a long pole. Beside him walked the Archdruid of Eire, barefoot, with spirals of woad covering every inch of his skin, his only garment a tabard of white bull's-hide. Behind them walked the White Horse Woman—whom Guinevere's ancestors had worshipped—the Lady of Apples, priests and holy people of every faith Britain held.

Before them walked The Merlin.

And behind them came Mordred, dragged by the last of Arthur's knights. His hands were bound with iron and silk and ivy, his mouth had been sewn shut, his body was weighted down with a hundred-weight of silver chains, each link carved with runes of blessing and protection. But his eyes were unblinded, and they flashed with fury.

The Merlin began to chant.

The knights pushed Mordred toward the oak—not with their hands, but with stangs made of sacred oak.

And when his body touched it, Mordred began to sink into the tree as if its wood were softened wax. He struggled, eyes wild with anger and power. Still, the knights thrust him backward, and still The Merlin chanted. In a moment more it would be done.

Then to her horror, Guinevere saw that Mordred had torn loose the sinews that had sewn his mouth shut. He roared out a single terrible word. The knights pushing him forward fell to their knees, their screams drowned in those of the holy ones who had come to see justice done.

But The Merlin had not fallen—and he shouted three syllables she did not understand, and did not want to. There was a flash and a roar. Brightness. Darkness. Guinevere cried out, fighting to control her panicked mount.

When she could see again, the oak's bark was seamless. The Merlin still stood before the oak, but his face was gray with terrible pain and weakness now, and he leaned heavily upon his staff for support. There was no sign of Mordred.

The Merlin staggered forward, summoning his failing strength. As he pointed at the oak, words of fire wrote themselves into the wood.

Oh Thou who wouldst meddle in the affairs of Light and Darkness, Touch Not the Sacred Oak sealed by Merlin's Own Hand, for herein lies imprisoned the traitorous son of the Great Bear: Medraut Kinslayer the Accursed. Flee, lest his undying evil take you for its own!

The Merlin turned at last, to look at Guinevere. "It is finished," he said, in a voice flat with exhaustion.

❧

Spirit shivered in the chill of the Girls' Locker Room, but as cold as it was, she still wasn't in any hurry to get changed for class. *I never thought I'd miss Mr. Gail and Mr. Wallis,* she thought ruefully. *But at least I guess I understood them. They might have been horrible, but they weren't killers.*

This wasn't the way it was supposed to go.

She'd thought—oh she'd been so naïve!—that once the kids had routed the Shadow Knights at the Sadie Hawkins Day Dance, the trouble would be over. Whatever the Shadow Knights had wanted to do on February 2nd, they'd failed. Nobody had died. People had gotten hurt, but nobody had *died*. They'd proved they could win.

It hadn't changed anything. And what was even scarier was, it was becoming more and more obvious that the Bad Guys weren't the secret society within Oakhurst called the Gatekeepers. They weren't a bunch of faceless Shadow Knights. They were the Oakhurst faculty.

At least the ones who were left. People kept vanishing here, and if you were smart you pretended you didn't notice.

I'd better get moving, she thought, closing her locker reluctantly. At least she wasn't the only one here trying to delay the inevitable. She turned to head for the gym.

"Hey, Spirit, 'scuze me—" Trinity Brown started to walk past her, then paused. "You know, when you got here you were, like, a waif. You *do* realize you've gotten all ripped, don't you?" Trinity chuckled. "Wish I was. Guess I was born to be a string." She held up her hand in a half wave and walked on.

Spirit blinked in surprise, staring after Trinity. She hadn't even realized Trinity—who was *not* a string, merely supermodel-lean—knew her name. It was kind of ironic . . . now that Oakhurst really *was* out to kill them, the kids were a lot kinder to each other than they had been when she had arrived in September. One of the first things she'd learned about Oakhurst was that friendships weren't encouraged.

But I have friends. Good friends. I don't know what would have happened to me without Loch and Burke and Addie . . .

And Muirin.

She just hoped Muirin was still her friend.

I'd better get going. She looked down at herself. Trinity was right: she *was* ripped. *If I live to graduate, the only job I'd qualify for is superhero,* she thought bitterly. *Or maybe government assassin. I sure don't know how to do anything else.*

❋

The class was *Systema*. It was a kind of Russian martial art that focused on controlling the joints of one's opponent. What it meant in practice was that they were all supposed to try to kill each other. When Anastus Ovcharenko started teaching the course, they'd worked out on mats. Now they worked out on the bare wood floor. Spirit and Trinity stood at the back of the group of students (not that something like that would save you). Muirin should have been here, too, but these days Muirin didn't spend a lot of time in her classes—and she saw plenty of Ovcharenko out of them.

He was already there, of course, smiling cheerfully as he waited for the last of them to arrive. Ovcharenko was always cheerful—especially when he was about to hurt somebody. He always picked someone to spar with while the rest of them paired off against each other. He said it was to demonstrate the proper techniques. Spirit was pretty sure it was more about punishment. Dylan Williams (the official ringleader of the rebellion back in February) had been his favorite chew-toy for weeks, but he'd managed to put Dylan in the infirmary yesterday, and Dylan wasn't here.

I don't care who he picks today as long as it isn't me, Spirit thought fervently.

"Now," Ovcharenko said, clapping his hands together and smiling. "Who wants to dance with Anastus today? Ah! I know! You! Come here—we will have fun together, eh?"

He smiled and nodded encouragingly. Everyone shifted uneasily, until they were all spread out in a ragged line. For one horrified moment Spirit thought Ovcharenko had chosen her after all.

But he was pointing at Trinity.

"You! Little girl! It is Trinity Brown, yes? You will come and dance with Anastus, yes? Come, come. I promise you I will be gentle."

Nobody laughed.

"No," Trinity said. She looked terrified—but utterly determined. Spirit glanced at her in shock. "I won't let you hurt me."

Ovcharenko smiled and began to walk toward Trinity. "Ah, but pain makes us strong, *dorogoi,* and we must all do many things we—"

Before Ovcharenko reached her, Trinity turned and ran. For an instant the sound of her bare feet against the wood floor was the loudest sound in the gym.

Then Ovcharenko began to laugh.

At least Ovcharenko was so amused by Trinity bailing that he hadn't picked out a new sparring partner, but the session had still been rough. *Even my bruises have bruises,* Spirit thought tiredly.

"Hey."

Burke was leaning against the wall as she walked out of the gym. Spirit looked around quickly, but there wasn't anybody in sight. Not that she expected there to be: Burke Hallows was a Combat Mage, and Combat Mages noticed *everything.*

"What are you doing here?" she asked. The five of them spent as little time together in public as possible. If Oakhurst had been a place where real friendship was discouraged in favor of competition before, well, now it was actually dangerous to show that you liked someone.

"The last class of the day is magic practice," Burke said, as if Spirit needed reminding.

"And I'm *still* the only student at Hogwarts West without any."

"You're lucky," Burke said gloomily. Then he smiled. "But the real reason I'm here is to grab a minute with my girl."

He reached out a hand, and Spirit moved gratefully into his arms. The only bright spot in the last two months was Burke. They'd started out playing boy-and-girlfriend as a ruse to keep Breakthrough's suspicion away. But Burke hadn't been playing, and neither had she.

Burke hugged her. "Ow," Spirit said ruefully, and Burke chuckled.

"Sorry," he said. He started to let go, but Spirit held on.

"Don't," she said. "It's going to hurt anyway. And I—"

"Shhh," Burke said, kissing the top of her head. "I know."

Spirit closed her eyes tightly, fighting to keep from ruining this brief moment of happiness with tears. Nobody dared go easy on anybody in *Systema*—not with Ovcharenko watching all of them. It was fight or . . .

Well, she wasn't completely sure of what "or" involved, except that she probably wouldn't like it much.

But if not for the fact Oakhurst was trying to kill her the way it had killed her family, this would have been the most wonderful time of her life. Burke was nothing like the kind of boyfriend she'd imagined for herself when she'd dreamed about someday dating and falling in love. But she *did* love him. And she knew he loved her.

And just think, I wouldn't have met him if I hadn't come to Thunderdome Academy.

"Do you think we can all get together after dinner?" she asked, deliberately keeping her voice low.

"Loch's making arrangements," Burke said against her hair. "I don't know the details. He hasn't been able to talk to Muirin, though."

"Funny thing," Spirit said snarkily, and Burke snorted.

Despite her mocking words, Spirit was honestly worried about Muirin. For as long as Spirit had known her, Muirin had chafed at the restrictions of life at Oakhurst—the dress code, the dreary school uniforms, the complete lack of social life. Breakthrough's arrival had changed all that. Madison Lane-Rider had started courting Muirin early, and Muirin had been more than willing to play along. As far as anyone with Breakthrough knew, Muirin Shae was drooling with the desire to become a Shadow Knight and join the international party crowd.

It was a good act.

At least Spirit hoped it was an act. So far Muirin seemed to love the glamour and excitement of playing double agent: the things she'd told Spirit and the others about Breakthrough's inner workings had saved them more than once. But eventually Muirin was going to have to pick one side or the other . . . and Spirit wasn't quite sure which one it would be.

Breakthrough's offering her money, freedom, glamour—and what can we offer her? The chance to get fed to demons. Not much of a choice.

"We have to get out of here," she said desperately. *Before Breakthrough makes us just disappear. Or worse.*

"I know," Burke said. "I wish I could say—" Suddenly he pushed her away. She opened her mouth to protest, but then she saw movement at the end of the hall. Someone was coming.

They didn't dare be seen together. If anyone knew about them, Oakhurst would manage to make both of them wish they'd never met.

She turned away, shrugging her bag full of sweaty gym clothes higher on her shoulder. She forced herself not to look back, not to wave, not to smile, as Burke walked away.

At least she could be pretty sure he'd still be here at dinner.

A few minutes later, Spirit opened the door to her room. She was lucky—having a free hour after *Systema* meant she didn't have to shower in the gym like everyone else—but right now the bathroom seemed too far away. She flopped down on the couch, wincing again at the pain of strained and bruised muscles.

I remember when I thought we could win, she thought tiredly. *I remember when I thought being here was just an accident—a horrible accident, but an accident.*

When Oakhurst had sent for her, they'd told her that her parents had arranged for Oakhurst to take care of her. Only it was just another lie. Her family—just like the families of every other kid here—had been murdered by the Shadow Knights. The bad guys found out you had magic, your family died, you ended up at Oakhurst.

We have to get out of here. They'd all agreed about that after the February dance, but it wasn't as easy as that. They had no money and no families, and they were in the middle of Montana. And Oakhurst wouldn't just let them walk away. Until they had a *good* plan, they had to hide right here, in plain sight, and pretend they didn't know what was really going on. It was hard, when Breakthrough was trying to subtly—and not so subtly—recruit them. They couldn't just blow them off.

But Muirin's taking things too far.

Sitting here worrying about it wouldn't change anything, and Spirit forced herself to her feet with a groan. If she didn't rehydrate, she'd feel even worse than she did now. She opened her dorm-fridge and regarded the contents with resigned disgust.

When she'd arrived here, you'd been allowed to choose what your fridge was stocked with. Now you took what they gave you—which was bottled water and sports drinks. She grabbed a bottle of Gatorade and flopped back down on the couch. But despite her best intentions, she couldn't stop worrying.

Merlin—Mordred—magic powers—Shadow Knights—we have to do something, but nobody's going to believe what's going on here even if we can get out and tell them.

Shower, Spirit thought firmly. If she didn't shower before dinner she wouldn't be able to stand herself—and all those bruises would stiffen up. *Shower,* she told herself again, pushing herself to her feet.

✦

She looked longingly at her bed as she walked back into the bedroom. She had half an hour before dinner, but if she lay down she'd fall asleep—and missing dinner would suck beyond the telling. She pulled her robe more firmly around her and sat down at the computer instead. *Email it is,* she thought with a sigh, tapping her laptop awake. *Who knows? Maybe there'll be another exciting Motivational Message.*

But what was waiting for her was worse.

I've been drafted? Spirit thought in disbelief, staring at her screen. The email in her inbox notified her she was now on the Dance Committee—along with Maddie Harris, Kylee Williamson, Zoey Young, Christopher Terry, and (oh joy) Dylan. She was replacing Ashley Fowler (you'd think, from the tone of the email, that Ashley had just resigned, instead of vanishing two weeks ago).

As if I didn't have enough to do! she thought.

It was bad enough she'd heard since the day she arrived at Oakhurst that Dance Committee was a seething cauldron of face-to-face flamewars and infighting—Addie had been on it through the New Year's Dance, and had told Spirit stories that made her laugh even as she winced in sympathy. And that was bad enough. But being on the Dance Committee would mean she was constantly aware of the countdown to the next dance. Today was March 2nd. The next dance was the Spring Fling on March 22nd. *Every dance so far has been the scene of some kind of magical disaster.*

She was terrified to imagine what was going to happen at the Spring Equinox.

Spirit scurried into the Refectory and took her place on the line that wound back and forth among the tables like a mutinous snake. There was a stack of plastic trays on a table near the doorway to the kitchen. When she'd arrived last September, Oakhurst had pretended it was grooming them to take their places as "the movers and shakers of tomorrow" and meals had been all about fine dining and company manners, with china, silver, crystal—and waitstaff. Even breakfast had been a field of etiquette land mines. Now Oakhurst was a school under siege. The food was still several steps up from school cafeteria food, but it was served cafeteria style—on plastic trays, with plastic glasses, paper napkins, and stainless steel flatware. Quiche and pâté were things of the past, and so were menu choices—unless it would absolutely kill you (literally), you had to eat it. The vegans were really suffering, because pretty much everything on the menu included an animal product of some kind. Some of them were still holding out, but a lot of them had caved. You ate what Oakhurst handed out, or you starved.

The line inched forward. Up ahead she could see a woman in the uniform of Breakthrough Security—Breakthrough didn't even *try* to blend in anymore—standing against the wall. It was hard to imagine what they needed protecting from in here. And it made Oakhurst seem even more like a prison.

It occurred to her that changing the food service meant Oakhurst didn't have to keep all the extra staff any more. There was still Housekeeping and Laundry service, but it had gone to weekly now, where before it had been daily. *But it all makes sense. Look at how much of the faculty isn't here anymore. I bet they've cut the Maintenance staff down just as far—and I bet Breakthrough doesn't want to spend its valuable time washing Burke's socks. . . .*

She could see him about a dozen places ahead of her in line, and knew he'd noticed her come in. But this time he didn't acknowledge her presence.

She let her mind drift—not much could happen while they were standing in line for dinner—when suddenly she was startled to alertness by a crash and a wordless shout. As she stared around wildly, looking for the source, she saw the front of the line scatter.

A fight.

Fights had gotten more and more frequent in the last month. There was more student solidarity now than there'd ever been before, but everyone was tense and on edge, and even before Breakthrough got here, Oakhurst had been trying to make them all into enemies. She didn't know the boys' names, but they clearly knew each other. The taller one swung at the shorter one. Nobody tried to stop them. She could see six of the Student Proctors in the watching crowd, and there were a dozen Breakthrough Security people here. No one moved.

This wasn't a case of punching and shoving. Maybe it had started that way, but they were all learning the kinds of martial arts skills that could be used to hurt somebody, and it quickly turned into the kind of fight where both combatants wanted to hurt each other. *Really* hurt each other. There was a swift flurry of blocks and counters and the other kids moved back even further to give them room. Spirit's stomach went into knots, but she knew she didn't dare show how sick this was making her.

One swept the other's feet out from under him. The one who fell grabbed his opponent and pulled him down. Both bounced to their feet a moment later. Their clothing was torn. *That's an automatic demerit,* Spirit thought half-hysterically. Both boys were bleeding now. She tried to keep herself from looking to Burke, but she couldn't help seeing him. He was standing motionless, head down, as if he was utterly weary, too tired to even think about interfering. Or maybe too intimidated.

Once he would have been one of the first guys breaking up a fight. The thought made Spirit feel like crying. Muirin always called Burke a "Boy Scout," but Burke was one of the most simply *good* people Spirit had ever known. Hanging back this way had to be killing him. *But we're all trying not to be noticed. And there's a bigger fight coming. An important one. He knows he has to save himself for it. Whatever it ends up being.*

She'd barely formed the thought when there was an ugly *cracking* sound, loud in the silence. One of the boys screamed. He fell to his knees clutching at his shoulder. His arm hung limp and useless at his side. His opponent grabbed one of the chairs. . . .

But now—finally—the security people moved in. Two of them grabbed the one with the chair. The other two picked up his victim. They dragged them quickly toward the Refectory doors. There must have been someone watching right outside, because the doors opened quickly. Two new security guards came in as the other four went out.

There was a moment of stillness. Then the line began to re-form. Slowly. And nobody wanted to get too close to anyone else.

∗

Spirit picked up her tray and stepped away from the serving counter. As she walked back into the Refectory (looking for her assigned seat, they all had assigned seats now, too) she saw the doors open again.

They're supposed to be locked by now, unless . . . Oh.

Muirin came sauntering in, looking like she was doing them all a favor by gracing them with her presence. Spirit stared. Muirin was wearing a black vinyl jacket over a hot pink mesh t-shirt, and a denim miniskirt with black fishnet stockings and black knee-high boots. Nothing could be further from the Oakhurst Dress Code. She'd even gone back to dyeing her hair a couple of weeks ago. Muirin had flaming red hair most girls Spirit knew would kill for. It was short (because it had been *blue* when she'd gotten here, and Oakhurst made her cut it) and now it was streaked with black.

"See what you can get if you play by the rules? Fewer rules!" Muirin sang, walking over to Spirit and striking a pose right in front of her. Her mouth was twisted in a mocking sneer, and it was pretty hard to miss the fact that she was wearing green lipstick and more eye shadow than the Oakhurst Code would ever have allowed. Anybody would think she and Spirit were enemies. It was a great act. At least, Spirit hoped it was an act.

Except for a few brief meetings, when Muirin passed on some piece of Breakthrough gossip, or a warning about a new school policy, Spirit had seen little of Muirin since the February dance. Addie and Muirin had been friends before Spirit came to Oakhurst, and Muirin was avoiding her too. Or . . . not "avoiding" so much as spending all her time with her new best friends—all of whom happened to be important Breakthrough people.

Muirin said she was spying on Breakthrough to protect them. Spirit hoped that was the truth.

"Hi, Muirin," she said unenthusiastically. "I didn't think—" *I didn't think you'd be here at all.*

"Demerits are a thing of the past!" Muirin singsonged tauntingly. She blew Spirit a theatrical air-kiss and turned away, walking with an exaggerated hip-swing. Ovcharenko had come in while Spirit was in the kitchen, and Muirin made a beeline for him.

"That's because none of us is going to live to graduate," Loch said quietly from behind Spirit. Spirit did her best not to yelp. Loch's main Gift was Shadewalking—it wasn't invisibility, exactly, but it was close. He brushed against her as he passed, and Spirit felt a tug at her pocket. Loch had just passed her a note. It must be about the meeting tonight. She'd see what it said later. When it was safe.

They'd all done their best to pretend they didn't want to know each other anymore. She didn't know who Addie was hanging out with these days—if anyone—but Loch's new "friends" were a bunch of boys Lachlan Spears might have known back in the real world; he hung with some of the ultra-rich trust-fund kids. Spirit didn't really hang with anyone, and acted shy and intimidated. It was an act—like Loch's, like Burke's, like (she hoped) Muirin's. They were all acting these days.

As she sat down at her table, she saw Muirin giving Ovcharenko some serious face time. *Ugh. He's almost old enough to be her father. That's just creepy.* That was another thing Spirit hated about the way things were now. When Breakthrough had showed up here, Ovcharenko had started making a big play for Muirin, even though he was years older than she was. At first Muirin had discouraged him—but that was a thing of the past now. She didn't know how Muirin could stand it.

Of course, consider the alternative, she thought, as she picked up her fork.

two

"Hail, hail, most of the gang's all here," Loch said quietly as Spirit entered.

The backstage area of the school theater smelled of dust and paint. Scenery for plays that hadn't been performed since Spirit had been here (and now probably never would be) was stacked against the walls. A couple of flashlights standing on end in the middle of the floor gave the only light.

"Where's Muirin?" Spirit asked, looking around. Muirin was the only one missing.

"She went back to Radial with Ovcharenko after dinner," Addie said, her voice flat with disapproval. "I don't know why she even bothered putting in an appearance tonight."

"To show the rest of us what we're missing, what else?" Loch said lightly.

Spirit sat down between Burke and Addie. Muirin's absence made her uneasy. She wanted to think Muirin wasn't, well, falling to the Dark Side. But it was hard to be sure *what* Muirin was doing when they all saw so little of each other. And the trouble was, Breakthrough seemed to know exactly how to offer each of them what they wanted most. . . .

"That fight tonight . . . ugh," Addie said, shuddering.

"It's just going to get worse," Loch said quietly. "This place was a pressure cooker to *begin* with."

"And now Breakthrough's turned up the heat," Burke said wearily. "It doesn't make sense. If they want us, why're they trying to kill us?"

"Survival of the fittest," Loch said, shrugging.

"Well I'm just about fit to be tied," Burke muttered.

"Maybe the lid will blow off the pressure cooker," Addie said thoughtfully. "The more rules Breakthrough makes, the more everyone rebels against them. Which reminds me . . ." Addie reached into her blazer pocket and brought out a pack of cigarettes and a half-pint bottle of vodka. "Courtesy of Muirin," she said, as the others stared at her. "It makes a good excuse, if we're caught together."

So at least Muirin's still helping, Spirit thought uneasily. She just wished she could be sure Muirin wasn't just giving them all enough rope to hang themselves. The four of them—the *five* of them—had been the ringleaders of what passed for a rebellion here since last October—and Muirin knew all the details. *If she rats us out . . .*

"Good for Muirin," she said, a little too forcefully. The others stared at her. *She won't turn us in*, Spirit thought desperately. *Muirin never does things just to please people.*

As she wrestled with her fears—it hurt to distrust Muirin, but things had gotten so bad lately that Spirit kept expecting them to get even worse—Addie lit one of the cigarettes. They handed it around the circle, waving it in the air so the place would smell of smoke. When it had burned down, Addie held it up carefully, concentrating. In the light of the flashlights, Spirit saw the paper go soggy, and there was a faint hiss as the ember went out. Addie's Gift came from the School of Water. There wasn't *much* water in the air, but there was enough that she could douse a cigarette.

She dropped the butt fastidiously to the floor and opened the bottle. "Time to become a teenaged alcoholic, I guess," she said. She poured a little into the palm of her hand and dabbed it on her cheeks and neck. "No way am I actually drinking any of that," she said, passing the bottle to Spirit. "I don't want to be off my game for even a second anymore."

Spirit copied Addie's gestures. The vodka was cold, and it smelled worse than rubbing alcohol. She'd thought vodka was supposed to be odorless and tasteless.

Burke slopped himself lavishly with it, and even ran his wet hands through his hair before passing the bottle to Loch. Loch carefully soaked his shirtfront in it, grimacing. "This stuff's never going to replace my *Cuir de Russie*," he said, forcing a smile. "So. Who wants to go first?"

"I will," Spirit said. "Ovcharenko picked Trinity for his sparring partner today in *Systema,* but she wasn't having any. She ran off. Anybody . . . seen her?" Spirit finished awkwardly.

"She's assigned to my table. She wasn't at dinner," Addie said. "I guess she could have just skipped it." There was a moment of silence. None of them wanted to say what they all knew: Trinity had joined the missing.

"I heard the *Systema* classes are going to be combined," Burke said. "They're going to be longer, too."

"But that means the advanced students are going to be in with—" Loch began.

"People like me," Spirit said, trying not to sigh. "Hey, if I get killed, maybe it will get me out of Dance Committee," she joked weakly.

"Not even death gets you out of Dance Committee," Addie said. "But they picked you? That's great! I kept telling Maddie you'd be good for it, but you know what she's like."

Spirit stared at her. "After everything you told me about Dance Committee, you think me being on it is a *good* thing?"

"Yes, considering how they're going to be doing the Spring Fling. There's going to be a general announcement on Sunday, but the Committee already knows, and Maddie Harris's incapable of keeping a secret, so *I* know. She probably already sent you an email about it."

"I must have missed it," Spirit said. "What secret?"

"This year, the Spring Fling's going to be a joint dance between Oakhurst and Radial. It's still going to be held here, but our Dance Committee will be combining with the Macalister High Dance Committee. And half the meetings will happen in Radial. So that means you can *spy!*" Addie said.

"On what? Because it's a little hard to spy if you don't know what you're spying about," Spirit said after a moment.

"Well," Loch said thoughtfully, "Leaving aside how hard it's going to be to escape from this place, running away doesn't do us any good if Oakhurst just drags us back again."

"Right," Burke said, nodding.

"So we need ammunition. Leverage. Something to make them back off—or even shut them down. We know the Shadow Knights and the Gatekeepers—Oakhurst's beloved 'honor society'—are the same bunch, so no matter what we've been told, the Big Bad is centered here, not something we're being protected from by being here."

Addie snorted rudely. "If this is protection, I'd hate to see what danger is like."

Loch grimaced in agreement. "So, since the one thing actually *in* Oakhurst that's weird . . . er—*weirder*—than everything else here is the oak tree in the Entry Hall, that's what we should be looking at." Loch went on. "Maybe it's a clue."

" '*Interfering stranger beware! Touch not the Sacred Oak sealed by the Druid Merlinus. Herein is imprisoned the son of the Great Bear, Medraut, Kin-slayer, Parricide, and Most Accursed. Turn you back, and flee,*' " Spirit said, quoting Muirin's translation of the runes burned into the trunk.

"Right," Loch said, nodding. "And everybody knows it was Merlin locked up in a tree, not Mordred—so what else do we know that isn't true? And how do we find out? We know there was a biker gang using Oakhurst as a clubhouse before the school was started here. The newspaper clippings all said 'local gang,' and I'm betting at least some of them are still in the area. I've thought for a while that if we could talk to them, we might find out something that would help. I just couldn't figure out a way to do that from here. So that's where you come in, Spirit."

"Me?" Spirit said. "Do I look like Lois Lane? Or Batgirl?" *Okay, maybe Batgirl,* she thought, remembering what Trinity had said in the Locker Room.

It was just a few hours ago. And now Trinity was . . . gone.

"The Spring Fling's in three weeks," Addie said. "And considering what's happened at all the dances lately . . ."

Spirit nodded reluctantly. "We have three weeks to either find a way out of here—or find a way to protect ourselves," she said.

"What we really need to make that happen is to know what the Shadow Knights are after," Burke said. He made a face. "Yeah, I know, they're evil—but if Oakhurst is a means, what's the end?"

"If Elizabeth Walker was right, and the Reincarnates are playing out the Arthurian Mythos over and over again, what Mordred wanted was Arthur's throne." Addie waved her hands, as if to underscore her exasperation with the ridiculousness of it.

The most unbelievable part of everything going on at Oakhurst wasn't even Merlin or Mordred. It was all of them—or *some* of them, at least. Just before the Shadow Knights arrived, Oakhurst had gotten a new student. For some reason, Elizabeth

Walker had come to Spirit to tell her a story Spirit had found nearly-impossible to believe.

✦

I t is all part of the curse that fell upon Britain when Mordred betrayed Arthur and sold himself to the Dark," Elizabeth said earnestly. "Everyone involved in any way with Arthur's kingdom is doomed to be reborn over and over until either the Shadow or the Grail triumphs. One must destroy the other."

"So why doesn't anyone remember all this?" Spirit wanted to know.

"The Shadow Knights do, but only if they turn to the Dark. Their master, Mordred, wakes their memories. I do not know about the Grail Knights. Possibly Merlin wakes theirs as well. But when they are reborn, they have no memories of their past lives."

"But—I don't get it. If they're reborn over and over and fight the war over and over, why hasn't anyone noticed until now?"

"Because until the spirit in the Tree was freed, they had no leader and no direction," Elizabeth said simply.

✦

E lizabeth had called them "Reincarnates." Elizabeth/Yseult's Gift had been precognition—she'd called it "prophecy"— and it had awakened early, causing her to dream her true life until she was forced to believe in it. She'd said there *was* no "Elizabeth Walker," only Yseult of Cornwall, wife of Mark, lover of Tristan. Sorceress, healer. A figure out of Arthurian Legend.

Only the legend was real. . . .

And if I'd believed her, instead of thinking she was crazy, maybe she'd be here now, Spirit thought miserably. Elizabeth had been terrified by what she knew, and the next morning she was gone, just the way so many Oakhurst students had vanished since.

"Elizabeth said Madison Lane-Rider and Muirin were sisters—or Reincarnate sisters, anyway," Spirit said. "And that Mark Rider was another one—Reincarnate, not sister. And probably Teddy, too."

"Huh," Loch said, frowning. "Didn't Muirin say the only reason Ovcharenko was interested in her was because she was Madison's sister?"

"Well don't remind her," Addie said. "I don't think she's put it all together. If she decides she's a Reincarnate, she'll probably decide that Guinevere isn't exciting enough and want to be Cleopatra."

"She's got the makeup thing down already," Loch said with a smile.

"Too bad you don't get to choose," Spirit said. *I'd choose to be in some other story.* "But Elizabeth said something else. She said none of the Reincarnates knows who they are until someone awakens their memories."

"So Ovcharenko makes five Reincarnates we know of," Burke said. "He wouldn't know about the others any other way. And that means Mordred has to be the one 'awakening' them."

"But if Mordred's doing that for the Shadow Knights . . . Where's the wizard to wake up the Grail Knights?" Spirit asked.

"I still want to know what Mordred—and everybody else who's trying to turn us into playing pieces—wants. Because

England is *that* way," Loch said, pointing. "And nobody ever mentioned Mordred wanting McBride County, Montana. But he's here—*if* he's here—so what does he want now?"

"I'd settle for knowing who the Knights of the Round Table are supposed to be," Spirit said. "Not everybody with magic is a Reincarnate. But some of them are." *Not me. Some of you,* she thought, looking at her friends. *Some of the people who actually have magic.* "If the Shadow Knights are the bad guys, that makes the Grail Knights the good guys. So where are they?"

And if Mordred is somewhere around here "awakening" Shadow Knight Reincarnates, and Muirin's a Reincarnate, how can we know for sure that Mordred hasn't awakened her too . . . ?

She really wished she hadn't thought of that.

❧

The wind cut through Spirit's winter coat as if she wasn't wearing one, and she wrapped her arms around herself tightly as she stepped out of the train. There wasn't even a platform, just a sign and some guardrails located at the top end of Main Street. The sky was overcast and, March or not, the air smelled like snow. Chris Terry said they were going to get snow again tonight—and he was a Weather Witch, so he certainly knew. *It'll probably be* August *before it all melts,* Spirit thought miserably.

The one good thing about the Dance Committee's first joint meeting was getting out of class for the afternoon (including *Systema*), because the rest of it—Spirit thought—was pretty much a recipe for disaster. There was a rumor going around

Oakhurst that after the Spring Fling Radial would be declared in-bounds. Considering everything Muirin'd told her about the hostility of the Townies to the students, letting the two groups mingle freely probably just wasn't going to end well. *Oh, well, I guess I'm about to find out,* she thought dolefully.

Spirit crossed the street to get to the sidewalk. Maddie Harris, Kylee Williamson, Chris, and Dylan were ahead of her. They were looking around as if they'd found themselves on an alien planet. Hoth, maybe. When they were all out of the car, the whistle blew, and the train moved slowly up the track so it wasn't blocking the road. It would stay here until it took them back to Oakhurst, unless someone called it back up to the school before that. The spur line connecting Radial and Oakhurst had been finished last week, and the new track ran in a big oval connecting the school and the town. At least the train meant all they had to do to get to Radial was schedule the trip. The "line" ran Oakhurst's single passenger car behind the switching engine normally used to bring Oakhurst's cars to and from the main line. It wasn't fast, but it didn't need to be.

"This has to be Hell," Zoey said feelingly as she hurried to catch up with them. Spirit had to agree. If her only two choices were join the Shadow Knights or spend the rest of her life in Radial, she'd give serious thought to joining the Shadow Knights.

Spirit had been hearing what a "one-horse" town Radial was ever since she came to Oakhurst. She'd been pretty sure it couldn't be that bad—she'd grown up in rural Indiana, where you could drive for miles without seeing so much as a gas station—but now that she saw Radial, she realized everyone'd been right. Radial was a one-horse town that didn't even have any horses.

Radial's main—and only—street was about two blocks long. It held a pizza joint, a combination newsstand and video rental place, a laundromat, a couple of empty storefronts with signs in the windows that said COMING SOON (though they didn't say *what* was coming soon), and something about the size of a 7-Eleven that proudly proclaimed itself the "Radial Superette." The second floors (of the buildings that had them) held lawyers' offices, the Chamber of Commerce, the *Radial Echo* (the local newspaper), and something that just said it was "County Services."

And that . . . was about it. The Association Library was out at the edge of town. Further out along the State Road was the little local hospital, and beyond that the high school all the kids in the county went to.

That was it.

"Hey, freedom! And the company of our fellow students! Hey, you know, guys, we should show them what we really do at Oakhurst!" Dylan spun around, waving his hands in "wizard" gestures. He was a dark-haired, green-eyed boy about a year older than Spirit was. His Gift was School of Earth: Dylan was a Jaunting Mage; he could *jaunt*—or teleport—objects. He used his Gift to make life unpleasant when he could. Or he *had*, before Breakthrough moved in.

"Do you really want to spend the rest of your life as Comrade Ovcharenko's chew-toy?" Kylee asked with deadly mockery. "Or maybe you'd like to be part of the foundation of one of the new buildings?"

"Nobody'd know," Dylan said sulkily.

He's right about that at least, Spirit thought, looking around. It was the middle of the day, but the only sign of life was lights on in some of the stores, and the people in the pizzaria.

Chris laughed as a sudden gust of wind made the others stagger. "Dyl, they *always* know. And what they don't find out, they make up."

"Oh my god, I thought it was cold on campus!" Maddie Harris wailed. "I'm going to die out here! Where are we supposed to go?"

"Town Library," Kylee Williamson said briskly. "It's this way." She pointed and strode off. The others followed.

Radial didn't look any better from close up. The thought of pizza made Spirit's mouth water, but—like Chris said—they'd know. After a minute or two, though, she was so cold she didn't care about anything but getting out of the wind. She tucked her chin into her scarf. It didn't seem to help.

"Look!" Dylan said, pointing. He'd stopped, so it was either stop and look or trample him. Spirit looked.

In the distance, the new Breakthrough Adventure Design Systems building was visible. Breakthrough made computer games: the building could have been dropped into any one of them and looked perfectly at home. It was a featureless cube of gray granite, and the top was crenellated like a medieval castle. There were flags flying from the walls, and each one had the Breakthrough logo on it—a black dragon coiled around a medieval tower. At first Spirit had thought it was right behind the Main Street buildings. Then she realized it couldn't be. It was huge. Bigger than the largest Walmart Superstore that had ever roamed the Earth—just the parts she could see were a terrifyingly impressive amount of work to have accomplished in barely eight weeks. How had they built all that so fast? And in the dead of winter?

"Just the building covers ten acres," Dylan said excitedly. "The business park covers at least fifty. They've nicknamed it 'The Fortress'—I was talking to one of the guys who's going to work there, and Clark said it's capable of being completely sealed off and locked down so nobody can get in from the outside—it's completely self-contained—you could live in there for weeks! That's why they put the outside walls up first, to hide the fact they're digging massive cellars that go down for miles—"

Clark. That's Clark Howard, the Breakthrough codehead who tried to make trouble for Loch at the Sadie Hawkins Dance.

"And it probably has its own nuclear power plant and an antigravity device and if they want to relocate it can fly," Kylee said derisively. "Dylan, you are so full of bull." Cold as it was out here, their first sight of The Fortress had stopped all of them in their tracks.

"It's got its own generators," Dylan said, unabashed. "Solar panels instead of a regular roof. It's like a whole city in there! Clark said they'd probably be able to sell electricity to the town once it's up and running."

Spirit wasn't sure how much of Dylan's information was true and how much was pure fantasy. She was sure he was repeating what Clark had told him, for whatever that was worth— Clark Howard would say anything Breakthrough wanted him to, and every sentence would be calculated for maximum damage.

They were still staring at The Fortress when a car—and not just *any* car, but a stretch-Humvee limo with a custom pearl-gray paint job—pulled up to the curb beside them and stopped. The back door opened.

"It's too cold to walk anywhere," Teddy Rider said. "Hop in! I'll give you a ride!"

"Oh, wow, you're about to save my life!" Maddie said enthusiastically. There was a chorus of agreement from the others. The last place Spirit wanted to go was into a limo with the chief Shadow Knight's baby brother, but if she didn't, she'd be the only holdout. Teddy pushed the door open wider, and they began to clamber in. Spirit went last. The door shut behind her automatically (or maybe by magic, how did she know?) as soon as she was in.

In the last six months she'd been in more limousines (three) than she had in her entire previous sixteen years, but even so, the inside of the Humvee was luxurious beyond her wildest imaginings. As she looked for a seat that wasn't too near any of the others, she felt completely intimidated by the opulence. *I can't believe people really live like this.* The floor was carpeted in a thick rug that gleamed like velvet. The back seat was a U-shaped couch upholstered in soft gray leather. There were jump seats along the interior walls between the doors, and a bar with a refrigerator in the middle. *What, no swimming pool?* Spirit thought, sitting down.

"Library," Teddy said into the intercom on the wall. It was

part of a whole control panel—probably how he'd closed the door. The car moved off.

"Wow," Chris said, not bothering to conceal his admiration. "This is—"

"Fully armored," Teddy said, smiling. "Customized by Grovemount International, the firm that does the limos for the oil sheiks. Armored glass, special tires—that's after the stretch customization—did you know they told me there are seventeen coats of lacquer involved in the paint job? I would've blinged out the wheels, too, but Grovemount wouldn't go for it. Hey, anybody want a Coke?"

There were enthusiastic sounds from the Oakhurst students. Teddy pointed something that looked like a TV remote at the bar, and the refrigerator doors opened on two sides. He gestured for them to help themselves.

Play along with the forces of evil, kids, and you too can get a car like this, Spirit thought crossly. She took the red-and-silver can Chris handed her. *It's even diet,* she thought in irritation, *most guys wouldn't think of that.* Chris was a nice guy, and smart, and if she could only be sure he wasn't a pawn of evil, he was the kind of guy she'd like to have for a friend. *Too bad you can't tell the players without a scorecard.*

"You never forget your first limo," Teddy said, with an engaging grin. Whatever he was selling, Spirit could tell Kylee and Dylan couldn't wait to sign up. Maddie and Zoey looked more doubtful. Spirit didn't know what Zoey's Gift was—though from her ring she could tell it was something from the School of Fire—and Maddie was a Water Witch. It was clear neither of them could imagine what Breakthrough could want with them. Chris was just quiet.

"I know you're all thinking about what you're going to do when you've finished at Oakhurst," Teddy said. "Worrying about the future, yadda. And I know you've all heard Doc A's speeches about you being 'part of the Oakhurst family.' I got them when I was there, too—and that stuff might have been great when dinosaurs roamed the Earth, but personally, I don't buy all that chick-flick crap. But there's one thing I *do* believe, and that's magic is thicker than water. If somebody has a Gift, they're a part of *my* family—mine, Mark's, Madison's, everyone at Breakthrough. And families take care of each other. None of you has a thing to worry about. My word on that. We've got a place for you. And if we haven't got one that fits you, we'll make one that does."

How can we fight that? Spirit thought with a sense of growing despair. *I can't even be sure Muirin's still on our side.* And Teddy was so handsome, so earnest, and so sincere. Who wouldn't believe him?

Dylan snickered. "In that case, we should make Spooky get out and walk. *She* doesn't have any magic."

Spirit gritted her teeth at the hated nickname. This was a perfect chance for Teddy to turn the others against her, playing the same Us vs. Them game Oakhurst played so well. But to her surprise, Teddy gave Dylan a stern look. "I didn't have a Gift while I was at Oakhurst, either. I didn't get my powers until I was twenty. But Doc A knew they were there, and Mark always believed in me. You all have to believe in each other." He smiled at Dylan, softening the lecture. "Doc A doesn't make mistakes."

It would be nice if that were true, Spirit thought. But there was no reason to think it was any more true than anything else Breakthrough was saying.

Because if "Doc A didn't make mistakes," where had all the Shadow Knights come from?

⚜

"A new town library's next on Mark's list of building projects," Teddy said as the Humvee pulled into the parking lot behind the Radial Association Library.

That was another thing Spirit would like to believe, because even by her old standards, the Radial library was a small and squalid place. It had obviously started life as a house; now the white clapboard siding was desperately in need of paint, and the clear plastic sheeting nailed up over all the windows was tattered and fogged.

Teddy looked out the window, frowning, then snapped his fingers as if he'd just thought of something (Spirit bet he hadn't). "I don't see any reason for you to be stuck here. Hey guys, are you up for a little adventure?"

"Hell yeah!" Dylan said, and even Chris nodded.

"Why don't you go on in and get the rest of the Dance Committee, Hailey?"

"Yes, sir." The voice of the chauffeur came over the intercom. Spirit watched as the woman walked into the library.

"What's the adventure?" Dylan asked eagerly.

"Hey, big guy, it wouldn't be much of an adventure without a surprise," Teddy said. "Patience!"

A few moments later, Hailey returned with seven Radial kids in tow. Spirit only recognized two of them: Juliette Weber and her twin brother, Brett (who was *so* not a member of the Committee). Brett and Juliette were clearly the king and queen of Macalister High, and they weren't really happy about being upstaged. Everyone scurried across the gravel and tumbled into the back of the limousine, which was big enough to seat all of them without crowding.

As soon as Hailey got behind the wheel again, she drove off. She obviously knew their destination without being told.

So this is what "normal" looks like. Even though she'd been to Billings only six weeks ago and Brett and Juliette had tagged along on that field trip, it had been a shock when Spirit realized the "magical" Oakhurst students really *were* different from "ordinary" kids, and the Radial Dance Committee might have been chosen to illustrate the difference. After she'd spent so long seeing nothing but other Oakhurst kids, the Radial kids looked as though they came from the cheap knockoff version of real life.

"Hey, wow, this is great!" a plump girl with terminal acne said.

"Big enough for your fat ass, Couch." The speaker was a skinny dark-haired girl, the only one of the seven Townies not dressed for the weather. She wore a denim jacket, and she must have been freezing. One of her eyebrows was pierced, and her makeup was as heavy as Muirin's—heavier. Her foundation and concealer were obviously worn to cover the pitting of acne scars.

As the Macalister High Dance Committee settled in (half of them overawed and trying not to show it, the other half chattering nervously) Spirit was able to match names to faces. "Couch" was Veronica Davenport—plump, *spectacularly* acne'd, and with a permanent nervously hopeful expression that made Spirit's stomach twist in sympathy. Veronica clearly knew the only way she could be included in anything was to agree with everything anyone else said. The girl who'd called her "Couch" was Kennedy Lewis. She was evidently the closest thing to a "bad girl" Radial could offer. (She did her best to be rude to the Oakhurst kids, but Teddy was pretending not to notice and everyone else was following his lead.) Erika Bass was the kind of pale sandy blonde who looked as if her eyebrows and eyelashes were invisible. She had a high nervous giggle—and she giggled *constantly*.

"Well, my dad—the Sheriff—says a one-industry town can have problems," Brenda Copeland said, and Spirit realized that she was continuing a conversation that the Radial kids must have been having when Teddy's driver went and got them. She was wearing a heavy shearling coat instead of a parka. "He says we should take a wait and see attitude." It was difficult to tell whether she was pretty or not, because she wore glasses with lenses so thick they could probably start fires. They made her brown eyes huge—and not in a good way.

"Well, I'm going to apply there just as soon as school's out," Bella said. "I'm class valedictorian, you know," she added, for the Oakhurst students' benefit. "I'm studying programming, too." She had frizzy brown hair, pale eyes, and braces—the full-on "Alien" kind, with the retaining wire and the neck brace. "I've always gotten straight As—I guess I could get a college scholarship if I wanted one, you know?"

"Oh yeah. Like an A+ in Home Ec is going to impress Breakthrough," Kylee said cuttingly.

"Well, I think having Breakthrough here is a wonderful thing—for us and for Breakthrough," Veronica said, her voice high and nervous. "Everyone knows they'll bring jobs into the county, right?"

" 'They' is sitting right in front of you," Dylan said with a sneer, waving toward Teddy.

"Well, it's still true, right?" Veronica said plaintively.

"Whatever you say, Couch. You better hope they hire you—maybe they could pay enough to afford even *your* grocery bills," Kennedy said.

Spirit watched Juliette's mouth settle into a thin angry line as the others did their best to impress Teddy. She wasn't sure whether she was more embarrassed *by* the Radial teens, or *for* them. At least everyone stopped sniping at each other to stare out the windows when they arrived at their destination—the Breakthrough construction site.

"Oh *awright!*" Dylan cried, bouncing up and down on the seat. He'd said the complex covered fifty acres. Looking at it now, Spirit thought it might even be larger. There was a gravel road leading up to the building in the distance, and as the limo drove along it, she could see foundations being laid for a wall that would probably extend around the entire park. Despite the weather, construction was going full speed ahead. Trailers were clustered like a besieging army at the foot of The Fortress's walls, and the roar of heavy machinery filled the air.

"This is only the tip of the iceberg," Teddy said, waving. "Once The Fortress is finished, we're going to start work on the apartment complex—I think Mark wants to put that right in town, if he can get zoning approval. Have to have places for everyone to live, right? We're relocating everyone who wants to come, of course, but we've really been romancing our key R&D staff. And Mark has plans for expansion, too. Come spring, we'll be able to start the landscaping, too. It'll look less like a big empty field then."

"Oh, you're so smart!" Veronica said.

Erika giggled.

"Mark knows all about the dangers of a one-industry town," Teddy said, smiling at Brenda charmingly. "Look at what happened when IBM crashed. He has plans to invest in the county's infrastructure in a big way. That way, even if Breakthrough goes bankrupt"—he laughed deprecatingly—"which isn't likely as long as people want to play electronic games of *any* kind— we'll be leaving behind us something of value."

Spirit glanced around at the limo's other passengers. She had the odd feeling Teddy was lying (but why would he bother with a big elaborate lie to a bunch of kids?) but she noticed none of the others looked as if they disbelieved him.

"That's where we're going today," Teddy said, waving off toward the left.

About a half mile from the main construction site were four high-end RVs—the Greyhound bus conversions like the ones rock stars used on tour. There were cars parked around them, mostly luxury SUVs, but Spirit saw a regular limousine too. The closest RV had the tower-and-dragon logo on the side. It was obviously the "office." Behind the RVs was a gigantic tent—the kind with inflatable walls and ceiling. A flag with the Breakthrough logo flew from its roof.

The Humvee drew up to the RVs and stopped. As it did, Mark Rider came out of the "office" RV. He was wearing a black leather stadium coat, but no hat. His dark hair whipped in the wind. As he looked at the Humvee, his face was expressionless, and Spirit was sure he was furious. But then he smiled.

"Oh my god he is soooooo handsome!" Bella said swooningly.

"Yeah, and his brother's right here," Kylee said blightingly.

Bella turned beet red, her eyes wide with humiliation.

"Ah, and I swoop in and romance the ladies who are struck senseless by Mark's beauty," Teddy said, seizing Bella's hand and kissing it theatrically. She blushed even harder, but now she was giggling.

Can't any of these guys pick on girls their own age? Clark Howard hit on her at the February Dance, Muirin and Ovcharenko were practically dating, and now Teddy was flirting with Bella. *Clearly the dating pool for Dark Lords is shallower than I thought.*

The back doors of the Humvee swung open automatically. Everyone climbed out. By the time Teddy finished introducing the Spring Fling Joint Dance Committee, Madison Lane-Rider had joined her husband. She looked as if she'd stepped from the pages of a very expensive outdoorsman catalogue.

"Oh, I've been looking forward to meeting all of you!" she said, coming forward and taking Juliette's hands in greeting. "The Spring Fling's going to be so much fun—and I hope you'll be willing to help me achieve a lifelong ambition, Juliette. And you, too, Brenda—all of you, really—at least the ladies. I've always wanted to open a little dress shop, and I think Radial's the perfect place for it. If I can talk you into borrowing some of my dresses for the dance, well, it will put me on the map! Please say yes!"

Spirit had thought things were already as weird as they could get, but the fact that everyone was taking Madison seriously was even weirder. *A little dress shop? Come on! If Madison wanted to do something with fashion, she'd be designing a collection in Milan or Paris!*

"Well I couldn't just leave them at the library, Mark," Teddy was saying. "That wouldn't be fair."

"Certainly not. But we can't exactly leave them standing around in the mud, either." Mark smiled at all of them again. "Why don't you folks use the rec center? Feel free to grab some snacks. Just be sure to take care of business before you get on the computers. Although I'd just like to mention we put the beta of *Final Battle: The Rise of the Black Dragon* onto the server this morning, and I'd really love it if you could do a little beta-testing."

"It's in beta?" Brett said in excitement. "It isn't going to be out for six months!" He looked toward the rec center eagerly. "Hey, *I'm* not on the Committee!"

"Come on then," Teddy said, clapping Brett on the back.

⋆

The door had a Breakthrough logo on it. (Everything here seemed to.) Everybody murmured appreciatively as they walked inside—it was *warm*. Even Spirit, who by now expected over-the-top excess from Breakthrough, was stunned.

"Wow," Veronica said in awe. "It looks just like a real house!"

"Yeah," Chris said blandly. "If your house has a sixty-foot-long living room."

The rec center was the size of two tennis courts. The floor was completely carpeted—a custom carpet with a repeating design of the Breakthrough logo (surprise). There were thirty computer stations—state of the art, of course—along the left wall and across the back. The screen savers all showed an animated version of the logo: the dragon coiled around the tower flapped its wings, arched its neck, spat fire. The right side of the room held half a dozen fridges, some tables and chairs, a counter with sinks, microwaves, coffee machines—and the biggest plasma television Spirit had ever seen. It was showing a football game. The middle of the room had several couch-and-chair "conversation groups," all upholstered in black leather.

"Enjoy!" Teddy said. He bowed with a theatrical flourish and left them.

Brett rushed over to the nearest computer and sat down.

Juliette rolled her eyes and shook her head. Zoey walked to one of the fridges and opened it. "Oh, man," she said. "There's everything in here! Hey, who's up for another Coke?"

"Potato chips," Kylee said feelingly, opening one of the cabinets. Spirit could see it was filled with every kind of junk food in the entire universe—cupcakes, pretzels, Cheetos, chips . . .

When Zoey closed the fridge she was holding two six-packs of soda and half a dozen tubs of chip dip.

"Okay, let's get this over with," Brenda said briskly. "The sooner we're done, the sooner we can get on the computers."

Even Juliette didn't argue. Looking at the faces of the Radial teens, Spirit realized that if he could read their parents the way he could read the kids, Mark was going to be able to buy the whole town out of pocket change—and everyone there would be eager to sell.

✦

Three

The Dance Committee got back to Oakhurst barely in time to make dinner—not that most of them would have cared if they'd missed it. The meeting had been brief and perfunctory—Juliette had wanted to set up a joint email list for planning, and had sneered when Maddie said Oakhurst didn't let them have Internet access—and then everybody had sat around stuffing their faces on junk food until Hailey and another driver showed up to bundle all of them into a couple of cars and drive them home.

Zoey and Dylan and Maddie had been loud and giddy with their sugar high, and even Chris and Kylee had been cheerful. Only Spirit had nothing to say. *Bread and circuses,* Mom's voice whispered in her mind. *Bread and circuses.* She hated to think that people could be bought off—or distracted—that easily from something (especially if it was *really bad*), but she was starting to realize the problem was actually that you didn't know how bad something was at first.

Maybe you didn't know until it was too late.

She had just enough time to dump her coat and things in her room and run to the Refectory. She got inside just before the doors closed. She scanned the room quickly and winced. The resemblance between Oakhurst Academy and a teen slasher movie had never been stronger, Spirit thought. Every meal, now, there were a few more missing kids. Spirit might not know all their names, but she could count. So could the faculty, so there was never an empty chair to let you be *sure* someone was gone. Between lunch and dinner, everything had been shifted around even further—a quick count told her two of the tables had been removed. Spirit shuddered: that was thirty places.

It didn't mean that many students were gone (yet): the chairs had all been crammed so close together at the remaining tables you probably wouldn't be able to reach for your glass without elbowing whoever was beside you in the ribs.

She wondered how many more of them would have to vanish to make the staff remove another table.

"Hey, White. Glad you could join us."

Spirit tried not to groan. If she'd had to make a list of "Oakhurst Proctors Most Likely To Become A Shadow Knight Upon Graduation," Joe Rogers would have been near the top. Ever since Breakthrough took over, he'd made it clear he was willing to play favorites—and look the other way—for a price.

"I had Dance Committee," she said briefly. "I was in Radial."

"You should keep track of the time better," Rogers said.

Spirit smiled at him coldly. "I'll be sure to tell Teddy Rider you said so, Joe."

She didn't need his glare to tell her she'd scored a point. "Go get in line," he said.

Sighing, Spirit took her place at the end of the long line. She was still cold—the Humvee had been warm, but the walk from the car to the building hadn't been—and the Refectory was chilly. As she waited, she glanced idly around the room, trying to spot the others, but didn't see any of them.

She frowned. Loch's assigned seat was at the table at the far end of the room near the back wall—but tonight he wasn't there. None of the usual kids were. Instead, Jenny and Kristi and Sarah were sitting where Loch and Noah and the rest of the "Platinum Spoon" kids usually sat.

"Hey, Spirit. Joe give you your new assignment?"

Kelly Langley, one of the Proctors, was walking up and down the line, casually ignoring the gun-toting Breakthrough thugs leaning against the walls.

"Oh god, not more homework," Spirit groaned before she could stop herself.

Kelly smiled and shook her head. "New seating assignment. You're at Joe's table. Seat Five."

Spirit felt like protesting, but this wasn't Kelly's fault. "Thanks," she said instead, and Kelly nodded and moved on.

Joe could've told me himself. He was standing right in front of me. He was probably hoping I'd sit at the wrong table and get a demerit, or have to go wandering around the room looking like an idiot.

When she'd come to Oakhurst, there'd been one Proctor

for every ten students. There were fewer students now, but there were still ten Proctors (though if they all lived until June, about a third of them would graduate). When Breakthrough had stuck everyone with assigned seating, they'd assigned a Proctor to each table (and had some left over). She'd had Gareth Stevenson before, and he was okay. Joe was a creep.

Just my luck, she thought sourly, and stopped. *Was it luck? Once is chance, twice is bad luck, three times is enemy action,* Dad used to say. She knew Joe was a member of the Gatekeeper "honor society"—he wore the pin on his jacket. And the Gatekeepers were Shadow Knights in training. So was it chance she'd been assigned to Joe? Bad luck? Or—

I won't know until I see who the others have, she told herself firmly.

She'd reached the serving window. She set her tray down and did her best to smile at the server.

A ll through dinner, Spirit kept her head down and did her best not to be noticed, but it was hard, since Joe Rogers apparently thought the table was supposed to be his personal cheering section, and if you were quiet for too long he started badgering you to "say something."

How about: you're a jerk and a bully and you've gone to work for Voldemort? Spirit thought crossly. She was more worried than she dared let on, because the only one of the others here at dinner was Loch. (Loch was at Kelly's table. Lucky him.) She wasn't worried by Muirin's absence—Muirin only showed up for dinner about half the time these days—but what about Addie? And *Burke?*

Oh please, please, please, he has to be okay. Breakthrough won't do anything really bad to him. They want him. He's a Combat Mage, and they're rare. Everyone says so . . .

She managed to get through the meal without attracting too much attention from Joe, but she was so worried that she risked approaching Loch after dinner was over.

"Not here," he said briefly, glancing at her face. "Library."

At least the Library was still a plausible destination even now. Most of their classes were either magic, folklore, or hitting things these days, but the one thing that had stayed the same was the crushing amount of homework. When she got there, Spirit took their usual table in the back of the Library, the one in the WiFi dead spot. Nobody sat there unless every other seat was filled.

A moment later, Loch sat down beside her. "Muirin was invited to eat in the Faculty Dining Room tonight," he said without preamble, his voice whisper-low. He didn't look at her as he spoke, and his lips barely moved. "Addie's got punishment drill—she's in the pool right now. Burke's in the Infirmary. I hear his magic practice today sucked beyond the telling."

"What happened?" She forced herself to speak calmly and quietly, even though she knew you only ended up in the Infirmary if something was *really* wrong—Healing was a Fire Gift, and Fire was the most common School. Even broken bones could be fixed in a matter of minutes by a Healer with a strong enough Gift.

"I'm not sure," Loch said. "I heard them saying something about a new Combat Mage. Burke's never faced one. If they've brought one in . . ." He shrugged.

"But he's . . . Burke's going to be okay?" she asked. She stumbled over the question, trying not to speak the one in her mind: *But he's going to be coming back?*

Loch glanced toward her for the first time since he'd sat down, and his expression was sympathetic. "Ms. Bradford says it's just for overnight."

Ms. Bradford was the School Nurse, one of the few members of the staff still doing the same job she'd been doing when Spirit had come to Oakhurst. Spirit let out a shaky sigh of relief.

"I never thought I'd see the day Adelaide Lake the Perfect would put a foot wrong," she said, to keep from saying anything more about Burke. She wasn't glad about Addie getting into trouble—she hoped she wasn't—it was just that . . .

"Maybe that's the problem," Loch said grimly. "Maybe they want her to screw up."

He looked so despondent Spirit impulsively put a hand over his. "Are *you* all right?" she asked.

He smiled bitterly. "The Spears family have always been survivors. It's just . . . Is this the first time you've ever been in love?"

Spirit stared at him. How could he? . . .

"It's kind of obvious," Loch said gently. "You and Burke. And I'm happy for you. Please believe that."

Spirit managed to nod. "I didn't expect . . ." she said. "I always thought, well, *you* were more my type. You know, before you— Someone who . . . Burke always seemed like he didn't know what a problem was," she finished helplessly.

"He does now," Loch said darkly. "I keep worrying he's going to crack. He knows Ovcharenko killed his foster family now, and we *all* know Ovcharenko's a Shadow Knight. And—Spirit—Burke's under a lot more pressure than we are. He's a Combat Mage. They really want him."

"He won't go over to them," Spirit said. "Not as long as we all stick by him." An idea struck her. "You should go see him, Loch. You're a Shadewalker. You could sneak into the Infirmary. He could use a friend."

"Yeah," Loch said, looking away. "I just . . . Spirit, you have got to swear to me you won't tell *anyone* what I'm about to tell you. *Promise.*"

"I promise," she answered, feeling suddenly terrified. What could be so bad Loch felt he had to swear her to secrecy? And what if it was something she thought she needed to tell?

"When I came to Oakhurst, I fell in love," Loch said quietly. "And I know he isn't interested."

She was so worried about Burke that it took Spirit a moment to work her way through to figure out what Loch meant. She knew he was gay. Clark Howard had thrown it in her face at the Sadie Hawkins Dance, but that was after Loch had already told her. Partly because he knew the Shadow Knights knew. Partly because the two of them were friends.

"You should tell him, Loch," she says. "Whoever it is. Maybe you're wrong. Maybe he's just scared of coming out . . . here. Like you are."

"Is it paranoia if they're really out to get you?" Loch asked with a sad smile. "I don't have to tell him to know I'm right, Spirit. I've seen the way he looks at you."

That was when it hit her—the realization of who he was talking about. *It's Burke. He's in love with Burke.* She'd thought things sucked for *her,* but at least she had Burke. Poor Loch! Spirit felt overwhelming grief and sympathy. "Oh, Loch," she says. "I'm so sorry. I would never—"

"I know," Loch said. "I know if it was the other way around you wouldn't try to get between me and Burke just because you loved him. Same here."

She smiled at him uncertainly. This was the sort of secret she would have no problem keeping . . . but why was Loch? . . .

"But you're wondering why I'm telling you this," Loch said, nodding as if she'd spoken aloud. "Because, as the saying goes, the best way to keep a secret is not to tell anyone. Simple. Radial's going to be declared in-bounds for the Good Children sooner than anyone thinks. In practice, the people who're going to get Town Privs will be just about anyone they're still trying to get at—or get rid of. I'm not sure which list I'm on, but it doesn't really matter: I'm pretty sure Oakhurst is going to set up something to . . . well . . . *out* me . . . and make sure word gets around in Radial. There's some other guys here that . . . well, let's say I won't be the only one. Unfortunately. And between small-town America and whatever the Shadow Knights do, well . . . I know I've been acting weird around Burke these last several weeks. I just didn't want . . . I hope you'll explain for me."

"You think you won't be here," Spirit said with a cold chill of horror.

"Do you think this whole 'oh, hey, I'm in love with your boyfriend' conversation is *easy* for me?" Loch said in exasperation. "Why the hell do you think I learned *parkour* in the first place? I've gotten really tired of being dragged off and beaten within an inch of my life! I've seen my friends— I saw David—" He broke off, struggling to control himself. "If it goes down the way I think, Spirit, I don't think they'll stop with a beating this time," he finished softly. "Maybe Breakthrough just wants me to be scared enough to join them to save myself. But I won't. So I just—"

"You listen to me, Lachlan Galen Spears," Spirit said fiercely. "We've gotten this far together. We'll get the rest of the way together. You're my friend, and you're Burke's friend, and . . . and nobody messes with my friends," she finished awkwardly.

"You tell 'em, Rambo," Loch said with a painful smile.

But she knew he didn't believe her.

*

We meet again, Guinevere," Mordred said.

His body was bound in a hundredweight of silver chains, and he stood in the center of a circle that had been drawn on the floor of her pavilion. The air was fogged with the smoke of sacred incense. Knights and priests and Druids stood along the walls, each poised to defend. The precautions were nearly enough.

"You will give me my title," Guinevere said austerely.

Mordred Kinslayer sneered. He would have swept her a mocking bow, but when he shifted, his shoulder brushed against the bound of the circle. Lightning crackled and flared, and the air was filled with the scent of an oncoming storm. He straightened with an effort.

"Shall I name you Queen? Arthur cast you out."

"Do you think so? Day after day you dripped your adder's poison in his ear, hoping to cause him to set me aside, for you know that he who is my husband—whoever is my husband—holds Britain. You meant him to imprison me in Glastonbury Abbey—did you think I would be so grateful to leave it that I would go with you when you came?"

"I think you would go with any man who offered you power . . . Lady," Mordred answered, his voice dripping with contempt.

Bedwyr stepped forward growling in fury, his hand on his sword. Guinevere raised her hand. He stepped back.

"Do not measure others by yourself, Kinslayer. My husband was no fool. The Lady of the Lake took me into her care—I went to Avalon, not to Glastonbury, as Arthur and I both intended. And there I prepared my army to fight you."

"An army which came too late!" Mordred cried. "Now Arthur is dead, and my time will come! Imprison me as you wish, False Guinevere! I have been steeped in blackest sorcery since I lay in the womb! My power is greater than any other—I have conquered Death, and I shall conquer Britain!"

"Greater than any, Kinslayer?" Guinevere said softly.

A figure stepped through the doorway of the tent. His hair and beard were white, and though he wore the dark plain robe of a scholar, he was still muscled like the blacksmith he had once been. In his hand was a staff hewn from the wood of the Sacred Oak, and at its top was fixed a shimmering green thunderstone.

He was The Merlin of Britain.

"You're dead!" Mordred shrieked.

The Merlin smiled coldly. "Did you not wonder where your wench Nimue went when she abandoned you? Do you not wonder into whose hands she gave your secrets? The trap you meant for my tomb could not hold me—but I—I will craft a prison that will hold you until the end of Time. . . ."

✦

Spirit woke to the shrill wail of her backup alarm. She felt as if she hadn't slept at all. Her head felt heavy and achy, and everything hurt. Only the sight of the time displayed on her laptop got her out of bed—she had twenty minutes to get to the Refectory if she wanted breakfast, and *didn't* want demerits.

But even as rushed as she was, she logged in to her email account first. Missing the morning Motivational Message would be dire. She grabbed an armful of clothes and dressed as she skimmed it quickly (important, leadership, the future, sacrifice, milestone, capacity, discovery, challenge, guidance, reward, triumph, yadda). She was about to dash out the door when she saw the next email in the queue was a memo from FACULTY. There hadn't been one of those in quite a while (since Oakhurst had given up telling them whoever wasn't at breakfast *this* time had "left to pursue other opportunities"), and it wasn't to STUDENTS but to SPIRIT WHITE, so even though she was running late, she opened it. The first paragraph was the usual puffery about Oakhurst students being the leaders of tomorrow; she skipped it. The next paragraph congratulated Spirit for being on the Approved List due to her exemplary (more boilerplate; she skipped ahead).

—in pursuit of our ongoing mandate to leverage our core competencies and reach out to the people of McBride County in an ongoing spirit of embracing the unique opportunities—

Radial was being declared in-bounds, just as all the rumors had said. Just as *Loch* had said. Students could work with their teachers to earn "Deportment Points," which could be used as skips for their academic classes—and to go into town.

Meaning we're all still going to be used as punching bags, but by working around the clock we can earn the chance to go to Radial and spend money we don't have on things that aren't there, she thought in exasperation. If they were "under siege" the way Breakthrough kept saying they were, giving them Town Privs was close to the stupidest thing she'd ever heard of. (At least next week's Dance Committee meeting was at Oakhurst so she didn't have to freeze to death while she argued with Juliette Weber about what colors the Spring Fling bunting should be.)

She slammed the lid of her computer to put it to sleep and headed for the door at a dead run. She got to the Refectory just as they were closing the doors. She skidded inside, panting just a little, and headed for the breakfast line. When she got there, she saw Addie was a few places ahead of her. She looked completely exhausted. She was talking to Maddie Harris (another Water Witch), and from eavesdropping, Spirit found out she'd been in the pool being drilled by Madison Lane-Rider until almost one this morning.

Spirit felt a spark of jealousy that Addie was talking to Maddie about her horrible night instead of to her, but she knew it was unfair. Addie *could* talk to Maddie without risking having her vanish. Or worse.

She got her tray and walked to her table. Out of the corner of her eye, she saw Loch at his new table. He looked as if he'd dressed in as much haste as she had. He was talking to a dark-haired boy Spirit knew slightly. Both of them seemed intent on their conversation, and Spirit felt a pang of . . . not jealousy this time, but worry. Oakhurst didn't like it if you made friends; Breakthrough positively loathed it.

She'd just picked up her fork—she had no appetite this morning, but if she didn't eat she knew she'd regret it—when Ms. Corby came in with her clipboard. *Ah, it's the morning announcements,* Spirit thought wryly. She took as much pleasure as she could from Ms. Corby's sour expression. She'd always acted as if dealing with a building full of teenagers gave her about the same level of thrill as cleaning up toxic waste, but since Breakthrough got here she looked about ready to spit nails. Spirit started to tune her out—anything really important would be in email—when the phrase "class reorganization" caught her attention.

Oh, that isn't fair! she thought a moment later, setting down her fork. Her *Systema* class had been moved to right after breakfast—and it was going to be one of the new extra long ones, too. Her Norse Folklore class had been moved to just before lunch (she was starting to wonder if Madison Lane-Rider ever slept), and in the afternoon, there was an Endurance Ride—which would take the whole afternoon, and kill her if Ovcharenko didn't manage it this morning.

I wasn't supposed to be stuck with Endurance Riding again until next week! she thought angrily.

The Endurance class could only accommodate twelve riders at a time, so they only had it every third day. The lucky class scheduled for a Thursday ride got four days between rides, not three—but thanks to "class reorganization" she had it again this afternoon!

I remember hating Mr. Wallis's gym class. I'd give anything if he were teaching it now, she thought dolefully. There was no point in eating breakfast now. She'd just end up puking all over the gym.

"Awww . . . *kitten*," Muirin said with fulsome mockery. "You've got to turn that frown upside down!" She leaned against the edge of the table.

Spirit just shook her head wearily. Muirin was dressed for *Vogue,* not for Oakhurst, and getting here in time for breakfast was clearly not an issue with her these days.

"Madison was telling me about her new boutique, and it's going to be so awesome—she says she's going to talk to the Fashion Institute of Technology about showcasing some of their student designers—light-years better than all those Sixth Avenue hacks!—and even have Breakthrough fund an FIT scholarship for Oakhurst students! She's going to completely redo one of those vacant shops in Radial as her flagship store and maybe even do a fashion shoot at the Spring Fling—you know, because just about everyone there's going to be wearing one of her dresses? I know I am—and it's going to be fabulous! No more of this tacky makeover crap from the Isle of Misfit Prom Gowns—and the Dance! I really don't know why you guys are bothering with the Dance Committee—Madison told me she'd consider it an *honor* to take over the whole design—"

"Madison told me." "Madison said." Don't you know any other words, Muirin? How can you think she's going to keep a single one of her promises? All this was absolutely insane. Why would anyone who intended to start a fashion line showcase their stuff at a hick town dance? Well, the answer, of course, was that they wouldn't, if starting a fashion line was really what they were doing. But if it was all part of a recruiting scheme, well, it didn't matter how crazy something sounded as long as the fish swallowed the bait. Madison Lane-Rider—and Breakthrough—were dangling everything Muirin had ever wanted in front of her, no matter how crazy it sounded to Spirit, and Muirin was smart enough to know she'd only get those things by doing what they wanted.

The question was—exactly what would Muirin Shae do to get all of her dreams handed to her on a silver platter?

QUERCUS told me we'd be safe if we kept our heads down and didn't stand out, but I don't think that's going to work much longer, Spirit thought as Muirin babbled on. She didn't seem to care whether Spirit was listening or not. *But things are getting really bad really fast, and I'm starting to think we can't escape—if we try it, we'll just vanish like all the others, and I really don't want to know where to. . . .*

QUERCUS was the only thing that let Spirit hold on to the hope that they might—possibly—live through this. In January, Oakhurst had arranged a field trip to Billings. Muirin hadn't been on the list of students authorized to go, but she'd stowed away, partly for the chance to pick up some contraband—she'd been smuggling harmless (but forbidden) items into Oakhurst since before Spirit arrived. She'd asked Spirit to sneak her items into the school with her own purchases—knowing Spirit's bags wouldn't be searched—and of course Spirit said yes.

That was when the Ironkey flash drive had mysteriously appeared. At first Spirit had thought it belonged to Muirin, but Muirin had never asked her for it, and when she plugged it in to her computer, Spirit could get past the Oakhurst firewall.

And more to the point, a chatroom opened where she could talk to QUERCUS.

Whoever he was.

At first she'd thought "QUERCUS" was just a name, but thanks to her hideous Latin Classes, she now knew "quercus" was Latin for "oak tree." And given the big honking Oak Tree in the Grand Foyer, she couldn't think the name was a coincidence. He'd told her to trust her instincts, to be kind, to seem as harmless as possible. It might be stupid to trust him without knowing anything about him, but she did.

Only how can it matter whether or not I trust him if I'm dead? And, oh, Muirin, I'm trying really hard to believe you're still one of us, but I don't think you'd be this cruel if it was just an act. . . .

It was all she could do to nod as if she was actually listening to Muirin.

She was afraid of what would happen if she looked like she wasn't.

❋

As she reluctantly changed for *Systema*, Spirit was still trying to decide what they should do, because the one thing she was sure of was that they needed to do something *fast*. The list of things they *should* do was staggering: find out whether Doctor Ambrosius was a helpless pawn of the Shadow Knights—or their accomplice. Find out what happened to Merlin. (*Because the one thing I know is he's sure not in that oak tree anymore*, she thought.) Find out what the Shadow Knights *wanted*—with all of them, and just in general.

And oh yeah, we have to stop them, too. Somehow. She slammed her locker door as hard as she could.

❋

She didn't know whether she was glad or worried to see Burke in class. *At least it means he's still alive*, she thought wearily. *For now.*

The new class was twice its previous size, and Spirit didn't hold out much hope of Ovcharenko keeping the beginning and advanced students separate during sparring. As always, he started by picking out a sparring partner. As usual, he picked Dylan.

Oh, come on! Spirit thought in indignation. *He just got out of the Infirmary two days ago!*

Dylan looked as horrified as Spirit felt. He looked around

wildly for allies, but even in a place that encouraged them all to hate each other, Dylan was especially disliked. Spirit swallowed hard, hating her own fear, wishing she were brave enough to offer herself in Dylan's place. Nobody else had been as brave as Trinity. She'd stood up to Ovcharenko.

Yeah, and she didn't even make it as far as the next meal.

"Why don't you pick on somebody your own size?" Burke walked up to the front of the room. He stopped directly in front of Ovcharenko. "You scared to?"

Oh Burke, no! Spirit thought in horror. *QUERCUS said we shouldn't draw attention to ourselves!* But Burke didn't know that. All he knew—all any of them knew—was that *Spirit* had told them not to draw attention to themselves. She'd been afraid to tell them about QUERCUS—she still remembered how hard it had been to get the others to take the danger they were all in seriously. Of course those days were past, but that just meant all of them were looking for someone to help them. If she told them about QUERCUS, they'd expect him to *do something*.

And how could she tell Loch and Burke and Addie about QUERCUS and not tell Muirin?

She wasn't sure she *dared* tell Muirin a secret that big.

Spirit whimpered softly as Ovcharenko smirked. He opened his mouth to say something—make one of his cheerful horrible jokes.

He didn't get the chance.

Burke Hallows—big, shy, sweet, *gentle* Burke—waded into him like an enraged pit bull.

The students scattered. Spirit heard screams. But she couldn't move, and she couldn't look away. Burke obviously meant to kill Ovcharenko—and Ovcharenko knew it. She could hear the fast hard slapping of flesh against flesh as attack and defense and counterattack moved too fast for her to see. Burke's nose was already broken; blood streamed down his face and soaked his shirt. It sprayed the floor as he shook his head.

Ovcharenko started forward. Burke spun and slammed an elbow into his face. The Russian spat blood and jumped backward. Burke sprang forward—and slipped on the blood-wet floor. The gym shook as he went down.

Spirit didn't realize she'd crammed her fist into her mouth until someone yanked it down.

"Suck it up, Spooky," Dylan hissed, squeezing her wrist hard enough to bring tears of pain to her eyes. "You want to show them he's your weak spot?"

She gave a tiny nod of understanding. Dylan stepped back, folding his arms across his chest. Spirit clenched her fists at her sides, digging her fingernails into her thighs.

Burke was up again, and for the first time, Ovcharenko looked worried. He was a master martial artist, a trained killer, *Bratva*—a member of *Russkaya Mafiya*. But Burke was a Combat Mage, he was finally facing the man who'd had his foster family murdered, and for the first time in his life he was completely committed to winning. In five minutes he'd taken the worst Ovcharenko could throw at him—and he'd learned from it. Now he bared his teeth in a feral grin and moved in for the kill.

Five seconds—ten—one of them had to tire soon. Ovcharenko's last kick had broken several fingers on Burke's right hand. Burke couldn't use it now. But he pushed forward, using his greater size as a weapon.

Ovcharenko grabbed his arm. Burke writhed and twisted, desperate to keep his elbow from being broken. Ovcharenko shouted in triumph as he flung Burke to the floor.

But Burke had grabbed Ovcharenko as he fell backward. The two bodies hit the floor with one impact, then Burke rolled up on one knee and—so fast it all seemed to be one move— whipped Ovcharenko over his head as if he were a rag doll and flung him the length of the gym.

Ovcharenko hit the wall with a crash and slid down it, limp and boneless.

No one made a sound. Not even Ovcharenko.

"Is he dead?" Zoey whispered into the silence.

"No! Only sleeping!" an unfamiliar voice boomed cheer- fully, and everyone jumped.

The speaker strode into the gym—he must have been watch- ing the fight from the other side of the doors. "But I can see that little Anastus is far beyond his skill here! Greetings, leaders of tomorrow! I am Beckett Green—and I promise, I will make you all cry and bleed!" He roared with laughter—as if this was a great joke.

Beckett Green was at least six-four, muscled like . . . Spirit wasn't sure what to compare him to. She'd never seen anyone who looked like him before in her life. Well, not in real life. On the TV, in movies, maybe. Cartoons, video games were even closer. He didn't look real, he looked like a special effect. He reached down to pick up Ovcharenko as if the man weighed nothing at all. He held him out at arm's length and shook him as if he was trying to beat the dust out of him. When Ovcharenko began to stir, Beckett dropped him abruptly. Ovcharenko staggered and sat down hard.

Burke was just getting to his feet. Beckett strode across the gym toward him. Burke wiped his face with the back of his hand—wincing—and regarded Beckett warily. Beckett reached him and clapped Burke on the shoulder, then pulled him into a warm embrace.

"Another Combat Mage! My brother—I had despaired of finding another like myself in all this wide world! We will have great fun together, you'll see!" He stepped back, hands on Burke's shoulders, holding him at arm's length and smiling at him. The smile looked honestly joyful. "You are wary. I understand. But I swear to you there will never be any tricks between us. It is unworthy between brothers and soldiers. I promise you this, my brother."

Spirit saw Burke relax and smile back. It was impossible not to believe Beckett was telling the truth—but that only made everything worse.

Had Oakhurst—had the Shadow Knights—finally found the one thing that could tempt Burke?

FOUR

In the middle of a ragged mob of her fellow sufferers, Spirit trudged wearily in the direction of the stables. With *Systema* right after breakfast—or whatever might be replacing it with Mr. Green as the new teacher—and Endurance Riding right after lunch, she was probably going to starve to death, because only an idiot would eat before either class. And if that wasn't bad enough, Mia Singleton—the Breakthrough riding instructor— had announced at lunch that they now had enough horses for twenty kids to ride at a time. That meant Endurance Riding was going to be every other day now, instead of every third day. And worst of all, she'd also said that from now on, certain Oakhurst courses were going to be open to Radial students.

"Looks like *glasnost* has come to McBride County," Loch said, so low she and Addie were the only ones who heard. "Do we call it the Montanan Spring?"

Burke was in the other Endurance Class, and of course Muirin hadn't shown up for any of the Endurance Classes for weeks. It was (just barely) safe for the three of them to talk to each other: during this class everyone was moving around so much it was likely they'd be overlooked. And a lot of it took place out of sight of the teachers.

"If they're letting the Townies in it's because Oakhurst wants more cannon fodder," Loch added. "You can bet on that."

But is that the real reason? Spirit wondered morbidly. *Or all of it?* It didn't make sense—at least if the point of Oakhurst was to train magicians to fight a wizard war. But on the other hand . . . If you wanted to take over an entire town . . . how would you do that? Wouldn't you start by getting rid of the people who'd fight you?

Sure you would. But you'd have to find them first. And what better way to do that than by convincing all their kids that Breakthrough was the best thing that ever happened to Radial? Once people like Brett and Juliette and Kennedy decided they wanted Breakthrough here, they'd complain long and loud about anyone who disagreed. Breakthrough would have its spies—and the spies wouldn't even know they were doing it.

Yeah, and if I tried to explain it to them, guess who'd be at the top of their Enemies List?

When she and the rest of the class arrived at the stables, the Radial kids were already there and on their horses. There were eight kids here from town. Spirit recognized Brett and Juliette Weber, Tom and Adam Phillips, and (of all people) Kennedy

Lewis, the Radial Dance Committee's token Goth. The other three—two boys and a girl—were kids Spirit didn't know.

"Looks like they aren't going to be getting the full meal deal," Loch whispered in her ear, and Spirit snorted. The Townies would run screaming from a typical class day at Fortress Oakhurst. (*"Fortress." Just like the one in Radial, right? Ha and also ha.*)

As usual, there was a big pile of equipment waiting on the ground in front of the stable doors, and twenty horses—one for each Oakhurst student—milled restively in the paddock. (It didn't matter if you had a favorite horse: you took what you could grab.) They were bridled but not saddled. Their saddles hung from the fence itself. Spirit shivered as she and the others came to a stop: it was cold out here, and the presence of the Townies meant none of them could cheat and use their magic to do things like make it warmer.

"Welcome to Endurance Riding," Ms. Singleton said, walking out of the stable. "As this is the first class for some of you, I'm going to go over the rules again. You are required to cover a marked ten-mile obstacle course. Oakhurst students must carry a full pack of equipment; Radial students must simply complete the marked course. As usual, Oakhurst students will be graded on success in choosing equipment and equipping their mounts. All participants will be graded on speed over the course and elegance in navigating obstacles. Failure to successfully complete all elements of the module will count as a failure for the day."

The Radial kids snickered. The Oakhurst kids didn't.

Ms. Singleton pulled out a stopwatch. Spirit felt tension

ripple through her fellow students like an electrical charge. "Oh my god," Addie breathed. "There isn't enough equipment for everyone—"

"Go!" Ms. Singleton barked.

"Get the horses!" Loch said, shoving Addie in the direction of the paddock. He grabbed Spirit by the arm and dragged her in the direction of the supplies.

The equipment list you were supposed to carry with you was everything you'd need to spend two or three days in the wilderness. Bedroll, shelter half, two canteens, food, medical supplies . . . Before she'd memorized the list, it had taken Spirit precious minutes to locate every item and get them on her saddle. Now collecting them was second nature.

Most of the kids headed for the paddock, to catch and saddle their horses, but a few of the more suspicious ones went for the equipment first. Spirit and Loch worked frantically, collecting three of everything—six of the things they needed in duplicate. At least the three of them weren't the only ones working together, Spirit realized gratefully. She knew Mia Singleton was paying close attention and watching everything.

By the time they were done, the first half-dozen students had their horses saddled and had begun to load them. That was when it became obvious to everyone there wasn't enough equipment, and so the stable yard was a chaotic jumble of shouting students, jostling nervous horses—and fights. It was like a bizarre and sadistic game of musical chairs. She wondered how much equipment was here. How many students would fail today? What was the penalty for failure?

Out of the corner of her eye, Spirit saw Kristi Fuller make a dash toward the pile of equipment she and Loch were guarding. Without stopping to think Spirit grabbed one of the canteens and swung it like a mace. It hit Kristi on the shoulder, knocking her sprawling. She scrabbled to her feet before she was trampled.

How could I do something like that? Spirit thought in horror, looking down at the canteen in her hands. . . .

"Loch!" Addie rode toward them, leading two saddled horses.

"You load—I'll guard!" Loch said.

Spirit grabbed a set of saddlebags and ran toward Addie. Saddlebags first, then you could lash down the bedroll and shelter half. If you didn't get the items onto your horse in the correct order, most of them would just fall off during the ride.

Addie brought the horses as close as she could, but controlling three animals (without having one of the Air Gifts that let you either talk to or compel animals) was a difficult task. Those of the students who were able to control their mounts with their Gifts (something the Townies wouldn't notice) were nearly ready to start.

"Come on! Let's go!" Loch shouted.

Spirit tossed him a set of canteens, then ran for her own mount. She paused long enough to hook her canteens over the saddlehorn—they were full, and weighed at least eight pounds each—then thrust her foot into the stirrup and vaulted into her saddle. Three months ago she wouldn't have been able to manage it, but since then she'd spent twenty hours a week—*every* week—on horseback.

Addie spurred her mount forward, out of the mob of struggling students, and Spirit and Loch followed. All three of them kicked and hit at the classmates trying to drag them from their saddles and claim their horses and gear. It was a relief when they managed to break free of the mob at the stables—at least now the only thing trying to kill them would be whatever was set up on the course.

There were four riders ahead of them—all from Oakhurst— and in the distance, Spirit could see a riderless horse running free. She couldn't decide whether it had thrown its rider or simply escaped. She wondered where the Radial kids were, and what they'd thought about the start of the class. *Welcome to Oakhurst,* she thought sardonically. *And you thought your high school was hell.*

A fluttering scrap of orange tape tied to a stake marked the official start of the course. The stakes marked the path you were supposed to follow, but they were spaced far enough apart that it would be easy to miss one. Any unplanned detours would cost the rider precious time. And the entire course was overseen by spotters—Breakthrough goons—on horseback.

Today's course headed due west. Uphill. The riders in front of them were drawing ahead quickly—the usual tactic was to go as fast as you could in a desperate effort to gain time, at least until you hit the first obstacle. *But if they're changing so many other things, maybe . . .* Spirit thought. She kept her mount to a trot; Addie looked at her with irritation, but matched her pace. Technically, March was early spring, and the constant wind had scoured the winter's snow from much of the ground, but that left patches of ice and—worse—places where the patchy snow had drifted into depressions in the ground, concealing them. The ground was treacherous. She was sure the Breakthrough people had done their best to make the footing worse than it would normally be, too.

Suddenly, one of the horses ahead of them went down. Its rider jumped free and rolled to her feet—it was Kylee—but when her mount lurched upright it was obvious he'd gone lame. Kylee was out of the running.

"Maybe she's one of the lucky ones," Loch said quietly.

"If she's at dinner tonight," Addie answered grimly.

❋

When they finally reached the ridge running along the top of the slope, the three of them could see the Radial kids a couple of miles ahead—they were easily identifiable by their motley winter wear, in contrast to the Oakhurst uniforms. Spirit counted quickly. They all still seemed to be there. Suddenly the Townies' horses begin to shy and plunge. A few moments later, the rattle of firecrackers reached Spirit's ears.

"This is too easy," Addie said slowly.

Spirit stared at her for an instant before she realized what Addie meant. "If the course was an obstacle course, it wouldn't matter if we saw them in advance—they'd still be just as hard. But what if it's a series of surprises, not obstacles? If we just kept the group ahead of us in sight, we'd know what each 'surprise' challenge was before we reached it."

"Breakthrough couldn't have made it that easy," Addie said slowly. "Could they?"

Loch laughed bitterly. (*Yeah, that's a "no,"* Spirit agreed silently.) A few minutes later they reached the place of the first "official" obstacle—but instead of another string of firecrackers, there was a low "chuff" and thick black smoke began to boil up out of the ground. In moments, they were blind.

"The only way out is through," Loch shouted, coughing, but it was quickly apparent the horses wouldn't walk through the smoke unless they were led. They dismounted, wrapping their faces in their scarves to shield themselves from the worst of it, and staggered blindly along the path. By the time they got through the smoke cloud, the kids from Radial were nowhere to be seen.

The temptation was to make up lost time, but this was hardly the first time they'd done an endurance ride, and carelessness or haste would cost them dearly. It soon became apparent that Spirit's first guess had been right: today's course had specifically been designed to spook the horses—everything from fire-pots spraying jets of fire into the air, to strips of tin strung on wires. It didn't matter what the riders ahead of you encountered; you'd almost certainly face something different. Keeping the horses from bucking—or bolting—was a constant challenge. "We're lucky nobody's buried claymores," Addie snarled as she fought her mount to a halt one more time. By now the Radial kids had left the course entirely. A couple of them had turned and ridden back toward town; the rest of them were paralleling the course from a safe distance.

"Don't give them any ideas," Loch said grimly.

He looked as tired as Spirit felt. Addie was the best rider of the three of them, and even she was having trouble. They had roughly two hours to cover ten miles, but they had to follow the course, and most of the time their mounts were going backward and sideways. By now the Oakhurst riders—the ones who'd made it out of the stable yard, at least—were scattered all along the course. Some of the students who hadn't been able to equip themselves back at the stables were making up for it by ambushing those who had. The course itself wasn't the only hazard.

Up ahead, Spirit could see a sheet of corrugated tin roughly thirty feet by four feet laid out on the ground. It flapped and wobbled; when the rider she was watching began to cross it, there was a combination of hollow booming and the nails-on-chalkboard sound of horseshoes on metal. But the horse and rider crossed it smoothly.

"How is he? . . ." Spirit said.

"Derek has Animal Control," Loch said bleakly.

The rider following Derek tried to do the same thing, but she didn't have an Air Gift (obviously), and her mount kept shying away from the frightening surface. She dismounted and tried to lead her horse across, but it refused to budge. Another student trotted past her, and at the booming clatter, the balking horse simply bolted back the way it had come. Its rider ran after it desperately.

"There's no way to get through this course without using magic," Spirit burst out.

"But with the Townies around—not to mention the spotters . . ." Loch said.

"I hate this— This hypocrisy!" Addie burst out. "First they

tell us it's forbidden to use magic to get through the course—and then they make it impossible for us to do it!"

"They're teaching us to cheat," Loch said with a crooked smile. "Isn't that special?"

"Well, there's more ways than one to cheat," Addie said grimly.

She dismounted and tied her scarf over her horse's eyes, then helped Loch and Spirit do the same with theirs. Then they waited until another rider with one of the Animal Control Gifts galloped his horse across the obstacle. Addie led all three horses quickly after him; Loch and Spirit defended her from other students who wanted to take her horse for their own.

After that there was a short stretch of the course where nothing was actively trying to *kill them*. There were flags flapping at the edges of the trail, some flashing lights, and a few simple jumps, but compared to what had gone before, it was a cakewalk. Some of the riders spurred forward, hoping to make up lost time. Loch pointed silently off to the right, where the course made a sharp turn and began to angle downhill. Only about half the riders saw the markers and made the turn—by now Spirit, Addie, and Loch were in the back half of the party, having lost so much time at the tin bridge.

"I vote we turn around and go home," Addie said, only half joking. The course so far had led them in a half circle; they were now only a mile or two from the stables.

Something small and black and furry skittered across the trail right under the feet of Loch's horse, making it dance and plunge—and then bolt. By the time he got it reined in and back on the trail, Spirit could see the black furry thing was just a piece of fake fur on a guide wire. She was watching it carefully as she approached the spot—and then her horse slipped and staggered, nearly throwing her. She looked back and saw a sheet of mirror-smooth ice gleaming where its hooves had disturbed its sawdust camouflage. She risked a glance at her watch. At least another half hour of this before the class was over. If they hadn't reached the finish line, at least they'd be able to ride off the course.

While she was still summoning her fortitude to ride on, there was a *crump* as if some kind of mortar had been fired, and the air was full of fluttering squares of paper. Spirit was about to scoff—compared to what they'd already gotten through, this was nothing—when the paper squares began to burst into puffs of flame. *Flash paper,* she realized after a shaky moment. Her horse was too exhausted to do much more than dance skittishly: if this had happened when he'd been fresh, he'd probably be in Radial by now. All their horses were exhausted. The next part of the course should by rights be something that called for speed and stamina.

They were passing the stand of trees now where the five of them had made their last stand against the Wild Hunt just before Christmas. "Remember when dealing with a demon lord of Hell was the worst we had to worry about?" Loch asked, smiling crookedly.

Spirit opened her mouth to answer, when suddenly there were screams from behind them. Not of surprise or anger or even fear.

Of utter terror.

Everyone Spirit could see ahead of them just kept going, and she wished desperately she could do the same thing—ride on and ignore whatever was happening behind them. It was the safest thing to do. The three of them had already stood out enough today—anything more would be even more dangerous.

But QUERCUS said kindness is my greatest weapon.

She reined in and turned back. Loch and Addie were riding behind her; they'd stopped, and Loch was looking back the way they'd come.

Oh please let that be an illusion oh please—she thought desperately. But she knew it wasn't. It was some kind of animal—huge, with pale tan fur mottled in gray. It didn't look like anything she'd ever seen in her life—except maybe the saber-tooth tiger CGI from the Discovery Channel. It had attacked one of the horses. The rider—it was Derek—was trapped under the horse, screaming as the animal ripped his horse to ribbons. His Gift of Animal Control wasn't driving it off—or he was too badly hurt to use it.

The horse thrashed weakly. The ground was dark with blood. Spirit could smell it.

There were only a few riders behind Derek—some of them had stopped to stare, others were detouring around the monster to continue on. At the edge of the trees, Spirit could see a Breakthrough spotter sitting motionless, watching the scene with interest.

What do I do? What do I do? Panic was a harsh metal taste in her mouth. She didn't have any magic—and neither Loch nor

Addie had anything that could attack at a distance. She looked from Loch to Addie. Both of them were staring at the monster in a kind of hopeless terror. In another moment it would be done with the horse—and then it would kill Derek. And there was nothing any of them could do but watch.

Suddenly there was the crack of a rifle shot. Spirit saw the spray of dirt kicked up by the bullet—it had struck near the monster, but it missed.

The next one didn't. Spirit saw a red mark appear high on its shoulder, and then its blood was flowing, staining the pale fur. It flung its head up and roared, then sprang away from the dying horse. For a moment it seemed to stare directly into Spirit's eyes. Its eyes were yellow-green, and its mouth was red with blood, and her first impression had been right: if it looked like anything, it looked like a monster tiger. Then it bolted in the direction of the pine wood.

"Hey! Get going or we're never going to be able to go on that pizza date!" Muirin cried. She brandished her rifle high over her head, like a cowboy in a Western. She was riding a pretty little black mare—*not* one of the horses supplied for the Endurance Riding course, and *not* fitted out for a cross-country hellride—and wearing brightly fashionable (nonregulation) winter riding gear.

Now that the danger was over, the Breakthrough goon was on his walkie-talkie, calling for a Jeep and a first aid team. Spirit could hear Derek sobbing as he pushed uselessly at the dead horse's body.

"Way to be inconspicuous, Murr-cat," Addie muttered.

Spirit hesitated, thinking she should dismount and do whatever she could for Derek. But she didn't get the chance.

"Come on!" Addie said irritably. She reached out and grabbed the reins of Spirit's horse, dragging it with her as she turned her own mount back to continue the course.

✦

Of the twenty students in the class, fourteen reached the finish point, and three of them were disqualified for not having the proper equipment. Of that fourteen, six had visible injuries—sprains, bruises, cracked ribs, broken bones.

But at least it was over.

And day after tomorrow we do it again, Spirit thought in exhausted incredulity.

Much to Spirit's surprise, four of the Radial kids—the Weber twins, Adam Lewis, and Kennedy—joined them at the rendezvous point to return to the stables with them. On the ride home, Addie and Loch prudently took the opportunity to distance themselves from Spirit and from each other, and Spirit found herself riding with Kylee (who was on a different horse than the one she'd started with) behind the Townies.

"I thought it was going to be, you know, a big deal," Spirit heard Brett said to Adam. "You know—something more than a few rags tied to sticks."

"Well, the tin cans were pretty noisy," Adam answered fairmindedly. "And I think somebody set off a couple of firecrackers."

"You have got to be kidding me," Kylee said quietly. She glanced sideways at Spirit, and the two of them shared a moment of perfect understanding. To listen to the Radial kids talk, there hadn't been any smoke bombs, any firepots—and certainly no prehistoric monsters.

What was that thing? Spirit wondered again. *And what is it doing* here? For the last six months, Oakhurst had been stuffing her brain with magic and spells and Gifts and Schools—and nowhere in any of that had been anything about saber-tooth tigers. She shivered—as much from dread as from cold and exhaustion. If they were going to start being attacked by monsters during every class, nobody was going to survive to attend the Spring Fling.

When she heard the sound of galloping hoofbeats coming up behind her, she didn't even look up. She knew who it was.

"Hi," Muirin said brightly, reining up beside Spirit. "Miss me?"

Spirit studied her critically. The rifle she'd defended Derek with was nowhere in sight. Maybe one of the course spotters had taken it away from her. "Yes," Spirit said honestly. "If you hadn't been there, Derek—"

"Pas devant les domestiques," Muirin said lightly, nodding toward the Townies. *Not in front of the servants . . .* Spirit took the hint and shut up. She wondered yet again if this "new" Muirin was really an "old" Muirin—Muirin the way she'd been before she was sent to Oakhurst. Was this witty callous stranger who took nothing seriously just an act she was putting on to fool Breakthrough?

Or to fool *them?*

FİVE

By the time they reached the stables, Spirit was ready to fall out her saddle with sheer exhaustion. They had to unload and unsaddle their horses, but at least they didn't have to do anything else—this was one area where staff actually took care of things.

Spirit signed the checklist saying she'd unsaddled her horse (it was probably possible to cheat and say you had when you hadn't, but she didn't think anyone would dare) and thought longingly of just walking into the stables and collapsing on the nearest pile of straw. She was so tired she didn't even care if she missed dinner.

But when she turned around, Muirin was standing at her elbow.

"Come on, come on!" Muirin demanded. "Come and see my surprise! All of you—Addie! Loch!"

After all the trouble we've gone to pretending we don't know each other, and she does this? Spirit cut glances with Addie and Loch, and both of them looked just as confused and upset. But there was nothing to do about it but follow Muirin—or risk being the center of an even bigger scene.

uirin's "surprise" was waiting in the motor pool parking lot. Among the half dozen Jeeps and big black SUVs, the bright blue "sport" SUV stood out like a peacock in a henhouse.

"Not very sexy," Muirin said grudgingly. "I mean . . . a Nissan. But it's got four-wheel drive, so I don't have to leave it parked until June!"

"Oh my god," Addie breathed. "It's a *car.* Muirin . . ."

"What did you have to do to get that?" Loch asked, disgust plain in his voice.

"Hey," Muirin said, tossing her head. "At least I can ask the date of my choice to the Fling."

There was a gleam of—triumph?—in her eyes as she looked at Loch. Loch simply looked weary.

"Well, don't think it isn't Topic A," Muirin said archly. "Everyone's talking about it. Guess it's a good thing you picked Burke, huh, Spirit?"

Spirit couldn't keep from wincing, even as she wondered whether Muirin was actually being as spiteful as she sounded—or was delivering a disguised warning. But at the same time she couldn't help but wonder—*would* she have fallen for Burke if she hadn't known Loch was unavailable?

"Anyway!" Muirin continued. "Having wheels of my own will make it a lot more fun to sneak out after curfew, right?"

"Oh, I don't know," Loch drawled mockingly. "You'll still be in Montana, sweetie."

"If you're going to be doing all that 'sneaking,' maybe you could help us out by doing some research down in Radial, Muirin," Addie said quickly.

That's right, Spirit thought. *I was supposed to track down any surviving members of those bikers once I got off campus. Not that easy with the Dance Committee meeting at The Fortress. . . .*

Muirin made a rude noise. "Research!" she scoffed. "Since I'm not gonna live to graduate, I've got to get in a lifetime's worth of fun right now."

I guess that's a "no," Spirit thought.

"So hey—who wants to go for a ride?" Muirin added.

Loch shook his head silently, turning away, and Addie was still outraged at Muirin's latest gift—obviously from Breakthrough. Neither one was going to take Muirin up on it, and Spirit saw the flash of hurt in Muirin's eyes—and the dangerous line of temper in the set of her mouth.

"Oh hey, Murr," Spirit said, forcing a laugh. "I didn't think *eau de wet horse* was your signature fragrance! I don't know about Loch or Addie, but I know I stink. And you probably don't want that smell all over your new car until the end of time!"

"Ha," Muirin said, smirking, the ugly flash of temper averted. "You have a point. Rain check?"

"Sure," Spirit said, forcing herself to sound as if she was looking forward to it. She wondered how long all of them could dance on this knife edge. Muirin had always had a sharp tongue and a quick temper, but she'd used to reserve her cruelty for other people. Not her closest friends.

She wondered if they were still Muirin's friends.

✦

When she walked into the Main Building, Spirit saw Burke in the first-floor lounge. She was about to detour over to him until she realized he was deep in conversation with one of the teachers.

He was talking to Beckett Green.

It felt like rejection, and it hurt. In a normal world, she and Burke could have gone on dates, spent time with each other. At Oakhurst, they had to pretend they didn't know each other, and every tiny scrap of time they'd managed to steal to be together (just the two of them) was precious.

But it also made her feel as if what she and Burke had could vanish at any moment—or be taken away.

They've given Murr a car. Now Burke has Beckett. What will they offer Addie? Or Loch? She had a good idea what they *could* offer Loch—the one thing he'd never really had. Safety. What would Loch give to know that no one would be coming after him, that his physical safety would be guaranteed? *Just sign right here, and no one will ever bother you again.*

Would he? And if he did, could she blame him?

As for Burke—

I just don't know what to think right now. She turned away and headed blindly back to her room. It was all falling apart, and there was nothing, nothing she could do about it. She closed the door behind herself and dropped down on the bed, pulling all the covers around herself in a kind of cocoon of misery.

At least she was warm.

❖

Hunger woke Spirit at last; she'd crashed hard once she'd gotten back to her room, and at the time she hadn't cared about missing dinner. She turned on the light and glanced at her watch. Two a.m. She might as well get up now. At least today was Saturday. That meant no *Systema* and no Endurance Riding. Just a lot of homework.

She pulled on her robe and opened her dorm fridge. Gatorade was better than nothing, she supposed. She chugged a bottle and brought a second one back to her desk. She opened the drawer of her desk, and her fingers slid under the litter of pens and loose papers to touch the Ironkey drive. Her link to QUERCUS, whoever he was. She plucked it out without hesitation and plugged it into her computer. The familiar book-shaped icon appeared once her computer recognized the device. She clicked on it, and the chatroom window opened.

Hello, Spirit, QUERCUS typed.

Hello, she typed back. She wondered how he'd known it was her—or if he was guessing. He always seemed to be right there whenever she opened their private chatroom. Maybe the Ironkey sent an alarm to his computer when it was plugged in. Or maybe he was more than one person, and they took shifts.

My riding class was attacked by a saber-toothed tiger today, she typed.

The sentence looked insane on the screen. What would he think? She wasn't sure whether she was trying to shock him or asking for help.

Tell me what happened, QUERCUS answered. No emoticons. No hesitation. Did he—she—it—even believe what Spirit was saying?

Right now she didn't care. She was so desperate to talk to someone—anyone—without watching every single word that she found herself telling QUERCUS everything. Not just about today, but about the last several weeks—things she'd held back before, still uncertain of whether he was the friend he seemed to be or a trap set by Oakhurst and Breakthrough. Sometime in the last week she'd stopped caring, she realized. If he wasn't a friend . . . then at least this would be over. She was so tired, tired of it all, exhausted by what Oakhurst was putting them all through, tired of living a lie, of weighing every word out of her mouth, of thinking everyone around her was a potential enemy. She just wanted to be able to talk to someone without having to imagine the possible consequences!

At last she worked her way back around to Muirin and her new car. —and Addie was horrified about it, but that didn't stop her from asking Murr to do some research for her. You know, when I got the Dance Committee gig, we figured I could poke around in Radial a little bit, but now I wonder if Teddy didn't have an even better reason for bringing all of us to The Fortress that day than I thought.

There was a pause, then QUERCUS replied, the letters coming up on the screen as if he was typing very slowly. You don't need to go to Radial to do research, QUERCUS typed. You can use the Internet.

Spirit began to scoff, but he was right: when this chatroom window was open, she could get out onto the "real" Internet. She hadn't even thought of it—partly because what she wanted to know about was right in Radial, and partly because the first time she'd taken advantage of the freedom the Ironkey drive gave her, she'd slipped up and accidentally let Muirin know she'd had Internet access, and she'd been afraid of repeating that mistake.

And Oakhurst is really good at teaching you not to think about things, she thought sourly.

Thank you. I will, she typed.

Her hands shook as she opened her browser window. She typed an address at random—ain't it cool news—and today's page came up. She let out a deep breath. It still worked. She chewed her lip, wondering where to start. Typing *biker gang survivors of magical gang war at the old Tyniger mansion* probably wouldn't get her very far.

She was right about that. It took her an hour of Googling before she hit pay dirt. To her surprise (she ended up stumbling over it by pure accident), the *Radial Echo*—Radial's dinky little hometown newspaper—hadn't just been microfilmed, it had been digitized. And the digital copy was available in a public online archive. The town had been incorporated in 1885, and all 125-plus years of the paper were archived. *Searchably.*

Muirin should be doing this, Spirit thought wearily, rubbing her tired eyes. Muirin was surprisingly awesome at research, as she'd proved time and again. But Muirin had already refused to help—and besides, Spirit would have to have let her in on the secret of the Ironkey if she was to do any online research. And she didn't dare. She heaved a sigh and got back to work.

Oakhurst had been founded in 1973, Spirit remembered, so what she was looking for was earlier than that. She remembered Juliette Weber saying the place had been a gang hideout in the seventies, but just to make sure she didn't miss anything she started with January 1960. By the time the sky outside her window began to lighten with dawn, she'd found what she wanted to know.

The gang everyone kept mentioning had been called The Hellriders. The first item—about them taking over Oakhurst—was from 1968. The last was from three years later—1971—and that was a big enough story that the *Echo* ran coverage for an entire month, and the story was picked up by several out-of-town papers.

It started the night of July 31, when a member of the Hellriders—Stephen "Wolfman" Wolferman—tore through Radial on his motorcycle doing over a hundred miles an hour. His joyride triggered a three-county chase that went on until he ran out of gas. The *Echo* just said he was "taken into custody," but the *Billings Gazette* included the information that Wolferman, a Vietnam vet, had been raving and disoriented when he was apprehended. *The Touchstone*—a monthly magazine published in Billings—gave even more information: apparently

Wolferman had been raving about the sun turning black, the moon turning to blood, and the dead rising up out of their graves. The local authorities assumed drugs, and went up to what was then still called "the Tyniger estate" to investigate. According to the *Billings Gazette*, they found several dead Hellriders, and evidence of "intergang warfare."

I doubt it somehow, Spirit thought. *If a second bunch of bikers had showed up, they would've had to go through Radial to get here. And even Radial would notice that.*

She frowned, staring at the page. August of 1971 to September of 1973 was barely two years. Not enough time to turn a derelict mansion that had been sitting vacant since 1939—when Arthur Tyniger died—into Dr. Ambrosius's showplace.

Then she shook herself. She was still thinking like a normal person. Nothing about this place had ever been, or was, normal.

Oh, don't be silly, Spirit told herself scornfully. *Of course it is. All you need is magic.*

Unfortunately, after that point, the regular papers lost interest in the story, but a Google Search using her new keywords turned up a page dedicated to the "Hellriders Massacre" on a site called Weird Montana.

And "massacre" was apparently the word for it. When the authorities reached the mansion on the morning of August 1st, 1971, they discovered "several" members of the Hellriders dead and the rest missing. There were some grainy black-and-white pictures on the Web page, but they were so blurry Spirit couldn't even make out where they'd been taken, though it had to be at Oakhurst. According to Weird Montana, the missing

Hellriders never turned up. The only survivor was "Wolfman" Wolferman, who never changed his story (such as it was).

Bingo. You were right, Loch. The authorities hadn't been able to charge Wolferman with anything more illegal than speeding, and he ended up going to the County Hospital. Weird Montana said he was released in the early 1990s and returned home to Radial to live. She went back to the *Radial Echo* and found a mention of his return in the "Local News And Views" column. He'd apparently moved in with his parents. The story gave the address.

She pulled out a pen and a piece of paper and jotted it down—dangerous, she knew, but she was afraid of forgetting it. She skimmed the next few years of the paper to make sure he hadn't moved or died. The only thing she found was the announcement of the opening of Oakhurst Academy in September 1973. Doctor Ambrosius—the paper gave his first name as "Vortigern"—was described as "a progressive European educator and philanthropist." Out of a vague curiosity, Spirit searched the rest of the *Echo* for mentions of either Doctor Ambrosius or Oakhurst Academy, but she didn't find a single one.

As far as Radial was concerned, Oakhurst Academy had simply ceased to exist.

<hr />

I am not cut out for this," Burke said, sitting up with a groan. The Nissan hit a pothole and bounced; Burke winced as he finished unwedging himself from the footwell in the car's cramped backseat, then reached down to lift Spirit up from the other side. She breathed a sigh of relief as she unfolded herself, and turned to glance out the back window. They were already off the school grounds; the school looked almost pretty in the dusk. *If you don't know what's going on there,* Spirit thought.

"Sweet, isn't it?" Muirin said, ignoring Burke. "Relax—we're outside the wards, and I'm the mistress of illusion, remember? Nobody's going to see anything I don't want them to see."

" 'Feel' is a different matter," Burke said.

"Which is why I snuck you guys out on the floor," Muirin said reasonably. "With the town in-bounds, you just know they're going to start searching cars." Muirin sounded cheerful. *And why not? No matter what bizarre new rules Oakhurst—and Breakthrough—come up with, it isn't as if she was going to be affected,* Spirit thought.

"It doesn't make sense," Spirit said, trying to keep from sounding (too much) as if she was whining. "First they declare Radial in-bounds. Then they set a campus curfew for dusk." The newest rule had been announced Saturday morning: after curfew, all students had to be either in the Main Building, or have a security escort to wherever they were going. And that meant pretty much from four o'clock on. "I wish they'd make up their minds."

Muirin just laughed. "Why should they, when they can drive you guys crazy by changing the rules every other day?"

"Mr. Green said the curfew's only until they can hunt down that whatever-it-was that attacked you guys on your ride Friday," Burke said.

"Whatever it is," Spirit muttered under her breath. You'd

have to be an idiot (or not going to Oakhurst) to think it was anything that belonged on this planet.

"Hope they catch it soon—this is cattle country, and something like that could do a lot of damage," Burke added.

"Burke the Selfless!" Muirin said mockingly. "Honestly—if you want to break the rules like this, why aren't you at least doing something fun? There's still time, you know—I could drop you guys at a No Tell Motel for a couple of hours. . . ."

"No thanks," Burke said. He looked wildly embarrassed. "This is a research trip. Spirit found someone who was actually there when Mordred got let out of the tree. If we're lucky, he can give us a lead on where Mordred is now."

"Yeah," Muirin said, detouring around another pothole. "You guys did a pretty good job of finding him. You didn't even have to leave the campus." Her tone was suspicious, and Spirit winced.

"I got lucky," Spirit said, hoping she sounded more convincing than she felt. She knew Burke thought it was suspicious, too—she wished she could tell him at least that she had a way through the school firewall, but right now none of her friends seemed any more reliable than Muirin. Burke was acting like Beckett Green was his new BFF, Addie was well and truly pissed off and might do anything out of spite, and Loch . . . well, Loch was convinced he was about to die and might want to use the information to make a grand fatal gesture.

Or make a deal for a get-out-of-jail-free card, and it wouldn't matter if he was including all of them in the deal. It would still be a disaster.

"You remember the other time, right?" she asked, hoping

she could turn her previous mistake to her advantage. "Well, I was poking around to see if there was anything on the school intraweb, and the firewall was down again. You know Breakthrough's been putting in a lot of new security. It was a lucky glitch."

"'Lucky,'" Muirin said dubiously.

"What else could it be?" Spirit said, mentally holding her breath. She had to get Muirin off the subject somehow. "But without you to help, it wouldn't matter what I found."

"Yeah, I *am* pretty fabulous," Muirin said mockingly. "But I still think you could've shared the love."

"Oh, like you have to worry about being stuck behind a firewall these days," Spirit said.

"True," Murin agreed smugly. "Hey, you sure you don't want me to drop you any closer than this?"

Spirit blinked. They were here already. She looked around as Muirin stopped in the town library parking lot—by unspoken agreement, she and Burke had been rather vague about Wolferman's address. It was Sunday evening, so the library was closed, and there weren't a lot of lights around.

"This is Radial, Murr-cat—how far away can anything be?" Burke said, making a joke of it. He pushed the passenger seat forward and clambered out of the backseat, reaching back a hand to pull Spirit after him. "We won't be long. Meet you at the pizza place?"

"I'll even buy," Muirin said. "Don't do anything I wouldn't do." She reached out and pulled the door shut, then gunned the engine and pulled out in a scatter of gravel.

"What is that, exactly?" Burke said softly, looking after her.

"I wish I knew." Spirit sighed.

Burke smiled and took her arm. "C'mon," he said.

"I still think I should've come by myself," she said. This far off Main Street there weren't any sidewalks; the two of them walked down the center of the narrow road. The sky was brilliant with stars. Back the way they'd come, the security lighting around The Fortress made a bright column of light shining up into the sky, but the only other lights she could see were the distant floodlights of the DOT equipment shed. In the distance, Spirit could see the lights of a few other houses, but if Radial were big enough to have a bad part of town, this would be it. Burke took out a flashlight and played the beam over the ground ahead of them. There was a full moon, but the light was deceptive—you were sure you could see better than you could, until you fell over something.

"And do me out of a chance to take you for a walk in the country?" Burke asked, smiling down at her. He put an arm around her shoulders and hugged her close, and for just an instant Spirit wanted *this* to be the reason they were here. A date. An ordinary thing two people did who weren't being stalked by evil wizards.

"Besides," Burke went on, "the guy's an ex-outlaw-biker. I think you're better off bringing a big scary jock with you. Because what if he's crazy? Or evil?"

"Or both," Spirit said helpfully.

"Right," Burke agreed. "I mean . . . I know he was in a mental hospital, but that doesn't prove anything. Not if he'd seen, well . . . *magic.*"

Spirit didn't quite wince. On her first day at Oakhurst, Dr. Ambrosius had turned her into a mouse and himself into an owl. Whether that had actually happened or not, she'd experienced it. If she'd been trying to explain what had happened to the local Sheriff's Department, they'd have said she was crazy too.

She wondered if it was worse to be locked up and told you were crazy when you weren't, or to be believed when you described things that you knew were impossible. *Tough choice.* After a few minutes' walk, they stopped at the only mailbox they'd seen. Burke shined his flashlight on it. 1642 PARK AVENUE ROAD was painted on the side in messy black letters.

"This is it," Spirit said unnecessarily.

The house was an old white farmhouse—or at least, it had been painted white at some point. Now it was mostly raw gray wood. There was just enough light to show the rusted-out junker half buried in snow in the front yard, the windows covered with ragged plastic sheets. The snow was deep and untouched; it had drifted up over the front porch and covered half the door. There were no lights anywhere to be seen.

I knew it was too easy.

Her shoulders slumped in disappointment. The place was obviously deserted, and she had no idea where else to look for Stephen Wolferman. "There's no one here," she said, but when she turned to Burke, he was smiling.

"You might have lived out back of Beyond, but I guess you didn't have much to do with farm folks," he said. "Let's try around back."

Their boots crunched through the snow as they walked up the driveway. The driveway hadn't been shoveled all winter, and Spirit couldn't see how Burke could possibly imagine anyone was living here. But when they reached the back of the house, she saw light gleaming through the cracks in the aluminum foil that covered the inside of the windows. There was someone here after all, but the sight of the aluminum foil made her hesitate—it didn't look very encouraging.

Burke ignored her hesitation and walked right up to the back door. He knocked firmly.

"Maybe he isn't home," Spirit whispered, when no one came to answer it.

"In Radial on a Sunday night?" Burke asked, and knocked again.

Eventually the door opened just wide enough for the house's occupant to look out. He regarded them silently.

"Mr. Wolferman?" Spirit said uncertainly. "Could we talk to you? I'm Spirit and this is Burke. We need your help."

"I can't help anybody," Wolfman said, sounding scared. He started to close the door.

"We brought you some presents," Burke said quickly.

Spirit glanced at Burke in puzzlement, but Wolfman opened the door, and for the first time, she actually got a good look at him. He was unshaven and potbellied and his long hair was nearly white. His appearance was a shock, and she realized she'd been expecting him to look the way he did in the photos from the old stories. But the "Hellriders Massacre" had taken place nearly forty years ago. Wolfman was in his sixties.

When they followed him into the kitchen, Spirit was suddenly very glad Burke was with her. The only light came from scores of big white jar candles clustered on every surface.

And the walls were covered with handmade wooden crosses. Dozens of them.

What have I gotten us into? she thought.

"You said you had presents," Wolfman prompted.

"Sure did," Burke said. He began digging through the pockets of his jacket and emptying their contents onto the kitchen table: a dozen of the big-size Hershey bars and a pint of whiskey. *Muirin,* he mouthed at Spirit.

"Sit down, sit down," Wolfman said. "Kitchen company's the best kind, right?"

Spirit sat down at the table. Burke took the chair beside her. She'd expected the table to be dirty, but it was so clean it squeaked. It was hard to be sure in the flickering candlelight, but the whole kitchen looked as if it had been scrubbed so hard and so long that the finish had been worn off of everything, including the faded linoleum. Everything she could see was shabby and ancient, as if she'd walked into some kind of weird time capsule of the 1950s.

"Would you like something to drink? I have water. It's good. From the well," Wolfman said. He seemed anxious to please them—and weirdly childlike.

"That would be great," Burke answered.

Spirit had assumed he'd been sent to the mental hospital because the story he'd told was unbelievable. Now she wasn't so sure. She looked around, trying not to seem as if she was, while Wolfman opened the cabinet and took down two glasses. He filled them at the sink, rinsing them carefully, then brought them to the table. Then he sat down, picked up the whiskey, and poured some into the coffee cup already there.

"What are you doing out so late at night?" Wolfman asked. It wasn't even six o'clock, but Spirit supposed if you lived by candlelight, you'd go to bed early.

"We wanted to talk to you about the Hellriders," Spirit said cautiously.

"You know the 'riders?" Wolfman asked eagerly.

"We want to know about them—about you," Spirit said.

"Aww, we were the best. The guys, they were really great guys—" Wolfman smiled and nodded happily.

It didn't take much to get him talking. A lot of what he said didn't make any sense to Spirit, and she didn't want to confuse him by asking too many questions. She got the impression that he and someone named Kenny had been in the Army together back in the 1960s and had decided to bike cross-country when they got out. They hadn't gotten further east than Radial. Somewhere along the way they'd become the Hellriders.

"So I guess you had a . . . clubhouse?" she asked awkwardly, when Wolfman showed signs of slowing down. She had to figure out how to ask him about Oakhurst, but the more she saw of him, the harder doing that seemed.

"Shhh!" he said sharply, looking around. "The aliens can

listen through the electricity. That's why I took out all the wires. But it's okay. We're safe here."

That was something Spirit doubted more by the minute.

"Sure we are," Burke said easily. "So it's okay to talk about it, right? Or else you wouldn't have let us in."

"That's right," Wolfman said, apparently completely willing to believe Burke. "Because Kenny said run. Kenny said run. I wanted to look for Kenny, but I never saw him again. Do you know where he is?"

"I don't. I'm sorry," Burke said. "Why did Kenny tell you to run?"

"I was in Vietnam. Me and Kenny. That's how it started. It wasn't a real war—it was a government cover-up because of the alien invasion. We got rid of them, you know, but then the government wanted to get rid of us, because we'd seen their secret ninja base, and we'd seen the aliens. They look like giant black snakes—with wings—and they can walk through walls but only when the electricity is on, so I don't use electricity anymore. The mansion was safe too, because it didn't have any electricity. . . ."

If Wolfman had seemed only a little confused when he'd let them into the house, he'd gone rapidly downhill. But they had to find out what had happened.

"But it wasn't safe, was it?" Spirit asked daringly. "Something happened."

"Kenny said run," Wolfman repeated, sounding forlorn. For a moment Spirit thought he wasn't going to say anything else, but when he began to talk again, the vague hesitancy was gone from his voice, and he sounded like the man he must have been almost forty years before. "The night of the big storm there was bad voodoo going down. We all knew it. Couldn't go for a run in the storm, and Bobby'd had a fight with his old lady, and Roadhog wouldn't let up. Only . . . I guess it wasn't Bobby after all, 'cause him and 'hog were friends. It was one of the aliens. They'd followed us back to our world. And it shot Roadhog, and that opened the interdimensional warp-gate to let the aliens out of the shadow universe and Kenny said run—Kenny said run, Wolfie, run, run, run—and there was blood everywhere and the shadows came out of the blood and Trace was gone, and Bobby was gone, and Preach was gone and I ran and I ran . . ."

His voice had gone high and shaky while he was talking; he drew a sobbing breath and scrubbed at his eyes. Under the edge of the table, Burke reached for her hand, and Spirit clutched his gratefully. It was easy enough to read between the lines: Bobby killed Roadhog—somehow freeing Mordred from the oak tree—and half the Hellriders ended up as Shadow Knights and the other half ended up dead.

How is this my life? Spirit thought bitterly. This wasn't even the creepiest thing that had happened to her this week!

"I'm the only one who remembers," Wolfman finished sadly. "And I will always remember, because if I remember, the ninja aliens can't win."

He got to his feet and walked over to the refrigerator. When he opened it, it was dark inside (no electricity), and he obviously used it for storage. He brought out a flat object wrapped in an old t-shirt and set it on the table in front of them.

"This is me and Kenny," he said, unwrapping it. "See?"

The framed photo was old and faded. It looked like something out of a movie. Two young men wearing jungle fatigues, arms around each other's shoulders, grinning at the camera. "Kenny was my best friend. Kenny said run, Kenny said run. You haven't seen Kenny, have you?" Wolfman asked again plaintively.

Beside her, Spirit heard Burke draw a quick startled breath.

What would you do if I said I saw Kenny this morning? she thought wildly.

One of the men in the photograph was clearly Stephen Wolferman, at a much younger age. And the man standing beside him—*Kenny*—could only be Doctor Ambrosius.

Kenny, who'd told Wolfman to run the night of the "Hellriders Massacre."

If Dr. Ambrosius had been Kenny then, had he had magic? If not, how had he gotten it? How had he become . . . him?

Was there any chance they'd found—Merlin?

They made their escape as quickly as they could after seeing the photo. Wolfman had told them all he could, and—everything else aside—if they spent too long here, Muirin might just go back to Oakhurst by herself.

"That was . . ." Spirit said as soon as they'd reached the road. It seemed darker and more threatening now than it had when they'd arrived. She had the feeling of being watched, even though there wasn't anyone in sight, but at least she wasn't sitting in a kitchen full of candles and crosses listening to somebody talk about an alien conspiracy.

"Poor guy," Burke said. "But I guess we've got our proof now."

Spirit shivered, but not because of the cold. "Maybe," she said hesitantly. There was something about Wolfman's story that didn't make sense, but she couldn't quite put her finger on it.

"Wish we could've taken the picture with us—you know, for proof," Burke said.

"Maybe we can find a copy of it somewhere," Spirit said absently. *Muirin could. If only I—*

There was a sharp crack, and she jumped and squeaked.

"Branch coming down," Burke said reassuringly, pointing. "Lotta ice still on the trees."

"I guess," Spirit said doubtfully. "Hurry up. I'm freezing," she added, walking faster.

They passed the library and walked on into town. Most of Main Street was closed up and dark, but The Fortress was lit up as bright as day (Spirit thought it would probably still be lit up at midnight; what a waste of energy), so there was plenty of light to see by. As they got further into town, she could see there were a lot of cars on the street, for some reason.

"Looks like they got tired of their fancy rec room," Burke said, sounding disgusted. He nodded toward the pizza joint, one of the few storefronts that was lit up. It was crammed with people. Spirit recognized Clark and Mandy from Breakthrough and a few other people she'd seen around Oakhurst but couldn't put names to.

"I guess they're boosting the local economy," she said darkly. Most of the people she could see were Breakthrough employees. "So much for nobody knowing we snuck off campus."

"Maybe that's a good thing," Burke said slowly. Spirit looked at him in confusion. "I'm thinking they might feel better if they think they've got something on us. And, well, it isn't as if they can do much worse to us than they're doing now."

"I hope you're right about that," Spirit said. She took a deep breath and followed Burke as he crossed the street and pushed open the door.

A couple of the Breakthrough people waved at them as they entered. Feeling oddly guilty, Spirit waved back. The noise— laughter, and a dozen different conversations, and music—was jolting after the quiet of the night outside. It sounded so strange, and after a moment Spirit realized why. Even at the school dances everyone was . . . careful. They all knew they were being watched—and judged. But there was no sense of that here.

Besides the Breakthrough wonks, there were a bunch of Townies, all within a few years of her age. She recognized Brett and Adam, and she'd have bet real money (if she'd had any) Breakthrough was picking up the tab for everybody's pizzas and Cokes here tonight. She saw some Oakhurst kids, too—Joe Rogers (of course), Sarah Ellis, and a couple of others whose names she wasn't sure of.

At least Burke and I aren't the only ones breaking the rules tonight, she thought. *But maybe the others aren't. Maybe they're being courted by the Shadow Knights. Just the way Muirin is.* Joe looked up when she and Burke walked in, but instead of the sneer she expected to see on his face, Joe just looked thoughtful.

"There's Murr," Burke said, pointing.

Muirin was in a booth near the counter. Spirit was relieved to see Ovcharenko wasn't with her, but she wasn't alone. There were three people—two men and a woman—sitting in the booth with her. All three of them wore red polo shirts with the Breakthrough logo embroidered on them where the pony or the golfer or the alligator went.

"Way to be inconspicuous," Spirit groaned quietly. Burke squeezed her hand understandingly.

"Hey, guys, ready to order?" Muirin called when she saw them. "Anything you want! Breakthrough's buying!" She waved a slice of pizza.

Thought so. "I kind of want to get back," Spirit said. "I need to study."

"Hey, you can't study all the time," one of the Breakthrough guys said. "Spirit, isn't it? Ken Abrams, Graphic Design." He smiled at her.

"I guess we've got time for a slice," Burke said. "C'mon."

Ken got up and brought a pie and an armful of Cokes back to the table. The other two Breakthrough people were Judy and Brian; all three of them worked in the graphic design department.

"These two geeks use Photoshop," Judy said, laughing as she punched Brian in the shoulder. "I'm a paper-and-pencils type myself."

The three of them were happy enough to monopolize the

conversation—mostly about how wonderful working for Break-through was, and how you didn't need to be a hotshot programmer to work there. It would have made a great recruiting pitch if Spirit hadn't known the truth. She concentrated on her pizza while Brian and Ken tried to convince Burke Breakthrough would be happy to hire him in their motion-capture department. Not as a programmer, but as a model.

"Face it, big guy, slap a horned helmet on your head and put a sword in your hand and you could storm the gates of any citadel we've got," Ken said.

"Nice to know," Burke said genially. "I'll keep that in mind."

Fortunately, Muirin was curious enough about what they'd found out to want to leave fairly soon, much to Spirit's relief. She'd had visions of having to spend hours pretending she wanted to hang out with Muirin's new friends.

But it was her idea to give Burke that stuff for Wolfman. So no matter what she acts like, she's on our side.

I hope.

❧

So. Give!" Muirin said, as soon as they got into the car. At least this time Burke could sit up front—there wasn't a lot of point to hiding when half of Breakthrough had seen them in Radial tonight. "What did he tell you?"

Maybe if I tell her about the photo, she'll realize it's too dangerous to keep leading those guys on the way she is. She always thinks she's smarter than everyone else, but they'll figure it out. And then what will happen to her? "He showed us—" Spirit began.

"According to Mr. Wolferman, Earth has been invaded by alien ninjas from the Shadow Dimension," Burke said. "I guess I wasn't counting on much once I saw he'd lined the house with aluminum foil."

So Burke doesn't trust Muirin either, Spirit thought in surprise. She wasn't sure what to think about that.

"Awww, too bad, Burksie," Muirin said, snickering. "Hey, I wonder why Ms. Groves hasn't suggested using aluminum foil against the forces of Eeeevil in magic class? Think I should tell her about it?"

"Yeah, even you would get detention forever if you tried that," he said. "Just so you know, the alien ninjas look like snakes with dragon wings and can walk through your walls when you have electricity," Burke continued. "Wolferman says he saw their secret base in Vietnam."

"Wow." Muirin shook her head. "That's messed up. But hey, at least you got a couple of hours outside the prison walls and a pizza out of it."

"It's the little things you treasure," Burke agreed gravely.

✦

Y ou shouldn't be out after curfew, Ms. Shae. It isn't safe."

Muirin parked up in the motor pool again. The three of them had just gotten out of the car, when one of the Security patrols showed up. There were two of them, wearing black uniforms and—even in the middle of the night—sunglasses. Both of them were armed—and wearing body armor, it looked like.

"Wanna see my pass, Dave?" Muirin said in her brattiest voice.

Dave laughed, lowering the flashlight he'd been shining in their faces. "Guess not. But you be careful. We still haven't caught that cat yet."

"When you do, I want seat covers," Muirin said, waving. Dave laughed and gestured to his partner, and the two of them walked away.

"It's okay," Muirin said when they were out of earshot. "They didn't see you."

"Thanks," Burke said. "I know they're going to know we were down in Radial—"

"—but why make things easy for them?" Muirin finished.

"Yeah, I try not to upset people carrying Uzis," Burke said dryly, and Muirin laughed.

SIX

It was actually a few minutes before curfew when Burke and Spirit got inside, and it was easy enough for them to mingle with the other students heading for their rooms. Their boots and coats attracted no attention—everybody just assumed they'd been outside for a legitimate reason. Still, it was more of a relief than Spirit had expected to reach her room and shut the door. From the moment she'd climbed into the back of Muirin's car with Burke earlier this evening, she'd been thinking: *This part isn't very dangerous—and this part isn't either.* But it all had been, and now that she was safe—as safe as anyone got at Oakhurst—she could let herself realize it.

She hung up her coat and the rest of her outdoor gear—hat, gloves, scarf—in the closet, then sat down on the bed to pull off her snow boots. At least by the time she'd reached the hall in the girls' dorm wing, her boots had been dry; there wasn't a single mark on the carpet to show she'd been outside.

Not that Oakhurst needed visible proof you'd done something—she was sure there were some Gifts they weren't being taught about in class, just so they could be used against them. And if one of the staff had Scrying, and thought about using it . . .

The five of them were screwed.

Either they don't have it or they aren't using it, she told herself firmly. *And if they haven't used it yet, why start now?*

It was cold comfort, but it was all she had. She pulled out the (red) sweater she'd bought in Billings and shrugged into it. Wearing something that wasn't in the school colors had never seemed more like an act of defiance, and the fierce joy she felt at defying Oakhurst disturbed her. It could so easily tip over into uncontrolled rage—and if she lost her self-control in this situation, she was doomed.

I need to talk to QUERCUS, she decided. She sat down at her computer, but she decided to check her email first. Just as well, as there were a dozen emails from Maddie about the Spring Fling. Spirit groaned as she skimmed them. *Who cares what music we pick? I bet Breakthrough's going to take over the entertainment just like they did at the Sadie Hawkins Dance.* At least the next meeting of the Committee wasn't until Wednesday. *And that means I get out of Endurance Riding that day!* she thought, and that actually was such a relief it made her feel almost happy.

She was just reaching for the Ironkey when there was a tap at her window.

She stifled a yelp and gingerly pulled back the curtain. Burke was standing outside in the snow. He waved.

"What are you doing out there?" she demanded, opening the window. She was glad she hadn't changed to her pajamas already—she wasn't quite ready to go there with Burke.

"Wanted to talk. Can I come in?"

Fortunately the windows in the ground floor rooms were large and low. She pulled it open as wide as it would go—the wave of cold night air was like opening a refrigerator, and she winced—and helped him climb through the window. He brushed off as much snow as he could before swinging his legs over the sill.

"Nice," Burke said, looking around her room. "Very, um, *pink*."

Spirit rolled her eyes. "I suppose yours is blue?"

He grinned at her. "What else?"

There was a moment of silence.

"So," she said. "How come we lied to Muirin?" She hadn't meant it to sound so much like an accusation, but she couldn't take it back now. "I mean—"

"We didn't *exactly* lie," Burke hedged. "I guess I wanted to talk to you first before we told the others—and I guess I wanted to tell them all together so we could figure out what to do next. I mean, we've found Merlin, so we just have to figure out how to . . . um, get him to help us, I guess."

"Are you sure?" Spirit said doubtfully. "About Merlin, I mean." Something still didn't seem right about Wolfman's story.

"You saw the picture," Burke said, sounding surprised at her question. "Stephen Wolferman's army buddy is Doctor A. With everything else Wolfman told us tonight, it makes sense: we know Mordred was in the oak, and he got out—the night of the 'Hellriders Massacre'—and the only survivor was Kenny's buddy Wolfman. And the only way that makes sense is if Kenny Hawking is Merlin. Wolfman should have been killed—or taken over like the others—I know I'm guessing about what happened to the Hellriders who vanished, but it makes sense, right?—but he wasn't. So Kenny—Doctor A—Merlin—must have protected him somehow."

"That makes sense," Spirit said slowly. "He must have been a Reincarnate—*the* Reincarnate, really. If Elizabeth was able to awaken her Reincarnate memories all on her own, then maybe seeing Mordred freed from the oak tree awakened Kenny's. So he chased Mordred away, or, or, or *something*. But"—the thing that was nagging at her was coming closer to the surface now —"why would he come back and found Oakhurst here? Around Mordred's oak tree?"

"That's the part that actually makes sense," Burke said. "You remember Ms. Groves telling us how magicians would put their spirit into something outside themselves—like a rock or a box—to keep it safe and make themselves more powerful? Maybe Mordred put his into the oak tree. Or maybe Merlin wants the oak tree so he can stick Mordred back into it again."

"Maybe," Spirit said doubtfully. "But if 'Kenny' is Merlin, he's supposed to be the good guy, right? So why is Oakhurst full of Shadow Knights? Why did he call them back here?"

"Maybe it's a trick," Burke said slowly. "Maybe he's called

them all back to trap them. Or . . . maybe he isn't really in charge. We wondered what the Wild Hunt was for. Maybe it was to keep Merlin helpless and trapped."

"But we got rid of it back in December," Spirit said, shaking her head. "So he ought to be . . . re-Merlinized, right?"

"Maybe he's trying. Maybe that's why he's seemed so weird lately. And I know December feels like a really long time ago, but . . . whoever called the Hunt and was making the sacrifices has only missed two so far—Midwinter and Candlemas—Imbolc. Maybe they have to miss a third one before the spell is really broken. And maybe Merlin can't figure out who's on his side any more than we can."

Spirit nodded slowly. Burke's explanation made as much sense as anything else, and she certainly didn't have one of her own. "But what if we're wrong about everything?" she said. "Burke, we're just guessing."

"I know," he said. "That's why I wanted to talk to you first."

Spirit bit her lip. "Do you think maybe we shouldn't mention the part about Merlin?" she asked hesitantly. "We know how Mordred escaped now. And we know the missing Hellriders became his first Shadow Knights. If we can find pictures of them . . . one of them has to be Mordred, right?"

"But you said yourself Merlin's the good guy," Burke said. "We can't know who he is and not tell the others. We need to help him."

"I guess you're right," Spirit said slowly.

"I hope I am," Burke answered. "Thanks."

"For what?" Spirit asked.

"For listening," Burke said. "For helping. I better go. It's after lights out and I don't have Muirin to make me invisible." He took her by the shoulders and kissed her on the forehead. "We'll get through this. You'll see."

He opened the window again and climbed out. Spirit reached to close it.

"And maybe Mr. Green can help, too," Burke said. He raised his hand in a wave and strode off.

Spirit closed the window very slowly. She'd been feeling better about everything—they'd found Merlin, and now he'd destroy the Shadow Knights and summon the Grail Knights—until Burke's last words.

The only people Mr. Green is going to help are the Shadow Knights! He's one of them! He's a friend of Ovcharenko's!

She pulled the curtains shut again and sat down on her bed. If Burke thought Beckett Green was on their side, what else might he be wrong about?

QUERCUS will know, she thought desperately. Her hands shook as she fumbled in the drawer for the Ironkey, but when she plugged it in and clicked the book icon, the chatroom window didn't appear. She opened her browser. Instead of the familiar intraweb home page, there was a white screen with the words SYSTEM DOWN FOR UPGRADES.

She was all alone.

❧

The day was cold. A raw gray wind whipped through the bare branches of the trees. It had been spring when Arthur drew the sword from the stone. It had been summer when they married. The years of Camelot seemed all too brief, as if the glorious reign of Arthur and Guinevere had only filled a handful of seasons. And now it was autumn. Arthur was dead and his kingdom was broken. All that remained were the magnificent white horses that had been her gift to him. Symbol of the king's justice and the rule of law.

There was one last sentence to see carried out.

"I will craft a prison that will hold you until the end of Time. . . ."

The memory of The Merlin's words gave her courage.

Guinevere heard muffled shouting and the clink of chains as Mordred Kinslayer was dragged to his prison. His hands were bound with iron and silk and ivy, his mouth had been sewn shut, his body was weighted down with a hundredweight of silver chains. Even such bindings would not hold him for long—but there was a stronger prison waiting.

Beside the sacred tree The Merlin waited, patient and terrible as the land itself. Arthur's knights pushed Mordred toward the oak with their wooden stangs.

The Merlin began to chant.

Mordred began to sink into the tree as if its wood were softened wax. He struggled, eyes wild with anger and power. In a moment more it would be done. The land would be cleansed of the terrible evil.

But at the last moment, Mordred tore loose the sinews that sewed his mouth shut and roared out a single terrible word. The chill gray of the day turned to howling darkness and killing cold—but The Merlin stood fast, and when the terrible darkness had passed, the oak's bark was seamless.

Mordred was bound.

The Merlin staggered forward, writing words of fire into the wood: a binding and a warning. Then at last, he turned to look at her. "It is finished," he said, in a voice flat with exhaustion. . . .

"Are you well?" she asked, and saw his mouth twist in a bitter smile.

"The Kinslayer made one last attempt to gain his freedom," The Merlin answered. "He cast a spell that will bind me to this aging flesh until the end of time. He means someday to escape his prison—and he means there to be no one left to fight him. But this prison will endure as long as the land itself endures. He has failed."

"But we will not fail," Guinevere said fiercely. "Hear my vow, Merlin of Britain: until Death itself claims Mordred Kinslayer, I pledge myself and my people to this task. When he comes, we will fight. And we will win."

"The land has heard your vow," The Merlin said. "And I pray the day you speak of never comes."

So do I, Guinevere said silently. So do I.

Spirit woke up feeling as if she hadn't slept at all. *Maybe I'm coming down with something,* she thought hopefully, before reflecting that even the flu wouldn't get her out of classes. They'd just Heal her with magic. And probably give her a demerit. Or a million demerits. When she'd come to Oakhurst, demerits had meant you were confined to your room between classes. Now . . . She shuddered. She wondered if enough demerits just meant you *disappeared.*

At least today she wasn't running late. She had time for a shower, even. When she finished dressing, habit made her check the computer again. The intraweb had been down last night. Did that mean they knew about QUERCUS?

Oh don't be silly, Spirit Victory White. If they did, you'd already be dead.

She winced as she played back her words in her mind. It was true. Loch wasn't the only one in mortal danger. Everyone at Oakhurst was—especially the five of them.

She took a deep breath. That ought to frighten her more than it did. It wasn't that she didn't believe it—she'd had plenty of proof in the last six months that it was true. It happened. It happened a lot. But the more she thought about it, the more she realized she was angry more than afraid. *It isn't fair. It isn't right. We've already lost our families. And nobody cared. And Oakhurst came and took us. And now it's trying to kill us.*

It wasn't fair. And she wasn't going to let them keep doing it. She didn't know how to stop them yet. She only knew she had to try.

The intraweb was back up this morning (of course it was, because she didn't have enough time right now to contact QUERCUS), and there was an email from STAFF saying students should expect intermittent outages for the next few days. *Great,* she thought, sending the email to TRASH. *And when it's working again, I bet it's going to be full of great new ways to spy on all of us. . . .*

Maybe they'd start turning on the web cameras without you knowing. She made a note to keep the lid of her laptop closed when she wasn't using it—the last thing she needed was for some Breakthrough nerd to be watching her in her under-wear.

She skimmed the other emails quickly. There was the usual Morning Motivational Message (she wondered who was writing them and if they were ever tempted to just recycle the old ones), and an email from the Dance Committee saying that due to construction on the school grounds, the Wednesday meeting would be held in Radial instead of at Oakhurst. *Rats,* she thought. *I'm not really looking forward to spending another three hours watching everybody drool over Breakthrough's shiny toys.*

She almost skipped the second email from STAFF, thinking the server had just hiccuped and sent the Motivational Message twice, but habitual caution made her open it to be sure. She was glad she had. She skimmed it quickly, then went back and read it more carefully.

Oh my god. Loch, you were right.

If you didn't have a suspicious nature—if you hadn't been at Oakhurst even as long as she had—it would have looked perfectly ordinary. It was the usual preachy "lets all get along" thing she'd seen so often. But this one was all about how the students of Oakhurst were the leaders of tomorrow, setting an example for everyone they met, and so they were reminded it was important to be tolerant of everyone's beliefs and lifestyles. Bullying or harassment of students on the basis of race, creed, or sexual orientation was absolutely forbidden.

"Sexual orientation"? Like if, oh hey, they just happen to be gay or something?

Oakhurst had been setting all of them at each others'

throats from the beginning. They didn't need to fight about religion (since Doctor A was doing his best to turn them all into atheists) or skin color (assuming there'd been anybody here who wasn't the whitest of white bread) when they could fight over who was the best *wizard*. Now Oakhurst was changing the rules. It didn't matter what it looked like on the surface: the email was telling them they were supposed to care about—and fight about—those things now.

I'm not your pet monkey, "Staff." I won't do it. And my friends won't either.

She wondered if Muirin knew what Breakthrough was doing. She was going to have to make up her mind about Muirin. About all of her friends, really. She couldn't go on just half trusting them, picking and choosing what she told them and doubting everything they did. *That's like being a little bit pregnant,* her mother's voice said in her mind.

I miss you, Mom, Spirit thought. *And Dad. And Fee. I wish . . .*

She didn't wish they were here. She wouldn't wish Oakhurst on her worst enemy, let alone on her family. She wished she was there—and even more than that, she wished Oakhurst didn't exist at all. She sighed. *Avast, me bucko,* Dad said in her mind. *Batten down the hatches and prepare to repel boarders!*

She smiled painfully. *I love you, Dad. I love you, Mom. I'll make you proud. You'll see.*

❧

In terms of what had become the "new normal," the day wasn't too bad. Mr. Green had taken over "gym class"—he worked them as hard as Ovcharenko had, but he wasn't a sadist about it, trying to *hurt them*. He actually seemed to care that they learn to protect themselves. Under other circumstances, she might have liked him.

If he wasn't one of Breakthrough's people.

If she wasn't afraid she was losing Burke to Breakthrough because of him.

There was another fight in the Refectory at lunchtime. Zoey and Maddie started screaming at each other about some Dance Committee thing, while Spirit did her best to become invisible so she didn't get dragged into it. The fight quickly got physical. This time Angelina Swanson and Daniel Stewart broke it up before the security guards could step in, but Angelina separated Zoey and Maddie by summoning a blast of air that knocked both girls sprawling.

That wouldn't have happened last September, Spirit thought, stunned. *Heck, that wouldn't have happened last month.*

"What the hell do you think you're doing?" Angelina shrieked.

Spirit tensed, certain something else horrible was going to happen—the School of Air had some of the most destructive Gifts of any of the four Schools: Weather Witchery, Transmutation, and all the forms of Communication and Control. They'd been taught the Communication and Control Gifts could only be used with animals, but Muirin had said once that if they were strong enough, they could be used on people too.

"Hey, hey, Angie, back it down," Daniel Stewart said. "Chill, huh?"

"Choose," Angelina said to Maddie and Zoey. "Demerits—or skip lunch." She smiled coldly. "I'd go hungry, if I were you."

Spirit finally took a deep breath when the three of them left the Refectory. *Wednesday's meeting is going to be fun,* she thought, wincing.

She didn't have long to worry about it. While she was waiting in the lunch line, Addie slipped her a note. They were meeting tonight.

What might happen there was a lot scarier than Dance Committee.

∗

Loch had found them a new hiding place. The Tyniger mansion was three stories high, but above the third floor there was a huge space—like an attic—where the servants' quarters were. The old servants' stairs had originally gone from the attic down to the first floor, but now they were blocked off below the third floor—and that meant, to get to the servants' quarters, you had to go all the way up to the third floor.

Before tonight, Spirit had never been above the second floor, where the Library, the lounges, and the Faculty Dining Room were. The third floor was the teachers' rooms, but despite the fact that they'd lost more than half the teachers since December, their Breakthrough replacements hadn't moved in to take their places.

Just as well, Spirit thought: if she or any of the others were caught up here, they'd really be in trouble. She breathed a sigh of relief when she reached the door at the back of the third floor—it looked like a closet—and ducked inside. It was dark and cold, and smelled of dust. She felt her way up the narrow wooden stairs by touch.

"This way," Loch whispered, when she reached the top.

She glanced around curiously. Spirit didn't know where the school maintenance staff lived (or had lived, before they'd mostly been replaced by Breakthrough thugs), but clearly it hadn't been here. The warren of tiny rooms under the eaves of the house had been deserted for a very long time.

There was a faint flickering glow coming from somewhere ahead, enough to light the narrow hallway. *Candles,* Spirit thought, and suddenly in her mind she was back in Stephen Wolferman's kitchen, listening to him rave and ramble and say things that were almost true. She swallowed hard. He'd been harmless. She'd known that. But somehow she was more afraid now, remembering him, than she had been at the time. Why?

When she reached the room, she saw it was barely bigger than the closet in her room downstairs. It was empty of furniture now, but there wouldn't have been room for much more than a bed here anyway. It was lit by candles stuck in bowls of sand. Not jar candles—tapers. Loch must have burglarized the kitchen, or wherever all the stuff from the formal dinners had been stored.

Guess it's safe. I don't think we're going to be having another of those anytime soon.

The others were already there. Even Muirin.

"The meeting of the Oakhurst Escape Committee is now in session," Muirin said sardonically. Despite herself, Spirit had to smile.

"How'd you find this place, Loch?" Burke asked as Spirit seated herself beside him.

"I've been spending my nights sneaking around the school seeing what I can find," Loch said. "If anyone catches me, all I have to say is I'm practicing my Shadewalking and I bet that'd get me off the hook. Oakhurst expects excellence—remember, an Oakhurst graduate who is merely average is one who has failed," he quoted in pompous tones.

Muirin snorted appreciatively.

"Couldn't you have found somewhere warmer?" Addie asked, shivering.

"This is the room farthest away from the rooms on the third floor that still have people in them," Loch said. "I'm not sure how well sound travels between floors. Also—window." He pointed.

"At least we might see them coming," Burke agreed.

"And without electricity, we're safe from the alien ninjas," Spirit said. Burke squeezed her hand.

"Yeah, okay, give," Muirin said impatiently. "You said you didn't get anything out of the guy—in which case, why am I here?"

"What guy?" Addie asked, confused.

Once upon a time, Spirit would have expected Muirin to pass on the information about her and Burke's trip to Addie—or she would have been able to tell Addie about it herself. Their desperate attempts to keep from attracting the Shadow Knights' attention were separating them almost as completely as the Shadow

Knights themselves. Spirit glanced at Burke, but he didn't look worried.

"Spirit found one of the bikers who'd been using this place as a clubhouse before it was Oakhurst, and we went and talked to him last night," Burke said.

"You *what?*" Addie exclaimed. "Without telling the rest of us?"

"*I* knew," Muirin said smugly. "Too bad it didn't do any good."

"I'm not completely sure about that," Burke said. "Stephen Wolferman—that's his name—was, um . . ."

"A few sandwiches shy of a picnic?" Loch suggested, and Burke grimaced in agreement.

"He was the only survivor of what the papers called the 'Hellriders Massacre'—the Hellriders was the name of their biker gang. On July 31st, 1971, half the gang vanished and the other half died. I don't know if he was crazy before he joined the Hellriders, or went crazy later, but yeah, like I said, he talked a lot about alien ninjas from the Shadow Dimension. But even so, I think we know how Mordred got out of the tree."

Muirin waved her hand impatiently.

Spirit sat quietly, letting Burke tell the story. He told the others what he and she had guessed, based on what Wolfman had said—and on the photograph he'd showed them.

"—and if Kenny Hawking isn't Doctor A, I'll eat that photo, frame and all," he finished.

Spirit had been waiting for some kind of blowup from

135

Muirin at the discovery they hadn't told her everything last night, but to her surprise it didn't come. "So let me get this straight," Muirin said. "We still don't know where Mordred is. But we've found Merlin?"

"He has to be, doesn't he? It's the only thing that explains Wolfman surviving the 'massacre' that night. He and Kenny were friends. Kenny has to have protected him, and only someone as powerful as Merlin could have stood up to Mordred. So Kenny must have been the Reincarnate of Merlin, and got Awakened, and protected Wolfman. Then I guess he must have run for it and hidden out for a while. Then he came back as Doctor A and started Oakhurst. He tried to get all the Round Table back together again."

"And ended up being held prisoner by the Shadow Knights," Loch said. "Which would explain a lot of things about Oakhurst. You know, we've been assuming the Gatekeepers and the Shadow Knights are the same thing, because the only Gatekeepers we've seen have been Shadow Knights. But it's possible they aren't. Maybe the Shadow Knights infiltrated the Gatekeepers at some point. And maybe Merlin—Doctor Ambrosius—never knew. And now they have him, and they've turned him senile or something."

"But that still doesn't tell us what Mordred wants," Addie said. "If he wants to be King of England—or just get his revenge on Arthur and the Knights of the Round Table—he's had almost forty years to do it. If Doctor Ambrosius can find every kid with magic, why can't Mordred find the Reincarnates?"

But he does—and he doesn't just find them, Spirit thought. *He kills their families—our families . . .*

"He probably has—and if you think I've forgotten that little Lizzie said Madison Lane-Rider was a Reincarnate and Anastus said I'm her sister, meaning I'm one too, think again," Muirin said. "But you know, it's a lot more fun to crushingly destroy everything the hero holds dear while he's still around to cry about it, which would also explain why Mordred didn't knock off Merlin when he got out of the tree. He's waiting until he's got everybody all together."

The others stared at her.

"What?" Muirin said. "I'm just saying. You know, I can't be the only one who's read *When I Am An Evil Overlord.*"

"In that case, we don't have a thing to worry about," Loch said blithely. "I haven't seen a single five-year-old child acting as an advisor to anybody."

"You make it sound like Mordred's *here,*" Spirit blurted out. "At Oakhurst." *Maybe Merlin doesn't know about our families, what happened to them. Maybe he thinks it was just accidents . . . maybe it was Mordred finding out where we were first, and then he saved us. . . .*

The silence that followed her comment was very loud, and she wished she hadn't said anything. But it was too late to take it back.

"I have a confession to make," Addie said after a moment. "Spirit, I never did apologize to you for thinking—for saying—you were being a drama queen about Oakhurst so you could be the person who solved the big problem. You weren't. You were right. And I wish I'd listened to you. But . . . you have to understand. Because you were right, it also means we're all in this way over our heads. Even if this were just a *normal* James Bond conspiracy—"

Muirin snickered, and Addie made a rueful face at her own words.

"—we know who some of the Shadow Knights are. Breakthrough is a huge and wealthy corporation. Anastus Ovcharenko isn't just their head of security, he's *Bratva*. And even if he weren't, Breakthrough has people who've been using their magic for years, not just months. Even if we got proof tomorrow that Mordred is, oh, say, Mark Rider—what could we do about it? Nobody will believe us—and we sure can't stop him ourselves. I'm just so tired of all of this," she finished in a whisper. "We're just kids. And we're up against—what? An immortal evil sorcerer? I want to be somewhere else. Anywhere else."

"We can't let them get away with what they've done," Burke said implacably. "Not to mention what they're *going* to do. There isn't anyone else we can bring in. Who'd believe us? We might just lead the Shadow Knights straight to a bunch of people they'll kill. It's down to us."

"We should sit tight and wait," Muirin said firmly. "This is the best place to hide. At least the Shadow Knights *want* us."

Muirin sounded as if she was trying to sell them on something, Spirit thought worriedly. What? Staying here and doing nothing until . . . whatever was going to happen, happened? Was it because Muirin thought that as one of the Reincarnates she'd be in a privileged position? Madison Lane-Rider was her Reincarnate-sister, and Madison was a Shadow Knight. Did that mean Muirin would become a Shadow Knight? Was she one already?

"So who cares if they're out to get Arthur's Round Table?" Muirin went on. "You keep saying they're evil, but isn't that kind of relative? OK, they want to bump off Merlin and any Reincarnates on his side that show up, but that's their feud, not ours. And we don't really know what they want to do after that. Maybe what they want to do isn't so bad. Maybe they'd be better at running things than Congress. Maybe all they want is to make video games. Maybe all that they want is England, and if that's all, I say let them have it."

"Your Russian boyfriend killed my parents, Muirin," Burke said, giving her a stony glare.

"Yes," Muirin said hastily. "And that was bad. Nobody says it wasn't. But look. Be smart. If we can make ourselves more valuable to Mark and Madison than he is, they'll turf him without a blink. You'll get your revenge. Meanwhile, we stay safe."

A month ago—a week ago—Spirit would have said Burke didn't want revenge, he wanted justice. She wished she was still sure of that. Seeing the way he'd attacked Ovcharenko had made her realize what he was capable of. It made her wonder if she knew him as well as she thought she did.

"And what if we can't . . . make ourselves more valuable," Loch said slowly.

"Then at least we don't get turfed *first*," Muirin said quickly.

"But Muirin, Burke's right. We can't just assume that—

aside from, oh, a few hundred murders—they're going to leave everybody alone. They're all *magicians*—and considering what they've already done just here, do you really want to let them . . . get away with whatever they're planning?" Spirit finished awkwardly.

"That's the trouble," Muirin answered. "We don't know who did what. We don't really know if Doctor A is *the* Merlin—or, you know, just some random Arthurian guy. We can't even be sure Mark Rider is a bad guy—remember, we're talking about people that lived in the Dark Ages, and they didn't work by the same rules we do. All we know about Mordred is from Arthur's gang. We don't know . . ." She trailed off, as if struck by something. "Hey, Spirit, didn't Lizzie say she wouldn't recognize any of the bad guys if she hadn't met them while she was Queen Guinevere?"

"Yeah," Spirit said. "But she was Yseult of Cornwall, not Guinevere. If she'd been Guinevere, she would have recognized everybody."

"Huh," Loch said. "You're right, Muirin. Good memory! And that tells us something we didn't know—Mark Rider can't possibly be Mordred."

Muirin beamed, and Spirit realized again how desperate Muirin was for affection. Desperate enough she'd even excuse Breakthrough's crimes just because they were nice to her?

She wished she knew.

"Did I miss something?" Addie asked.

"Elizabeth told Spirit she recognized Mark as one of Mordred's Shadow Knights. Which means Mark is the Reincarnate of someone Yseult of Cornwall met. And Yseult never met Mordred. So Mark isn't Mordred," Loch said.

Muirin made a face. "But he *is* a Shadow Knight. There goes my theory that he's possibly not a bad guy." She looked as if she had bitten something sour.

"Too bad," Burke said. "Maybe Merlin—"

"No, wait," Spirit said. "Guys. Why are we concentrating on Merlin?"

"Well *duh!*" Muirin said. "He stuck Mordred in a *tree!* Hel-*lo!*"

"But *Merlin* isn't Mordred's main enemy. *King Arthur* is. So where's Arthur?" Spirit asked.

"You mean *who's* Arthur, right?" Loch said.

"It's like *Where's Waldo?*, except now with added mortal peril," Muirin sniped. Even Burke smiled at that.

"You know," Addie said thoughtfully, "we're being offered courses in Norse Mythology, and Egyptian Mythology, and Greek and Roman Mythology, and Chinese Mythology . . ."

"And Serbo-Croatian Mythology and Finnish Mythology and it's not just a class, it's a mythadventure," Muirin said. "Your point?"

"My point is, the Arthurian Mythos is pretty big. So why aren't we getting it?" Addie said, frowning. "We get Celtic Mythology, yes. But that isn't the same thing."

"Grail, grail, the gang's all here," Loch said. The others winced at the pun. "It makes sense if we're living it, though."

"That's my point," Addie said. "We aren't being taught it because we'd find out something they don't want us to know."

"But everybody already knows it, don't they?" Burke says hesitantly.

"No," Spirit said decisively. "It's huge. My—" She swallowed hard and went on. "My sister was really into it. The stuff in the movies and on TV? That's just a tiny piece of one of the stories. Since we were homeschooled Mom even got Fee college books about it. People have been writing about Arthur and Camelot and the Round Table and . . . everything . . . for more than a thousand years."

"So which one's the true story?" Burke asked.

Spirit shrugged. "All of them. None of them. I don't know."

"The real question is: how much of it do *you* know?" Addie asked.

"Not enough," Spirit admitted sadly. "I always thought it was silly." *Oh Fee, I'm so sorry for all the times I teased you!*

"Silly or not," Burke said, "we need to know more than we do. Muirin's right. We don't know who did what. And we need to."

"Anybody want to bet that one-horse library down in Ice Station Radial's got a couple of books on the subject?" Muirin asked.

"Maybe," Loch says thoughtfully. "Don't you have Dance Committee on Wednesday, Spirit?"

Spirit groaned. "Oh god, don't remind me. Maddie and Zoey tried to kill each other at lunch today. And if Maddie isn't being ditzy and Dylan isn't trying to start trouble, Chris is bending over backwards to be helpful—which comes across as patronizing—and Juliette Weber patronizes him right back, and she can barely get a sentence out before Bella and Veronica are falling all over themselves to say 'Oh my god, you are so right, Juliette,' and—"

Burke chuckled. "Welcome to high school."

Despite everything, Spirit found herself smiling back. "Yeah. That's it exactly."

"Well maybe you could see what the town libe has," Loch said, resolutely ignoring the byplay.

"Nuh-*uh*," Muirin said. "She'd have to steal the books. And when we're talking about stealing library books, that's a job for . . . Super-Muirin!"

"Isn't that a bit below your pay grade?" Loch teased gently. Muirin stuck her tongue out at him.

"And once we've done the research, we decide whether we've got any chance at all of stopping Breakthrough and Mordred ourselves—or even of finding out what they actually want to do," Addie said, firmly dragging the discussion back on track. "I *still* say we should try to find someone who can help. I'm not denying Breakthrough is big, and the Shadow Knights scare me to death. But you know . . . Breakthrough is just a computer game company. Prester-Lake BioCo could buy it out of small change. And *I'm* Prester-Lake. You guys keep forgetting— maybe we're kids, but a couple of us are important kids, or at least, we're the heirs to important stuff. At the very least, I can get my trustees to investigate Oakhurst."

"If you can get to them without going on the run," Loch said. "Remember, once we run, we become runaways, and everyone knows bad things happen to runaways. Nobody would ever suspect Breakthrough if you ran and you . . . vanished."

This hasn't solved anything! Spirit thought wildly, as the others chattered excitedly. *We were supposed to come up with a plan tonight, think of something to do now that we know who Merlin is! Instead, everybody's talking about stealing library books, and Addie still wants to get somebody from outside to help, and . . .*

. . . And we think Doctor Ambrosius is Merlin. But what if Murr is right and Merlin isn't actually the good guy?

Suddenly the thing that had bothered her ever since they'd visited Wolfman came clear in her mind.

Wolfman was there when Mordred got out of the tree. Mordred had to have seen him. Why didn't he kill him—or take him over? We assumed his friend Kenny—who is now Doctor Ambrosius—protected him, but if he did, why is Wolfman so crazy now? Why didn't Kenny help Wolfman later—when he came back and founded Oakhurst? Why didn't he bring Wolfman to Oakhurst when he put the school together?

And why isn't "Kenny" using his own name? The other Shadow Knights are.

She didn't have any answers. And looking at her friends, she was afraid to even ask the questions.

SEVEΠ

Spirit was still mulling over the problem when the Dance Committee met again on Wednesday. She hadn't been able to talk to QUERCUS—the intraweb had been down again when she got back to her room Monday night, and it had stayed down all day Tuesday. She wasn't even getting out of Endurance Riding by being on Dance Committee anymore. The class had been canceled until further notice, so *nobody* had to deal with it. Spirit was guessing it was because of the monster, but she didn't know. For the first time, Oakhurst's news blackout was more than a minor annoyance. If the monster was still out there—and hadn't just vanished back to the same place things like the Wild Hunt had—it had to be attacking the local livestock. If it was . . . That would be proof, but proof of what even she wasn't sure.

Maybe proof that Merlin and the Grail Knights are somewhere

*nearby. Because whatever that thing is, it doesn't seem to be a part of
Breakthrough's plans.*

At least today she didn't have to deal with being at The Fortress. She guessed Mark Rider had really been annoyed with
Teddy for bringing them all onto the site last week. This time
nobody showed up to whisk them off anywhere, much to Kylee
and Dylan's disappointment, and they were meeting at the library.

The Radial Association Library had been remodeled when
it was turned from a house into a library, at least as far as knocking out some of the interior walls and turning doorways into
archways. But it still wasn't very big. The front room had the
checkout desk and the low shelves that held the children's
books. The back room had tall metal shelving (antique, cast iron,
and heavy) and a couple of battered wooden tables. The Radial
committee were gathered around one of them. There was a
huge goody basket on the table. Courtesy of Breakthrough. Of
course. The Radial kids had already opened the basket and
shared out the contents among themselves. The table was covered with cans of soda, cookies, cupcakes, candy bars . . . Chris
sat down and grabbed two Cokes, passing one to Zoey.

"Hey!" Erika said. "Those are ours!"

"You wish," Dylan sneered. He grabbed a Coke and plucked
the gift card out of the nearly empty basket. "To the joint Radial-
Oakhurst Spring Fling Dance Committee, with the best wishes
of Breakthrough Design Systems," he read out, sneering. "So
it's half ours—and you're half thieves."

He skimmed the card back into the basket and grabbed a

bag of chips and a handful of candy bars. He tossed them to Chris and Kylee and Maddie and Zoey, then grabbed an armful of sodas to pass around. He even gave Spirit one—not because he was suddenly her new best friend, but to irritate the Townies.

"So anyway," Brenda said, tossing her hair back and ostentatiously turning her back on the five from Oakhurst, "Dad was out at the Wolferman place all day dealing with County, and the Fire Marshall, and everyone. He said we were just lucky the fire didn't spread to the DOT barn—it took out that whole patch of woods."

"The Wolferman place." Wolfman.

"Was— Was anyone hurt?" Spirit asked hoarsely. Kylee frowned at her in puzzlement.

"Just the crazy old guy who lived there," Juliette said dismissively. "He was probably the one who started it. He was an ex-con or something."

"Crispy critter," Brett said, and snickered.

"The Fire Marshall said it started because of candles," Brenda said, happy to provide inside information. "Everybody knows the place hasn't had electricity for years."

The fire was obviously the most interesting news right now, and nobody seemed in any hurry to get down to Dance Committee business. It had apparently started early yesterday morning and ripped through the entire house. By the time the Fire Department arrived, all they could do was keep it from spreading.

Wolfman is dead, Spirit thought numbly, staring down at the unopened can of soda in her hands. *Burke and I went to talk to him, and a few hours later there was a fire.* She glanced at Zoey. Zoey was a Fire Witch. It was one of the more common Gifts— more than half the Oakhurst students had gifts from either the School of Fire or the School of Air. She didn't think Zoey had set the fire at the Wolferman place, but any Fire Witch could have done it.

Wolfman hadn't had a chance.

"We've got a lot of stuff to cover today," Maddie said, interrupting the gossip ruthlessly. She took out her spiral notebook (with the Oakhurst coat of arms printed on the front, naturally) and opened it to a blank page. "Especially the song list for—"

Suddenly the front of the building . . . exploded. *Wind attack!* Spirit thought automatically. In that instant she was grateful to Ms. Groves for teaching them things they thought they had no possible use for. She might not have any magic of her own, but Spirit knew every Gift and every spell any of the Schools could wield.

Shadow Knights! But why here?

Everything seemed to happen in slow motion. The windows, the door, the front wall itself sprayed across the floor into the back room, all reduced to tiny fragments. She winced and ducked—the air was full of blowing debris; it was like being an a wind tunnel. *Oh my god there were* people *in the front room. . . .*

The Radial kids were frozen in their chairs. The Oakhurst kids were up and moving.

Maddie screamed.

The figure striding through the hole that had been the front wall of the library was twelve feet tall, wore gleaming black armor, and had glowing red eyes. Spirit stared at it for a stunned moment because it seemed so familiar. Then she placed it: it was straight out of *Rise of the Black Dragon*. She'd seen it over at The Fortress last week when the others had been playing the new game.

An illusion. It has to be. But the damage the Shadow Knight could do was very real.

The assessment had taken her mere seconds, but it was long enough for a second and third armored figure to join the first. *The door—there has to be a back door—* Spirit thought frantically.

"Get up! Come on! Move!" she screamed. *They'll never cover this up. . . .* she thought inanely. Her ears were still ringing from the blast; she could hardly hear herself. Chris was standing next to her. She shoved him so hard he staggered into the table. "Get them!"

The Radial kids were finally starting to move. At least Juliette and Kennedy were. The others were still staring at the impossible—unbelievable—sight. Spirit grabbed the person nearest to her—it happened to be Dylan—and started dragging him toward the back of the room. There was a back door—she remembered now she'd seen it the other night when Muirin had parked in the library parking lot.

Spirit felt as if her mind were racing, as if she wasn't thinking, but remembering things she already knew. Maddie was a Water Witch, Kylee an Energy Mage, Zoey a Fire Witch, Dylan a Jaunting Mage, and Chris a Weather Witch. If they wanted to fight back, the only one whose Gift would be much use was Kylee's.

The wind was rising. She tripped over flying books, staggering sideways as much as forward. There was so much dust in the wind she couldn't see where she was going, and its howl was so loud she couldn't hear anything else. One of the Shadow Knight illusions picked up a chunk of debris and threw it; it struck the side of the arch and fell to the ground, sucked into the back room by the inexorable force of the wind. If the wind got strong enough, it would pin them against the walls, and they'd be battered to death by flying furniture. It was already swirling around the inside of the building like a tornado.

Like a tornado . . .

"Oh god!" Spirit cried.

She heard a ripping sound, saw light where there shouldn't be light as the roof tore away and walls collapsed. The floor shook. She didn't dare look back. She'd gotten to the door. She slammed her body against the crash bar with all her strength.

The door was locked.

She tried to turn back, tried to call for help, but there were people behind her, pushing her against the door. "It's locked! It's locked!" she screamed as she clawed her way through them going back the other way.

The front of the library was gone. Its ceiling and most of the front porch had been flung into the back room. She saw Zoey struggle out from under the fallen table, only to be struck and buried by a falling bookshelf. Zoey screamed. If the table hadn't still been half on top of her, she would have been killed instantly.

The room exploded into flame as Zoey panicked and lashed out with her Gift. Anything burnable carried by the mage-born cyclone sparked and sizzled; water droplets spattered Spirit's skin as windborne snow melted in the onrush of heat.

Kylee knocked Spirit sprawling as she ran past her toward their armored attackers. She held up her hands; Spirit felt a pang of vertigo, as if she was trapped in a plummeting elevator, as Kylee used her Gift to suck all the energy out of the room. The fire died. Even the wind died. The sudden silence was deafening.

"Come on!" Dylan screamed. Spirit dragged herself to her feet and staggered toward the back door—or where it had been. It was gone, and she didn't care how as she slipped and skidded on the steps. They were covered with fresh snow. The day had been clear a moment before. Now they were trapped in a blizzard.

Spirit tried to count—who was here, who was still inside? There were twelve Committee members, plus whoever else had been in the library. She saw Brett and Juliette ahead of her, but the snow was so thick she wasn't sure where the rest of the Townies were. She was here, and so was Dylan—

"*Chris!*" Dylan shouted, and ran back up the stairs.

"Stay here!" Spirit shouted to the others, and followed him.

The momentary calm was over. As she neared the door, she was hit by a blast of wind; she staggered, gripping the door frame to drag herself back into the building again. Books and pieces of wreckage slammed into the walls, making thudding sounds audible even over the howl of the vortex. She held up her hands to protect her face. The floor beneath her thrummed; the whole building creaked and shivered as if it was going to come down at any moment—or take off.

Near the center of the room, Chris was trying to lift the bookshelf off of Zoey, wincing and ducking as flying debris struck him. Dylan was dragging at Chris's arm, trying to get him to leave—Spirit could tell Dylan was Jaunting everything he could to keep it from hitting the two of them—the three of them. She lurched forward—there was a calm spot in the center of the ring of wind—and grabbed Chris.

"It's a storm! Chris! Stop the storm!" He stared at her, wild-eyed, then nodded. She only hoped his Gift was strong enough to do it.

Where's Kylee?

Kylee was standing in the wreckage of the outer room, facing down one of the Shadow Knights. The monstrous armored figure wavered as she sucked enough energy from it to make the illusion start to break up. Then it reached out and swatted Kylee—or seemed to—sending her flying. Kylee hit the wall of wind behind her as if it were an actual wall, but fell through it an instant later to land sprawling on the floor.

Spirit ran toward her, staggering as she entered the tornado again. Kylee was already up before Spirit got halfway across the room. She was bleeding from a dozen minor injuries, and beneath the blood, her face was a mask of rage. Suddenly Spirit was as afraid of Kylee as she was of the Shadow Knights. The power of an Energy Mage could kill: they manipulated energy—including life energy. Kylee started forward, clearly intending to renew her attack on the Shadow Knight.

"No!" Spirit screamed.

She didn't dare touch Kylee. The air around Kylee was so cold it smoked; she was drawing the energy out of everything around her, and if Spirit touched her she'd be dead instantly.

But before Kylee could reach the doorway, it burst into flame.

This wasn't the panic-stricken lashing out of a half-trained teenaged Fire Witch. This was fully controlled power. The sudden blast of furnace heat made Spirit stagger backward. The fire was licking over the walls, sucked along them by the vortex—in a moment everything in the room would be on fire.

"Stop it!" Spirit shouted, gasping for breath. She knew she couldn't make herself heard over the noise, but Kylee glanced toward her, lips drawn back in a fierce smile. She nodded as if she understood.

Spirit looked around wildly. Brett and Juliette were outside—who was still in here?

There.

She saw two figures huddled in the corner—Kennedy and Brenda. She ran to them. When she tried to pull Kennedy to her feet, Kennedy fought her.

"You're going to die!" Spirit screamed into her face. She couldn't hear the sound of her own voice over the roar of the wind and the fire. Despite all Kylee could do, the fire was gaining. "You're going to die if you don't move!" She grabbed

Kennedy and threw her as hard as she could. She was stronger than she'd been a few months ago. Kennedy went sprawling. She skidded through a puddle of water. Everything here that wasn't burning or covered in ice was soaking wet.

Brenda grabbed Spirit's arm and used it to pull herself to her feet. Her eyes were wild with panic. "Please," she said. Spirit read the word from her lips. She dragged Brenda to the doorway and just *shoved*. Brenda went sprawling down the stairs. Spirit turned back. Kennedy saw her and scrabbled for the doorway.

Two more safe. Out of how many?

The room was filled with fog now, as fire and ice clashed and filled the room with blowing, billowing steam. The flames turned the steam clouds red and gold. Spirit couldn't see anything. Not Kylee. Not Dylan or Chris. She groped back to where she'd seen Zoey, moving by touch.

Chris had his jacket off, using it to protect his hands as he and Dylan struggled to lift the bookshelf off Zoey and the table. *We're all going to die right here,* Spirit thought, in a moment of shocking clarity. The words in her mind seemed to come from outside herself. She couldn't imagine leaving Zoey here. And they couldn't move the bookshelf. It was too heavy to move. Zoey was trapped. *But we don't have to move the bookshelf . . .*

"Dylan!" she screamed at the top of her lungs. "Use your power!"

"Too heavy!" he shouted.

"No! Jaunt *Zoey*!" She didn't know the limits of Dylan's ability to Jaunt, or how much he could carry. From the despairing look on his face, he didn't think he could do this. "Dylan!" Spirit shouted again.

Suddenly time seemed to slow. Even through her pain and panic, Spirit felt an uprush of . . . *something*. It was like when she'd faced the Wild Hunt, like the night of the bonfire—she felt as if she was a conduit, a pipeline for a force so powerful she had no name for it. She reached down and gripped Dylan's shoulder. If the power was real, she willed it into him.

He stared up at her, white-faced, and reached for Zoey's hand.

The two of them vanished. Mist skirled into the place they'd been.

Chris lurched to his feet, gasping for air. "Tornado—" he said.

Suddenly the fire flared brighter. In seconds the temperature skyrocketed, baking away the fog. Kylee staggered toward them, beating at her burning clothes.

"Run!" she screamed.

The three of them reached the door together. Kylee vaulted the stairs, landing in a snowdrift and rolling—her skin was steaming from the energy she'd sucked away from the fire. Chris and Spirit skidded out after her.

An instant later, the building exploded.

They would all have been caught in the fireball, but it didn't swell outward the way it should have. It tried to, but before it could, it was sucked skyward, into the twisting black vortex of the monster tornado filling half the sky.

In a moment the funnel would drop down, and Radial would be gone.

"I can't— I can't—" Chris gasped, staring skyward in horror.

"You have to!" Spirit cried. She clutched at Chris's arm, desperately reaching for the power she'd felt before. *From me to you,* she thought dazedly.

Chris flung his head back and sank to his knees in the snow. There was a moment where everything was balanced on a knife edge. Spirit clenched her fists, *willing* Chris to succeed.

Then the wind dropped, going from gale to breeze to stillness in a matter of heartbeats. The temperature began to rise. The black whirlpool of clouds overhead stopped spinning and began to break up.

Chris began to laugh with sheer relief.

Spirit staggered to her feet and looked around. The parking lot was filled with drifts of rapidly melting snow. Dylan was curled up on his side, groaning and gagging. Zoey lay beside him weeping and clutching at her leg. Maddie stood in the middle of the parking lot, staring at the charred wreckage of the library with wide eyes. Juliette and Brett were nearby, also on their feet. Brenda and Veronica were with them. Veronica was crying; Brenda just looked stunned. Kennedy was standing at the far end of the lot, her back to everyone.

There were one or two other people standing in the street. Spirit couldn't tell whether they'd been inside the library or not.

"Where are Bella and Erika?" Spirit said slowly.

Juliette began to laugh hysterically. She jammed her fist into her mouth. Her twin put his arms around her. Her yelps of hysterical laughter turned to sobs.

Oh no. No!

In the distance, Spirit could hear the wail of sirens. The Fire Department would be here in seconds—and probably Breakthrough too.

"Listen," she said—not just to the Radial kids, but to everyone, "whatever you saw, whatever you *think* you saw, don't tell anyone. Especially anyone from Breakthrough. Stay away from them. Just— Stay away."

The others stared back at her silently, their faces blank with shock. Then Spirit saw Brenda's eyes fill with determination. "That's right," Brenda said loudly. "We don't know what happened. Kennedy! Get over here!"

Kennedy turned around. Brenda called her again and she began to walk toward them. Brenda stared into Spirit's eyes. Spirit tried to will belief. Acceptance. *I don't have time to explain, I can't explain, but please please please believe me and do what I say.*

"We don't know what happened in there," Brenda repeated when Kennedy reached her. "We were inside the library. Then we were outside. That's all we know."

"But—" Brett said.

"We didn't see anything," Brenda repeated meaningfully. "We don't know what happened."

"Where are Bella and Erika?" Kennedy asked. Her voice was hoarse and shaking.

"We don't know," Brenda said. "We hope they got out."

Spirit bit her lip and saw Brenda shake her head fractionally. They both knew the other two hadn't escaped.

She knew Brenda was going to want a real explanation.

And soon.

She wished she knew what she was going to say.

⬦

It was almost dark by the time Spirit, Chris, Kylee, and Maddie finally got back to Oakhurst. Breakthrough had gotten to the library even before the fire truck and Sheriff Copeland arrived. They'd sent for an ambulance—Breakthrough had its own, of course—and took Zoey and Dylan away immediately. The rest of them weren't as lucky. The pizza parlor was turned into an impromptu command center while Sheriff Copeland tried to find out what had happened. Nobody was sure how many people had died in the explosion. It might be as many as six.

To Spirit's relief, Brenda, Brett, Juliette, Veronica, and Kennedy stuck to their story. They didn't know what had happened. There was an explosion. They ran outside.

No one else in town had seen anything. (They certainly hadn't seen three characters from a video game trash the town library with magic.) After an hour or so the theory Spirit heard most was of there having been a freak tornado dropping a couple of tons of ice on the town and then ripping the library to shreds. It was as good an explanation as any, especially if they couldn't tell the truth. The hardest part was hearing Sheriff Copeland praise them for keeping cool heads in the emergency. Spirit had never felt so much like a hypocrite. They were being trained for this at Oakhurst—trained to be soldiers. And when a real attack came, they'd choked. And people had died. *At least we don't have to worry about what to tell them up at the school,* Spirit thought bleakly. *They'll probably just pretend it never happened. Just like usual.*

And the worst part was, none of them knew *why* it had happened. Why had the Shadow Knights attacked in broad daylight—in Radial—with witnesses?

Finally Sheriff Copeland let them leave. Ms. Corby and Mark Rider had come for them personally in one of the Breakthrough SUVs. But in all the confusion of the attack, Spirit had forgotten that while she and her friends all knew Breakthrough and the Shadow Knights were one and the same, Chris and Kylee and Maddie didn't.

"Are Zoey and Dylan okay? Are those the same guys that attacked us a couple of weeks ago?" Chris said as soon as the three of them were in the car.

Spirit winced mentally. She hoped the Townies did a better job of keeping their mouths shut, or they were all going to be in hot water.

"What happened down there?" Mark asked. He and Ms. Corby were in the front seat; the four of them were in the back. "Are you sure it was an attack?"

"I guess we just assumed it was magic," Kylee said smoothly, glancing sideways at Spirit as she did. "It was so freaky. There was this big explosion, and—wham!"

"So none of you saw anything more than you told Sheriff Copeland about?" Ms. Corby asked.

"I saw Dylan Jaunt Zoey out from under a bookcase," Maddie said. "Are they okay?"

"They're going to be just fine," Mark said. "Thanks to your quick thinking, nobody was hurt."

"Aside from the people who *died*," Spirit said.

"It's certainly a tragedy, Spirit," Mark said gravely. "And one we'll be able to prevent a recurrence of, fortunately. At least, once The Fortress is up and running. Naturally I'll have my people look into it to discover what really happened. But whether it was a freak storm—or not—I promise you, it won't happen again. We'll keep you safe."

Even Chris had nothing to say to that.

⁂

They'd all been checked out by the EMTs in Radial, so once they reached Oakhurst, they were sent directly to their rooms. Ms. Corby phrased it as a suggestion—*I know you'll be happy to get back to your rooms and rest*—but Spirit (at least) knew it was less concern for their well-being and more in the nature of damage control. If they were in their rooms, they wouldn't be telling their version of the afternoon's events to the other kids (Spirit had never quite figured out why the Oakhurst staff so consistently overlooked the gossip-spreading powers of the intraweb chat rooms). They'd missed dinner, but Ms. Corby said they'd be given trays in their rooms. Clearly that had been arranged beforehand, because when Spirit reached her room, there was a tray already waiting for her. She changed into fresh clothes before investigating it—the stuff she'd worn down to Radial was damp, muddy, torn, and reeked of smoke.

Now let's see what's on the menu for good little cannon-fodder. . . .

She lifted the cover off the meal tray and regarded its contents in disbelief. *No way did La Corby authorize this.* Instead of the usual "healthy menu," the tray held a sandwich, chips, a slice of chocolate cake, a can of soda, and an apple. She tucked the apple and the soda into the back of her chest of drawers for later, grabbed a bottle of water out of her fridge, and took her sandwich over to the computer. To her relief, the intraweb was up again. She didn't bother looking in to any of the chatrooms—the school might take the system down again at any moment—but scrabbled for her Ironkey and plugged it in.

The familiar window opened, and she breathed a sigh of relief.

Hello, Spirit. How are you this evening? QUERCUS typed.

I have a lot to tell you, and I don't know when the intraweb will go out again. Typing as quickly as she could, she told QUERCUS everything that had happened in the last few days: talking to Stephen Wolferman, identifying Kenny as Doctor Ambrosius, the fatal fire a few hours later, the attack at the library today.

—and it was Shadow Knights, right out in front of everyone, and if nobody saw it but us that would be one thing, but the Radial kids saw them too. And now Bella and Erika are dead, and I don't know how long the other five are going to keep their mouths shut about what they saw, and if they talk, what's going to happen to them? Now that we've found Merlin, we have to talk to him and tell him what's—

She didn't even get to the end of the sentence before QUER-CUS began to respond.

Do not approach Dr. Ambrosius under any circumstances. Do not tell him what you know. Do you understand?

Spirit stared at the line of text and the blinking cursor at the end of it for a long time before she responded.

Yes. But—

She didn't get to finish that sentence either. The special chat-room window vanished. She checked, and it wasn't because the intraweb was down again—when she checked, she could get out onto the Internet just fine. (The Radial Chamber of Commerce home page had a brief story about the "freak storm." It mentioned the dead and missing, but there were no names listed. Probably because their families hadn't been notified yet.)

She unplugged the Ironkey from her laptop and sat staring at the Oakhurst home page.

"I don't understand," Spirit whispered to herself. Why didn't QUERCUS want her to talk to Merlin? Why had QUERCUS signed off without letting her ask any questions?

And why had they been attacked in the first place?

Since she couldn't talk to QUERCUS, she logged into the main school chatroom and watched the conversations scroll by. She groaned. *Can't any of you morons remember for five minutes at a time the Staff and the Proctors read every word of this?* Chris and Maddie were both giving a full account of the attack at the library, including detailed descriptions of their attackers. At least

Dylan and Kylee weren't in-channel, and Zoey was probably still in the infirmary. Spirit could only be grateful her own name didn't come up. She closed the window before somebody could PM her to demand her version of events—because as of now, her choices were to agree with the story the others were telling, or call them liars, and neither option seemed that good. She got to her feet with a growl of frustration. *I'm going to go crazy sitting in here talking to the walls.*

She looked around the room and frowned, then checked her watch to be positive. *Nope. Nowhere near lights out.* There was no reason she actually had to stay in her room if she didn't want to.

She wasn't going anywhere in particular—she just wanted to be somewhere there were people—but when she passed one of the lounges and saw Loch, Burke, and Addie inside talking, she was confused and curious enough to investigate. *I thought we all agreed to stay away from each other in public. . . .*

"—so I really think that's best. It will take a couple of weeks to make the arrangements," Addie was saying.

"Arrangements for what?" Spirit asked.

Addie's face lit up with relief at the sight of her. "I'm so glad you're okay!" she said in a rush. "I heard about . . . what happened today in Radial. I was outside when it happened—you could see the explosion all the way up here—so I went and found Muirin. She'd been listening to the Radial police band up in the Security office, and told me what was going on and, well . . . I went to see Doctor Ambrosius. I've asked him to contact my trustees. He says he'll have me moved to a different school.

163

Somewhere I can actually—help. He says that's where he's sent all the kids that have been going missing—he says they weren't safe here, so he's sent them away."

Spirit tried not to look as shocked and betrayed as she felt. Never mind that Addie was suddenly buying into this story of the missing kids being "sent away somewhere safer"—Addie wanted to *join* them.

"You can't just leave!" Spirit said incredulously. Was that the real reason she'd cautioned the other members of the Dance Committee not to say anything about the attack, she wondered? Fat lot of good it had done!

"I am not Wonder Woman," Addie snapped. "I did not sign up to save the world!" She got to her feet and stalked out of the lounge.

Spirit looked at the two boys helplessly. Burke was already getting to his feet. *Oh good,* she thought in relief. *He's going after Addie. He'll talk her out of this stupid idea.*

"Hate to run out on you," Burke said, "but I've got an extra practice session scheduled with Mr. Green. At least we got one good teacher out of this whole mess, right? Maybe he can help us with . . . the thing."

"Sensible—in Burke's tiny mind—means he isn't actually getting *hit,*" Loch snarled as soon as Burke was out of earshot. "Do you know Green's changing all the PE classes around again? One of the new buildings going up is a shooting range. It won't be ready until Spring, but hey, that's okay, because we can do trap-shooting outdoors, right?"

"That's always been an elective," Spirit said slowly. She knew how much Loch hated guns of any kind.

"Not anymore," Loch answered grimly.

Before she could think of anything to say, Loch was on his feet and moving, too. "No, wait!" she called after him. "Loch!"

Loch kept on walking as if he hadn't heard.

Spirit stood looking after him forlornly. After what had happened this afternoon, this was the final straw. *This isn't how it's supposed to go! Don't all of you see—they're trying to break us up again! Only this time they're doing it by making us think breaking up is the way to fix things. They're scaring Addie—and being nice to Burke— and making you think anything's better than staying here. . . .*

And she couldn't figure out how to convince the others their plans simply wouldn't work.

✦

W hat are you doing in here, Nancy Drew? Looking for clues?" Muirin asked, walking in and closing her door. She was dressed for outside, though not (of course) in anything like the school uniform.

Spirit got to her feet. She didn't need to look at her watch to know it was well after lights out now. She shouldn't have been in Muirin's room at all.

"I was just waiting for you. I didn't touch anything."

"Good," Muirin said. She walked into her closet to hang up her coat.

Spirit wondered what Muirin had been doing out so late

after curfew, and—worse—who she'd been doing it with. They all *knew* Ovcharenko was a murderer now. Breakthrough's pet hitman. Was Muirin so desperate for safety that she didn't care?

Or was she one of them now?

"I wanted to talk to you," Spirit blurted out as Muirin came out of the closet again with her arms full. Not one thing in that pile of silk and lace would have passed the Oakhurst dress code.

"Hold that thought," Muirin said, vanishing into the bathroom.

She came out again a few moments later. Her face was scrubbed clean—thinking back, Spirit wondered if she'd ever seen Muirin without makeup before—and she was wearing a black velvet floor-length robe that looked as if it ought to belong to Elizabeth the First—or maybe Vlad the Impaler. The lapels and cuffs were red satin stitched in gold thread, and there was a double row of gold frogs down the front.

"Don't gawk," Muirin said, smirking. "Secretly I've got on Hello Kitty jammies under this."

"Your secret is safe with me," Spirit said, smiling back hopefully.

"Yeah, well, I've got an image to protect," Muirin said. "Hey. We heard about what happened down in town today. That had to suck."

"Six people dead—and oh god, Murr, two of them were on the Dance Committee, and that shouldn't make it worse, but . . . I *knew* them. And now Addie's asked Doctor Ambrosius to move her to another school, and Burke thinks Mr. Green—he's Breakthrough, Muirin, a *Shadow Knight*—is the greatest thing in the history of ever, and Loch . . . Loch's just giving up."

Muirin sat down beside Spirit on the bed. "Well, you know, that's probably for the best," she said consideringly.

Spirit glanced toward her in surprise. This wasn't the reaction she'd expected.

"Look, I don't want to hurt your feelings or anything. You've been a good friend. You trusted me when nobody else would. That means a lot to me. But it's only in bad movies where a bunch of kids can destroy a giant international conspiracy of Eeeevil. Addie was right. We can't do it, we're only kids, and it isn't our fight in the first place. Who cares what they want? They're after Merlin and Arthur. Big whoop. So Evil wins: it'll all be a bunch of behind-the-scenes stuff and people like you and me will never see any difference. There's no way we can beat the Shadow Knights, or stop what they're planning, and . . . I don't want to die, Spirit. I really don't. I'm going to go along with whatever they want until I can get the hell out of Dodge. You and Loch were supposed to be the Midwinter Tithe to the Wild Hunt. Remember? You two were the only ones who heard the hunting horns. He's on borrowed time. Both of you are. And that was before the Gatekeeper Army of Darkness got here."

"Don't you care about all the people they've killed?" Spirit asked desperately. *And you're a Reincarnate, Muirin. They aren't going to just let you walk away. They'll make you choose. One side or the other.*

167

"Always with the high horse!" Muirin mocked. "I bet you they haven't killed as many people in the last forty years as die in car crashes on one holiday weekend. Read my lips: *I want to live*. And . . ." For a moment Muirin hesitated. "Like I said. You've been a good friend. You want to stop your preaching and stick with me, I'll see what I can do for you."

I'm not going to cry, Spirit told herself wildly. She wasn't going to call Muirin a sellout or a coward. "What about Burke?" she asked. *What about Burke and Loch and Addie and anyone you've ever thought of as a friend? They killed Seth—doesn't that matter to you anymore?*

Muirin didn't answer, her jaw set in a stubborn line. "You let me know when you've made up your mind," she said finally. "Just don't wait too long."

Could I do it? In the Library, Spirit stared blindly at the row of books on the shelf in front of her. *Everyone else is giving up. It's not like I'd be letting them down. Should I tell Muirin I'll do it?*

She'd gotten through the day in a daze, too stunned by Addie's defection and Muirin's offer to do more than go through the motions. She couldn't stop thinking about them. This was the end. The end of everything. Loch had given up, Addie was willing to hand herself over to Oakhurst and let them do whatever they wanted, and Muirin had as good as told her she was going to throw in with the Shadow Knights to stay alive.

And Burke . . . What about Burke? Muirin hadn't been willing to make any promises about Burke's safety.

He'll be safe. Mr. Green will protect him. And Burke . . . he already thinks Mr. Green is a friend. If I say we should trust him and go along with whatever he says, Burke will be happy to. We'd be safe . . .

She shook her head, even though there wasn't anyone there to see it. Even though she didn't know what it would involve, she couldn't take the easy way out.

Easy? When has anything at Oakhurst been easy?

It was late afternoon. The kids with magic were doing their magic practice. She . . . was doing her homework. She stared down at the pile of books and papers on the table, remembering when the most horrible thing in her life had been homework. Now homework was practically a vacation.

Was it just three months ago the five of them had been huddled around this exact table trying to figure out a way to destroy the Wild Hunt? She remembered how scared she'd been. How hopeless it had seemed. She'd never imagined she'd look back on those days with longing, but even as scared as she'd been then, she'd still believed it was possible to win. . . .

And now she knew they couldn't. Muirin was right. Addie was right. They had two choices: die, or give in to what the Shadow Knights wanted—and live.

Despite herself, Spirit began to cry. She would have gone back to her room, but she'd have to go through the halls and the Entry Hall to get there, and everyone would see her. She buried her face in her hands and did her best not to make any noise.

"You're far too young to be weeping in corners, Miss White."

The voice came in the same moment a hand descended on her shoulder. Spirit jerked upright with a gasp.

Ms. Groves was regarding her solemnly.

"I—" Spirit began.

"Come with me," Ms. Groves said.

EİGHT

"*N*ow we can talk without being disturbed," Ms. Groves said, closing the door behind them.

Ms. Groves's room—*rooms*—were up on the third floor. Unlike Spirit's bedroom, it was divided into two separate rooms, a bedroom and a sitting room, with a door between. The furniture was the same style as in Spirit's sitting room, but there were more and different pieces—Ms. Groves's sitting room was filled with bookcases and books, and there were pictures on the walls. Photos, mostly: some of kids in Oakhurst uniforms, some of Ms. Groves herself in what looked like exotic foreign places.

"Tea, Miss White?" Ms. Groves asked matter-of-factly. "I find it loosens the tongue." Without waiting for a reply, she walked into the other room, returning with an electric kettle. A few moments more, and she was setting a cup on the table beside Spirit.

"Perhaps you're still upset by your experience in Radial yesterday," Ms. Groves said, though not as if she actually believed it.

For a moment Spirit froze. Ms. Groves—acerbic, demanding Ms. Groves, her History of Magic teacher—wanted to know why Spirit was upset. Wanted her to explain—just the way Ms. Smith always did, going on at everyone in Math Class to "share" their fears and nightmares until half the class ended up in tears—or vanishing.

She shouldn't. It was insane to think even for an instant of trusting Ms. Groves. She'd been a teacher here at Oakhurst for years—and she was *still* here, when nearly all the other teachers had vanished, replaced by Shadow Knights.

But the need to confide in her—the sense it was something right to do—was almost overwhelming. It should have terrified her (no one knew what School Ms. Groves belonged to, only that she was a Mage), but it didn't. The feeling was more like the rush of power she'd felt at the library. It was strong, compelling—but it felt *right*.

"It's not that," Spirit said. "Well, it *is*. But it's more— everything!"

The words came tumbling out of her as if she was confiding in someone she trusted . . . as much as she'd trusted Mom. Or Dad. She found herself telling Ms. Groves that Addie was leaving, Muirin was making unwise (dangerous) choices, Loch was giving up, Burke was trusting the wrong people. *It's odd*, she thought while she was talking. *Ms. Groves has always been snarky and strict and gave us extra homework if we even blinked in class, and Ms. Smith is always telling us we can talk to her and saying it's all right to be scared and everything, but I'd rather talk to Ms. Groves. . . .*

"—and they know about the—about the *bad people* who are here, and people keep dying—or vanishing—and—"

Ms. Groves set her teacup down and drew a quick shape in the air. Spirit felt a sensation like her ears popping from overpressure and broke off, blinking at Ms. Groves in surprise.

". . . and you're afraid that when the Day of Reckoning comes—as it will—you won't be able to cope with it all by yourself, aren't you?" Ms. Groves said calmly.

Now Spirit found herself gaping in astonishment, too stunned to be scared.

"My specialty—as you are well aware—is the History of Magic, which *some people* should take into account," Ms. Groves said, with a touch of her usual barbed tones. "Yes, you're in danger. Yes, so are your friends—any of the students who won't fall under the Breakthrough *glamourie* are in danger. And now you're wondering, Miss White, why if I know all this, I haven't helped you, or done something, or warned anyone. And the fact is, you don't know who I may have helped or warned, and I don't intend to tell you, either."

"I— But— I— You—" Spirit stammered.

"Do put your thoughts in order before speaking, Miss White," Ms. Groves said severely. "Babbling and stammering is *most* unattractive, as well as evidence of a disordered mind."

"But you're one of the teachers!" Spirit burst out, blushing furiously.

"Indeed I am," Ms. Groves said. "But flattering as your implied opinion is, I must inform you I am certainly not powerful enough to oppose the forces arrayed against us by myself. Even saying as much as I am puts us both at risk."

"Then why are you doing it?" Spirit asked carefully, choosing her words with care.

"Because you haven't come into your Power yet. And that is a very good thing. The spells being woven around Oakhurst and the other children here can't affect you as strongly. They're keyed to Gifts, you know. They draw their power from one's innate magic—a thing which you have not yet manifested. Yes," Ms. Groves continued, nodding in answer to Spirit's unvoiced question, "that's one of the reasons why, from the very beginning, you've noticed things about Oakhurst that no one else has. When you tell people what you see, you can break the *glamourie* that keeps them from seeing it—you have done a great deal of that without being aware of it. But in future I would be very careful about continuing to do so, if I were you. They know which of the students are not . . . fully bespelled. And they are watching all of you."

She drew another symbol in the air, holding a finger to her lips to warn Spirit to silence, and the ear-popping sensation came again.

"Now," Ms. Groves said briskly, as if the last few minutes hadn't occurred at all, "you've showed a great deal of promise in your studies, so I'm inclined to think you'd benefit more from an independent study program. Do you have any ideas about what you'd like to study?"

As she spoke, she walked over to one of the bookshelves and took down a book about the size and thickness of a dictionary. She walked back to where Spirit sat and handed it to her. The book weighed at least two pounds, and it was so old and worn there was no title on the front or the spine. When Spirit opened it, the title page said: *The Matter of Britain: Arthur, Camelot, and the Grail 1100–1500.*

Spirit hesitated for only a moment. "I've gotten really fascinated with the folklore and mythology of the British Isles, Ms. Groves, so I'd really like to study that," she chirped brightly.

Ms. Groves smiled at her approvingly. "A very good choice, Miss White. Let me know if you have trouble finding what you need in the Library. And now, I believe it is almost time for you to report to the Refectory for dinner."

Spirit got to her feet. "Yes, ma'am. Thank you, Ms. Groves."

"Don't mention it, dear child. I certainly won't," Ms. Groves said.

◆

Friday was miserable. Spirit had tried to talk to Addie at breakfast, only to have her turn her back and walk away. When she got to Gym Class (it wasn't *Systema* now, Mr. Green was just calling it "Training") she saw Burke and Mr. Green standing together, waiting for the others. Mr. Green said something she couldn't hear, and Burke laughed. Mr. Green put an arm around his shoulders, beaming at him proudly.

It made her stomach hurt. She guessed this was what love was—to miss someone when you were just standing across the room from them, to think of everything that happened as something you wanted to share with them, to ache with worry when you thought they were in trouble. *I don't have time for this!* she thought in mournful exasperation. How could being in love make you happy and miserable at the same time? Without knowing Burke loved her, she would have despaired a long time ago, but . . .

It was distracting her, keeping her from focusing on anything else. And that wasn't just inconvenient right now.

It might be fatal.

All that was bad enough. But because the class was larger now and ran longer, Loch was in it too. He was standing next to Noah, one of the other "Platinum Spoon" boys, and Spirit thought nothing of it—until she saw a couple of the other boys nudging each other and pointing at them when they thought nobody else was looking.

Loch looked miserable.

Spirit didn't see Muirin anywhere at all that day. Not in the Refectory, and not in the halls. She had a sense of what Mom would've called "waiting for the other shoe to drop," and Spirit wasn't quite sure what was causing it. It was almost anticlimactic to hear (at dinner that night) they were going to a new schedule. There'd be classes on Saturday now, as well as a half day of classes on Sunday.

Who needs magic to keep us from noticing things? They'll just work us all to death.

She went back to her room right after dinner and read the book Ms. Groves had loaned her until she fell asleep. She didn't even try to talk to QUERCUS. Why should she? He'd started acting as weird as everyone else.

✦

As some of you know from experience—ha!—there is 'escaped tiger' at large," Ovcharenko said, striding back and forth in front of the clump of miserable students gathered on the shooting range. "It is necessary for you to be able to protect yourselves at all times. This we will now learn!"

He beamed at his audience in a way they'd all learned to distrust. The two men in Breakthrough Security uniforms behind him stood perfectly still, as if they saw and heard nothing.

The morning email had included the schedule of Saturday classes. Most of them were combat-oriented, and because the same email went to everyone, Spirit knew that Saturday afternoons would now involve "combat drill" in which two teams, chosen by Ovcharenko, would compete against each other using their Gifts. Spirit shuddered. She'd never been happier to be a Muggle.

But that didn't get her out of her new Saturday morning class. She was scheduled for "Introduction to Shotgun and Rifle," meaning she'd been told to report to the range right after breakfast. There were about twenty kids here—this was the "beginners" class, for anyone who'd never taken skeet or trapshooting before. That let Burke and Addie out, and Muirin obviously knew how to shoot a gun plus having a free pass with regard to everything.

That just left her and Loch. She kept glancing toward him. Loch had his head down, ducked into his scarf, and his shoulders hunched. It wasn't because of the cold—the Skeet Range was actually pretty warm. There were a bunch of giant outdoor heaters set up, but Spirit was willing to bet the main heating element here was (duh) magic.

The Skeet Range didn't look anything like the firing ranges Spirit had seen in movies or on television. It just looked like an open field. There wasn't anything to stand behind to shoot— the only table here was covered with shotguns. Halfway across the field were two large boxes, one set at either edge. Spirit wondered if they were supposed to shoot at them.

"And so, we teach you the use of weapons," Ovcharenko said. He walked over to the table and picked up one of the guns. "A shotgun—completely harmless, eh? *Pull!*"

One of the security people pulled out something that looked like a television remote. Suddenly both of the boxes out in the field started flinging disks into the air. Spirit knew from what Burke had said that the disks were made of clay— like a flowerpot—and weighed over two pounds each. It seemed a little eerie to see them zipping into the air like Frisbees.

Ovcharenko swiftly flipped the gun to his shoulder and began to fire. When it was empty, he grabbed a second one and continued shooting. Every shot found its target. Every target disintegrated into a spray of dust.

Harmless? Spirit thought. *Anything that can do that to a big clay disk doesn't look harmless to me.* "I thought Ovcharenko wasn't a Combat Mage," Spirit muttered.

"Ovcharenko's an Air Mage. He's using a form of Kenning Magic," Loch said, moving toward her. "He can Know something so thoroughly he can quickly become an expert."

She wondered how he knew. Loch's Gifts were School of Air. Maybe that was how.

The security guard who didn't have the remote control finished reloading the shotguns Ovcharenko had fired. When he was finished, Ovcharenko picked up the nearest one and walked toward Spirit. He was grinning.

But Spirit wasn't his target.

"Take it," he said, pushing the shotgun at Loch. "Take it! Only *pidoras* would be afraid of a little shotgun, eh?"

Spirit saw Loch clench his jaw and grab the shotgun out of Ovcharenko's hands. Ovcharenko gestured for him to follow, and walked forward until Loch was standing about ten feet in front of the class. Then Ovcharenko went back to the rest of them, choosing students seemingly at random. He handed each of them a shotgun and lined them up next to Loch.

The last one he chose was Spirit.

"Come! Come!" he said, thrusting the shotgun at her. She clutched it, terrified she'd drop it and it would go off. It was heavier than she expected it to be. She took her place at the end of the line. *Maybe this will be over soon,* she thought hopefully. She hoped so. She'd never seen Loch look so furious. And she had absolutely no interest in firing a shotgun.

"We shoot from left to right," Ovcharenko said, brandishing his own weapon. "Pull!"

That means Loch shoots first and I shoot last, Spirit thought. *I just hope Loch doesn't decide to shoot Ovcharenko.*

A movement out of the corner of her eye caught her attention, and she looked toward it. Mr. Green was walking up around the edge of the crowd. Behind her, she heard the *whing!* of the trap, followed by a thud as the clay disk hit the ground. She looked back quickly. Ovcharenko was leaning close to Loch, speaking so quietly she couldn't hear. Loch's face was white with rage.

Ovcharenko stepped back. "Pull!" he shouted again.

She saw Loch raise the shotgun and looked away quickly. It seemed wrong to watch.

There was the sound of a shot.

Loch screamed.

Spirit turned back quickly, almost dropping the shotgun she held. She saw the shotgun in Loch's hands slew around as if it was dragging him. It swung back and forth—as if he was fighting with it but was unable to drop it—and Loch didn't look furious now. He looked terrified.

The other students holding shotguns shifted uncertainly, milling about in place and bumping into each other. They weren't quite scared enough to run—or maybe they were as scared as Spirit was of the shotguns they held accidentally going off. While everyone was still shifting nervously, Loch stopped moving.

The shotgun in his hands was pointing straight at her.

He's going to shoot me, Spirit realized numbly. She wanted to run, but she was frozen in place.

Then . . .

There was the sound of a shot.

Spirit screamed and clutched the shotgun in her arms, too terrified to drop it.

Everything happened so fast.

Beckett Green jumped in front of her. The load of heavy steel shot struck him, knocking him backward. He fell against her. She staggered backward, and would have fallen if someone behind her hadn't caught her.

Mr. Green took a step, then fell to his knees. Then he collapsed, facedown, on the ground. Everyone was screaming.

Loch, Loch, what about Loch—

She looked up just in time to see Loch take his shotgun by the barrel and swing it at Ovcharenko as hard as he could.

❧

Spirit was huddled on one of the couches flanking the fireplace in the Main Hall. She'd chosen the one facing the oak tree that formed the central pillar of the space. Sitting with her back to it—now that she knew what it was—gave her the creeps. Muirin and Addie both seemed to agree; they were sitting on either side of her. Burke was standing in front of the fireplace, not looking at any of them.

Only Loch was absent.

Loch was in Doctor Ambrosius's office with Bethany Mitchell and Thomas Carter, the two detectives from the Sheriff's

Office who'd investigated—or *not* investigated—the disappearance of Nick and Camilla last October. Spirit had been angry then, thinking they just didn't care. Now she was pretty sure they'd been bespelled into dropping the case.

Spirit knew Addie and Burke—if not Muirin—had places they were supposed to be right now, but as soon as the word had swept through the school about the disaster on the shooting range, they'd shown up. They'd been waiting with Loch when Spirit finished giving her statement. She'd kept it brief: *I was waiting to shoot. I heard someone yell. Then Mr. Green jumped in front of me.*

It was the truth. It just wasn't all of it.

"Why couldn't someone save him?" Addie asked, her voice nearly a whisper. "A Greater Healing can do everything short of raising the dead."

"There wasn't anything to Heal," Muirin said flatly. "His body started dissolving almost immediately—and what it dissolved into was sticks and mud."

It was true—or at least it was what Spirit thought she'd seen before someone had thrown a tarp over the body and hustled them all into the gym. (This was Oakhurst; even when you saw something, you couldn't believe your eyes.)

Burke winced slightly at Muirin's words. Spirit felt sorry for him and angry with him at the same time. He'd lost a friend. But he shouldn't have had . . . *that* friend. *But maybe Burke was right and I'm wrong. Mr. Green sacrificed himself to save my life . . . I think. Would a Shadow Knight have done that?*

"That isn't possible," Addie said, shaking her head. "It must have been . . ."

"An illusion?" Muirin asked. Her tone was mocking, but Spirit could tell it was a put-on. "Ads, Dave Griffin came and got me to talk Anastus down off the ledge—and incidentally keep him from going after Loch, you can thank me later. *I saw the body.* You know a Gift can't fool someone with the same Gift. I might not be able to see through an illusion, but I'd know it was there. That means—"

Suddenly the door to Doctor Ambrosius's office opened. Loch stumbled out, white-faced, looking as if he'd been crying. He saw the four of them—his face twisted in revulsion, and he turned to head off the other way. But he wasn't fast enough. Burke was across the expanse of the Main Hall before he'd taken more than a few steps. He put a hand on Loch's arm, and Spirit thought Loch might have shrugged it off if the two detectives hadn't come out next. Ms. Corby was with them. She looked over at Spirit, Muirin, and Addie, giving them all a venomous glare.

"Mr. Spears, you can't blame yourself for any of this. Mr. Green's death was a terrible accident, but that was all it was—an accident," Detective Mitchell said. She waited a moment, but if she was expecting a reply from Loch, it didn't come. Detective Mitchell shook her head and walked quickly after her partner.

❧

Spirit was on her feet before she thought. As she neared Burke and Loch, she could hear what Loch was saying. "—I'm fine.

If you want to be a little friend to all the world, there are a number of more suitable—" He broke off as he saw Spirit. "Is there any possibility you'll all go away?"

"Look, I have to talk to all of you," Muirin said. "It's important, and it can't wait."

"Yeah, well, I'm not really in any mood to hear about your new friends and your new clothes right now," Loch snapped waspishly.

Burke looked irritated, obviously thinking Muirin was just trying to make herself the center of attention at the worst possible time. Even Addie—Spirit glanced toward her—looked long-suffering.

Muirin looked at all of them and her face lost all expression. "Fine. See you guys around," she said coldly. She turned to walk away.

For an instant, Spirit wondered if they should just let her go. Was Muirin taking advantage of Loch's grief and misery to make another pitch for the Shadow Knights? But . . . no. If that were the case, she wouldn't have asked to talk to all of them. *And didn't Ms. Groves say the whole place is full of "don't think" spells? This is the first time Muirin's asked for a meeting since before we defeated the Wild Hunt.*

"I think we should listen to her," Spirit said quickly. She turned and ran after Muirin.

"Wait, Murr!" she said, catching up to Muirin. "You're right. If you say it's important, I believe you."

"Why should I bother?" Muirin said. Her voice was harsh, but her expression was lost and unhappy.

"Because we're friends," Spirit said. "Because we believe each other. Because we believe *in* each other." *That's what faith is,* Spirit realized in surprise. *And if we don't have faith in each other, who will?* "If we don't all stick together, what's going to happen to us?"

To her relief, Muirin let her turn her around and walk them both back to the others. "This is a good time, really. Nobody's going to think much about the five of us being together right now," Spirit added.

"Right," Muirin sniped. "We can go off and practice our Care Bear Stares and that'll give them time to figure out how they're going to off you next time. Because if you can't see the way this was supposed to play out today was with you dead and Loch killing himself—or *supposedly* killing himself—in remorse, you're even stupider than most people from Indiana."

"Hey," Burke said, hurt.

"Okay, so was that it? Are we done now, Muirin?" Addie asked coldly.

Muirin gave her a sneering look that didn't go past her lips. Behind the sneer, she was terrified. Spirit saw the fear in her eyes. "We haven't even started yet. Hope your fancy company makes a lot of Androstenediol. You'll get even richer. Come on."

She stalked off, clearly expecting them to follow.

"Androstenediol?" Burke said blankly. "What's that treat?"

"Radiation poisoning," Addie answered.

It was only the fact that whatever had happened on the Skeet Range had knocked Breakthrough for a loop that let the five of them slip away from their watchers so easily. Muirin led them to the basement level under the classroom wing. It was a part of the school Spirit had been in only rarely, because it held the soundproofed magic practice rooms where you practiced your magic if you happened to have some. If one of the rooms was occupied, the light over the door was red. Today none of the lights was lit.

"Come on," Muirin said, leading them to the room at the end. When they were all inside, Muirin picked up a heavy wooden bar and slid it through the braces on the door.

"I didn't think there was a room in the entire school you could lock," Spirit said in surprise.

"This is the practice room for Jaunting and Apportation," Muirin said. "You don't *want* to be able to open the door accidentally."

Spirit looked around curiously. There was no furniture. The floor was covered with heavy rubber matting, and the walls . . . looked as if people had been throwing things at them. Heavy things. Hard. A lot.

She leaned against the wall and slid down it to sit on the floor. Burke lowered himself to sit beside her and put his arm around her shoulder. Addie and Loch stood.

"As you know, I've been spending a lot of time with our new Breakthrough overlords," Muirin said. "But what you don't know is that Teddy Rider and Anastus Ovcharenko don't get along at all. I've been using that. I flirt with Teddy, steam starts coming out of Anastus's ears."

As she talked, Muirin paced back and forth, practically bouncing. Her tone of voice was chirpy and upbeat, as if this was all a big joke, but looking at her, Spirit knew she had been right about what had been behind that sneer. Muirin wasn't just unhappy.

Muirin was terrified, too afraid to stand still.

"I don't care—" Addie began.

"Wait!" Spirit said quickly. "Addie, you owe it to Muirin to listen. You know you do."

Addie nodded shortly, her black hair swinging forward over her face to hide her set expression.

"And I wouldn't bother to tell you all this—since you're so fabulously interested in my life and all that—except for the fact you'd probably want to know how I ended up all on my own in The Fortress."

"'Alone' is the part I have trouble with," Loch said.

"I love you too," Muirin shot back. "But listen you guys: Mark and everyone keeps pretending there's a lot of work still to do on The Fortress. They're lying. It's almost finished. And it really is a fortress—it's set up for people to live in there, at least for months—maybe years. And I know why. You remember how none of us could figure out what Mordred and the Shadow Knights wanted?"

"Yes," Spirit said quickly, before anyone else could speak. "Because nothing they've been doing has seemed to make any sense."

Muirin gave her a grateful look.

"Get to the point," Loch snapped wearily.

"They're going to start a war," Muirin says. "A *big* war. Missiles, bombs. Like their *game*, for god's sake: *Final Battle: The Rise of the Black Dragon!*" She plucked a copy of the advance CD out of her jacket and waved it.

"Oh, Muirin. You're getting this out of a computer game?" Addie said reproachfully.

"No!" Muirin said. "They put it *in* their game—you've met Mark, do you really think he wouldn't take the chance to gloat?—but they're working to make the game scenario really happen! Breakthrough is hacking its way into the computers that launch the missiles. There are missile silos all over this part of the state, and some of them still have missiles in them. And before you ask, Smart Boy," she said to Burke, "they're going to hack the software so they can't be called back or destroyed in flight."

"That's ridiculous," Addie said. But she didn't sound as convinced as she had a moment before.

"Okay," Muirin answered, "*you* come up with a good reason for there to be stacks of Department of Defense documents all over Hacker Heaven and the whole place set up like the Pentagon. Once they crack the encryption, it's all over."

"It can't be," Burke said, sounding sick. "You must be wrong, Murr. You—"

"No," Spirit said quickly. "Muirin's right. We wanted to know what Mordred wants, and this is it. Muirin, what's that saying you're always quoting? About technology and magic?"

" 'Any sufficiently advanced technology is indistinguishable from magic,' " Muirin said. "Arthur C. Clarke."

"So . . . any sufficiently advanced magic is indistinguishable from technology, too," Spirit said. "Burke, you've always said if the Outside World knew about Oakhurst and Magic, they'd grab everyone they could and make them be soldiers for them, and we wouldn't have much choice. Because there's a lot of Outside World, and it's full of technology, and—if we're the grand total of all the Magicians in the world, we're outnumbered."

"Right," Burke answered cautiously. "The side with the most guys usually wins. Basic tactics."

"But Mordred's been stuck in a tree since the fall of Camelot. He doesn't care about the modern world, and—like you said, Muirin—he can't possibly declare himself King of Earth. Not the way it is now. But if he's the only one with real power . . ."

"Then Magic replaces Technology, and Mordred and the Shadow Knights are the only ones with Magic," Loch said, sounding horrified. "And they rule . . . everything."

The silence that followed Loch's words was heavy with fear—and belief. Burke stretched out his free arm, and Muirin stumbled toward him gratefully. She sat down beside him and he wrapped his arm around her, hugging her.

Loch crossed the room and sat down with his back to the door. His face looked bruised, and he rubbed his eyes. "They can do it," he whispered, as if to himself. "A Kenning Mage, a good one, one that's a computer expert too, that's all they need. What he can't hack, he can magic his way into, and what magic can't do, hacking can. Add a little luck, and they're in."

"Can't we *do* something?" Addie asked, shaking her head desperately. "It's a construction site—there has to be dynamite around. If you blow up their computers . . ."

"No can do," Muirin said bleakly. "Mark tore a strip off Teddy for leaving me alone in Hacker Heaven. I don't think I'm getting back in there any time soon. With or without explosives."

"We have to tell Dr. Ambrosius," Burke said.

"No!" Spirit burst out. She closed her eyes, but even so, she could feel the others all stare at her. She finally said it. Said what she had been thinking all this time, and hadn't said aloud, because she knew the others had all been pinning their hopes on the idea that at least Dr. A could wake up and save them all. "I mean, what if he isn't Merlin? Or if he can't help? We need—"

"You need to tell us why you think he isn't, Spirit," Burke said slowly. "You were there. You saw that picture. It was Doctor A."

"Yes it was," Spirit said. "And so we know he was there the night Mordred got out of the tree." She took a deep shuddering breath. "And we know Wolfman escaped, and he and Doctor A—Kenny Hawking—were friends, and so we assumed it was *Merlin* who helped Wolfman escape, because Kenny Hawking was a Reincarnate who got Awakened and realized who he was. But . . . that doesn't make sense. Wolfman was crazy—at least when we talked to him he was—so why wouldn't his friend have done more for him? And Wolfman was murdered after we talked to him."

"You didn't tell us that!" Addie exclaimed.

"Brenda was talking about it on Wednesday when we showed up for the Committee meeting," Spirit said. "Then the Shadow Knights attacked the library, and . . . But that's the point! If Kenny is Doctor Ambrosius, and Doctor A is Merlin . . . he isn't in control of anything, because why would he let the Shadow Knights kill Wolfman if he was? So either he's *not* Merlin—or he is, and he's being completely controlled, and has been since right after Mordred got out of the tree."

"Okay, so maybe Doctor Ambrosius isn't Merlin," Addie said slowly. "But we don't know—unless you can tell me how we spy on what's probably the most powerful magician in the school."

"I've got an idea," Muirin said slowly. "But you aren't going to like it."

The next day was Sunday, and that meant Sunday Service. With everything else going on, and so many classes being dropped, you'd think it would be one of the first things Oakhurst would ditch, but no. Spirit had never liked the chapel or its bland nondenominational decor—and services—but now the stained glass windows with their depictions of knights in armor all seemed horribly meaningful instead of just weird.

She'd spent all night reading Ms. Groves's book, as much to blot out what Muirin had told all of them as in hopes somewhere in it there would be a solution to their problems. All she'd found was confusion piled on confusion. All the stories contradicted each other—in some, Arthur's court was in France. In some, he went to war with the Roman Emperor. In some he was married to someone who wasn't Guinevere. And less than half the stories in the book were about Arthur and Camelot anyway. Galahad and Percival and Gwalchmai and Gareth—her brain was stuffed with weird names and weirder stories until she couldn't even *think*.

It's hard to believe the Dance is next Friday, Spirit thought numbly. *And oh yeah, Mordred's going to bomb the world back to the Stone Age.* There was one more meeting of the Dance Committee before the Dance itself. Of course, a few deaths were no reason for Oakhurst to cancel an event, but she hadn't heard about Radial pulling out either.

She sat up straighter and did her best to pay attention to the service. It had actually included a memorial to Beckett Green, for a wonder—but then, he hadn't just vanished like most of their teachers did. He'd been murdered—by Anastus Ovcharenko, or whoever had forced Loch to point the shotgun at her. But if Mr. Green had been memorialized (if that was even a word), this sure wasn't a memorial service.

Usually Doctor Ambrosius picked two or three holy books to read to them out of—by now she was pretty familiar with the Bhagavad Gita, the Qur'an, and the Tanakh as well as with a number of lesser-known scriptures. He always had a way of doing it that seemed to say all religions shared an underlying spiritual truth—and those "truths" were all equally false. Spirit usually found it more boring than anything else, but today Doctor A was sticking with the Bible. The Book of Revelations, to be exact. And it wasn't at all hard to pick up the subtext. *And Lo! For there will be a Final Battle of Good and of Evil and maybe a* few other things too, and in that battle the Special Kids will be saved and the Bad Kids will be cast into a burning lake of fiery fire to experience permanent fatal death. Great. Way to be subtle, Evil Overlord.

I should have told everyone about QUERCUS when I had the chance, she thought. Now it was much too late. They were all on edge. If the others found out she'd been keeping a secret—a big secret—from them for *months* . . .

She wasn't sure what would happen.

At least she'd managed to convince them to try to find out more about Doctor Ambrosius without having to flat-out say why she distrusted him so much. She glanced over at Dylan. Dylan caught her looking and smirked at her. Spirit wasn't sure whether to glare, pretend she hadn't noticed, or just close her eyes and pretend she wasn't here at all. She wasn't sure what Muirin had told Dylan to convince him to help, but she'd gotten him to agree.

Loch had a digital recorder. It wasn't even contraband; he used it to make notes for studying. It could record for about a day before it ran out of charge, and it was about the size of a cell phone. Dylan knew the layout in Doctor A's office as well as any of the rest of them did: he'd Jaunted Loch's recorder to the top of the bookshelf behind Dr. Ambrosius's desk today before the service, and he'd retrieve it the same way tomorrow. And Spirit hoped it would have something *definite* on it. Because if it didn't, then Burke was going to go to Doctor Ambrosius, and Spirit couldn't come up with a really good reason not to, even if she was desperate enough to reveal QUERCUS. *I can just see how that would go: "Oh hey, my invisible friend who appeared mysteriously says you shouldn't trust Doctor Ambrosius. And I've been keeping him a secret because I don't trust you."* Yeah, how about not?

She stifled a yawn.

❋

Ms. Smith and Ms. Corby were standing on either side of the doorway as everyone filed out. Spirit barely had time to register that they were pulling kids aside when Ms. Corby summoned her. She found herself standing beside Zoey, Kylee, and Maddie. On the other side were Chris and (Spirit's heart sank) Dylan. A moment later, Burke and Loch joined them.

"What's this all about?" Spirit whispered to Maddie.

"You've been chosen to attend afternoon tea, Miss White," Ms. Corby said without turning around.

Back when Oakhurst was at least *pretending* to be a real school where the student body was going to live to grow up, one of the things on the curriculum was "Genteel Deportment," which was what the formal dances and the formal dinners and the afternoon teas were for. Afternoon teas were held by Doctor Ambrosius every Sunday for the faculty and four boys and four girls chosen at random. Spirit had just assumed the teas had been discontinued, since she'd been picked during her first month at Oakhurst, and you couldn't be picked again until everyone else had been picked once.

Surprise.

Then again, how many of us are left? Maybe my number just came up again.

Yeah, right.

✦

Afternoon tea was even more grueling this time than it had been the first time, and even getting out of her new Sunday afternoon classes couldn't make it any better. She was supposed to be doing two hours of Horsemanship (held in the paddock near the stables for safety) followed by her "Fencing" Class (they hadn't worked out with anything as light as a foil in weeks). If they were all being prepared to survive in some kind of post-apocalyptic wasteland, their bizarre curriculum finally made sense. *Lucky us, to be the Oakhurst class here when Breakthrough decides to carry out its evil plan. I bet all Mark and Teddy Rider and Madison Lane had to take was French and Calculus.*

She kept her face very still as a sudden thought struck her.

What made her think any of them had actually gone to Oakhurst at all? She had only their word for it they were alums. No one had bothered going through the files down in the secret basement to verify that.

But they weren't old enough to have been Hellriders . . .

. . . were they?

No.

That had been forty years ago. Wolfman had been, well, Doc A's age. It would have had to have been Mark and Teddy's *father* who'd been one of the Hellriders. But that would mean they weren't orphans.

Even though her brain really hurt right now, Spirit tried not to close her eyes and make a face. Somebody would be sure to see and ask why. *Every time I think I've managed to disbelieve*

everything Oakhurst's told us, I realize I'm still believing part of some-
thing we've all been told. And what if I'm still believing the thing that's
going to get us killed?

She felt a little better about the Sunday Tea when she realized why the eight of them had been chosen. Six of them were
on the Dance Committee, and Loch and Burke had been involved in the shooting—Loch directly, Burke as Mr. Green's
protégé. So it was probably just Doctor Ambrosius wanting to
see if any of them were going to do something interesting (like
freak out and gain access to their Reincarnate memories, because at least *some* of them had to be Reincarnates, and that
was one more thing to worry about).

Or maybe it was the staff he was watching. None of the
Breakthrough people were here, not even Mark and Madison,
and in comparison to the other time Spirit had been here . . .

Last time there'd been twenty people besides Doctor Ambrosius and the students. Today there were six.

She was starting to wonder if Breakthrough wanted *any* of
them. At all.

⁂

Monday evening. Less than an hour until she found out if their
attempt to bug Doctor Ambrosius's office had gotten them
anything that could convince the others he wasn't to be trusted.

Two months ago—a month ago—the events of the past
thirty-six hours would have driven her to screaming hysterics.
Today she just thought they were funny—in a really horrible
way.

Sunday afternoon Addie almost drowned during practice when one of the other Water Witches thought the pool was empty and froze it into ice. Sunday night Spirit used the Ironkey to log into QUERCUS's chatroom, but QUERCUS still wasn't there. Monday morning they found out they had Ovcharenko back teaching *Systema* again, and now Burke was his designated chew-toy. Burke was good enough to take the worst Ovcharenko could throw at him, and Ovcharenko knew it—but the implacable patient anger on Burke's face when he looked at Ovcharenko was frightening. In the afternoon, Mia Singleton had the Endurance class doing jumps in the Paddock—and Spirit took what could have been a bad fall when the saddle on her horse just slipped off as he was clearing a jump. Just before dinner, Loch caught up to her to tell her Noah Turner had said the Breakthrough guy he was dating (wow, surprise) said there was a memo with a list of all the gay and lesbian Oakhurst kids that was going to be "accidentally leaked" this week to the entire student body. Noah wasn't on that list. Loch didn't have to say anything more.

That's how Breakthrough's buying Noah's loyalty, just the way it tried to buy Muirin with makeup and clothes and . . . freedom. Or Burke with friendship. They promise you whatever you want most. Whatever it is.

I want my family back, she thought fiercely. *Give me that, Breakthrough, and we'll talk.*

But while even Breakthrough couldn't give her that, it didn't mean it couldn't offer her something she wanted. She hadn't had a moment alone with Burke since he'd snuck in through her window the night they'd gone to see Wolfman, and that hadn't exactly been a romantic tryst. She'd been trying not to think about him too hard, so as not to give anything away if someone was watching, but when she did think about him, it was with an ache of *want* so bad it nearly made her cry.

If Breakthrough could give her Burke? Safe and happy and free?

Would that buy her?

I have to make sure they never know it could.

ПÏПE

That night, Spirit and Burke and Loch and Addie went up to the attic as soon as they could sneak away after dinner. Spirit hoped Muirin would be joining them, but she hadn't seen Muirin all day, and considering what Muirin had told all of them on Saturday, Spirit was more worried about her than ever. Muirin was self-centered and occasionally spiteful, but she was also generous, brave, and loyal. Spirit could only hope Muirin was taking her own advice and keeping her head down, especially around Breakthrough.

When Spirit got there, Addie had already lit the candles for light and for heat, but it was still freezing. But even shivering in a corner, Spirit felt better than she had all day.

No, not better. *Safer.*

I can't go on like this much longer, she thought. She hadn't had a lot of patience with Addie just wanting to leave, but now she realized she'd been unfair. You just couldn't go on being this scared day after day. Eventually you'd do anything to make it stop. And the penalty for that was disappearing to wherever Breakthrough disappeared people to. And that made everything worse all over again. She wanted to think, to plan, to imagine what they'd find on Loch's recorder and what they could do about it, but her mind just kept going in a tiny circle saying: *escape, escape, escape* . . .

Maybe they could. Loch had Kenning and Shadewalking; those Gifts were enough to guide them if they decided to strike out cross-country. Burke could protect them, Muirin could make sure they got away undetected—they could even use her car, if they could figure out a way. . . .

But this was the point at which Spirit's imagination always failed. Where could they go? And who could they trust?

Burke came in—glancing around the room watchfully before stepping inside—then crossed the room to sit beside Spirit. He put an arm around her.

"I'm so sorry!" she blurted out, even though she couldn't say what she was apologizing for. For not being sorrier about Beckett Green's death? For being angry Burke had liked him?

"You don't have anything to apologize for," Burke told her quietly. "Not to me. Ever."

His words should have made everything better. Instead they just increased her silent panic. *I'm not that girl, Burke! Whoever you think I am, I'm really not! I'm not brave, or noble, or—or—or smart enough to figure out a way out of this mess. . . .*

"Showtime," Loch said quietly, at the sound of footsteps in

the hall. To Spirit's relief, Muirin walked in—but with Dylan right behind her.

"What's he doing here?" Burke rumbled, tightening his arm around Spirit.

"Blackmail," Muirin said brightly as she pulled the door shut behind her.

"Nice place," Dylan said, looking around.

"Feel free to make it your own," Loch said, gesturing grandly. "We won't be using it again after tonight."

"Why not?" Dylan asked, sounding puzzled.

"Because *you* know about it, moron," Muirin said. "So. I brought you here. That was the deal. Where's the recorder?"

"Right here." Dylan held out his empty hand, and the small silvery oblong appeared in it.

Muirin reached for it, and Dylan snatched it out of her reach. "Uh-uh," he said. "You're spying on Doc A, and I want to know what you've found."

"The deal was you hand it over, Williams," Muirin hissed.

"So I'm changing the deal," Dylan said. "Either I get to hear what's on it, or I Jaunt it up to the roof, and good luck getting it back from there."

"Oh, let him," Addie said wearily. "What can it matter?"

Dylan took a step into the room and leaned against the doorway. Muirin walked past him and sat down on the floor beside Addie. After a long moment, Dylan stepped forward and sat down in the last empty space, between Muirin and Loch. He set the recorder on the floor in the center of the impromptu circle. Loch reached for it, and Dylan snatched it back suspiciously.

"If you can figure out how to run that without power, great," Loch said in a flat voice.

"That model doesn't run on batteries," Dylan said. "You have to charge it in a USB port."

"Yes," Loch said, with exaggerated patience. "And I have two identical recorders. And this is the power pack from the other one. Fully charged." He held out his hand. On the palm was a small black square. "So let me change out the power pack, or Jaunt it to the roof. I don't really give a damn."

Dylan blew out a shaking breath.

"We're just scared," Spirit said softly. She thought Dylan was probably just as scared as they were. He'd been in the town library last Wednesday when the Shadow Knights attacked it. *And they looked like characters out of that stupid game, the same one Muirin says they've put their whole plan into. But who'd believe anybody would be that crazy in real life?*

Dylan nodded sharply and handed the recorder to Loch. With deft motions Loch changed out one power pack for the other, then switched the recorder on and set it in the middle of the circle again.

They all stared at it as if it was a television—or might explode. At first Spirit thought it wasn't working, but then she heard the opening and closing of drawers.

"It stops recording when there aren't any sounds," Loch said quietly. "So we shouldn't have to listen to twenty-four hours of nothing."

Even so, they had to listen to at least ten minutes of chairs and drawers and Ms. Corby saying things like "Here's the report you asked for," before they reached something interesting.

"I hope you've brought me good news, Mark."

Spirit glanced up at Burke, frowning. It was Doctor Ambrosius's voice, but suddenly it sounded different. Not like him at all. It was deeper. Almost . . . younger.

"Yes, my lord. I've done a complete scrub-through of our computer systems. The girl didn't find anything."

And Mark sounded almost . . . scared. The corner of Muirin's mouth quirked up, but aside from that she did nothing. She was listening too intently. They all were.

"Yet she could have. Tristan is a liability. You cannot afford liabilities, Mark."

"Tristan is my sworn knight. I will not cast him out for a meaningless mistake. We will need him."

"No mistake is meaningless, merely overlooked by our foes. You seem to enjoy surrounding yourself with fools. The other matter could have been settled by now if Agravaine did not have such a penchant for drama. If he'd handled things quietly, Spirit White and Lachlan Spears would be dead now."

Spirit flinched at the sound of her name. She heard Loch draw in a slow breath.

"These things take time, my lord," Mark said. "I assure you—"

"You're too used to living a masquerade for the mortal cattle I will soon rule. Do you really think it needs to look like an accident?"

Listening to that voice, Spirit thought about the first time she'd seen Doctor Ambrosius, and what he'd done. He'd turned her into a mouse. He'd attacked her. And he'd gloated about it afterward. *He was like this all along and I just—we all just—forgot about it. . . .*

She reached for Burke's hand. He was reaching for hers, too. She wound her fingers through his and squeezed tightly.

"If Agravaine just shoots them in their beds, *Master,* even the englamoured sheriffs will notice. There'd be an inquest. And worse, the others will talk. It is possible even my liegemen will let something slip where it should not be heard if Agravaine is so blatant. This is no isolated kingdom where you can shoot a messenger. There are telephones, computers, even mail—a thousand ways to reach the outside world."

"You overstep yourself, Mark of Cornwall," Doctor Ambrosius snarled.

"Truth serves you better than empty flattery, my prince," Mark answered. "We aren't ready yet. Some of your liegemen have not arrived. The rest of our supplies aren't here. And aside from our most pressing obstacle—though Tristan assures me his vassals will soon have the information we seek—we have not yet located your great enemy. We've questioned Yseult as much as we dare—she doesn't know anything about Merlin, nor does she know the identities of the Grail Knights."

"They must be near! There have been signs—portents. Have not the Palug Cat and the Boar of Triath returned to the world? Did not the Green Knight himself come to our court? That is the first luck we've had, for he came seeking Gawain—

none of the others I've identified among the children here is possessed of such a strong allegiance: Nimue, Morgaine, even Gaheris can be brought to the Shadow. It is a great pity Agravaine slew the Green Knight before we discovered who Gawain is in this life—but I have my suspicions, and with luck, Gawain will lead us to Arthur . . ."

"Does it truly matter if—when—your plan bears fruit, my lord?" Mark asked. "Arthur and his knights—and even Merlin—will have lost. Again—and this time, for all time."

"And do you think I can lie quiet while they breathe?" Doctor Ambrosius snarled. "The whole purpose of this place was so I might gather up all the Mages born into the world to sift through them for my ancient enemies reborn."

"And ancient allies," Mark said.

"You always preferred the winning side, Lord Mark," Doctor Ambrosius said.

"I prefer it to being the vassal of a weak do-nothing king. As you know," Mark answered.

"And I prefer competent help," Doctor Ambrosius snapped. "See that your liegemen suffer no further lapses of judgment."

"As my lord wills," Mark said.

There was the sound of a door opening and closing, and after that nothing but the sound of doors opening and closing, scraps of sound sandwiched between the "dead air" sound of the recorder shutting down in the absence of sound.

"Is this some kind of a joke?" Dylan demanded.

Spirit jumped. She'd been listening so intently she'd forgotten he was here.

"No . . . I can tell it isn't. All this means something to you guys."

Loch grabbed for the recorder, then yelped, shaking his hand. Dylan bounced to his feet and backed away, brandishing the recorder he'd Jaunted out of Loch's hand.

"So tell me everything—or I take this to Doc A and tell him where I got it and what was going on."

"Or you could hand it over and keep your teeth," Burke rumbled. He let go of Spirit's hand and started to get to his feet. Dylan tensed, preparing to run.

"No," Spirit said, putting her hand on Burke's arm. "Wait. We can't fight among ourselves. That's what they want. Dylan, if you take that to Doctor Ambrosius, you'll die. He'll kill you. And he'll kill us."

"Oh come on," Dylan said uncertainly.

"No, it's true," Spirit said. "Didn't you just *hear* him? He wants Loch and me dead! Ovcharenko planned for Loch to kill me, then to murder Loch—and that's what would have happened if Mr. Green hadn't interfered—and he *died*, Dylan! Doctor Ambrosius won't waste a second thinking about whether to kill you, too—he'll just *do* it. And . . . I don't know if I like you, but . . . I trust you, Dylan. You didn't have to save Zoey at the library. But you did." And he'd saved her from giving too much away when Burke had been fighting Ovcharenko, too. QUERCUS had told her all along to trust and be kind, and even though she wasn't entirely sure right now whether or not she trusted *QUERCUS*, there was no one else giving her advice to follow.

"I guess I . . ." Dylan said, and stopped.

"So we'll tell you what's going on," Spirit said, plowing stubbornly onward even though she could feel the other four around her hating the whole idea of involving Dylan. "Just . . . don't say we're making it up, okay? Because we already know how dumb it sounds."

Dylan grimaced, but didn't say anything. He leaned against the doorway, regarding her suspiciously, the recorder in his hand.

Spirit took a deep breath. *I hope I know what I'm doing,* she thought. She spoke quickly, telling him about the Tithing, the Wild Hunt, Elizabeth Walker's story about the Reincarnates, deciphering the carvings on the oak tree in the main hall. Dylan's face was set in a sneer of disbelief, but Spirit didn't let that discourage her.

"—and it didn't make any sense for everyone here at the school to have magic, because if we were all the Legacies of Oakhurst graduates, some of us would have to be non-magical. But then we found out we had it backward. You don't come to Oakhurst if you're an orphan. If Doctor Ambrosius wants you here, he *makes* you an orphan. He's been using Ovcharenko to kill the families of the kids he wants. For years."

"It's true," Muirin said, speaking up—it was the first time any of them had said anything since Spirit had started her explanation. "Ovcharenko told me that himself. And I don't think he just did it to impress me, you know, because he was really really drunk. Ovcharenko killed Burke's family himself. And I don't know if Ovcharenko personally killed yours, but I know for sure Doctor A *had* them killed and probably used Ovcharenko's *Bratva* Family to do it."

"He . . ." Dylan said slowly, and there was belief in his face and his voice for the first time. "He killed my family. He killed my *sisters*."

"Yeah, welcome to the Dead Parents Society," Muirin snarked.

There was a moment of frozen silence, then—shockingly—Dylan put his hands over his face and began to cry.

Suddenly Spirit heard Kylee's voice in her memory.

"*—everybody ought to know about Mister Dylan I'm-So-Hot Williams. See, our last names are so close our files keep getting mixed up, so one day I got ahold of his. Family vacation right? Mom, dad, three kids . . . so they ditched him at an amusement park in Florida. Took the police three days to track them down. Found 'em all dead. They'd run off to commit suicide rather than have him around anymore. . . .*"

Dylan had always insisted they'd been murdered—but down deep inside maybe he hadn't been sure. Maybe (Spirit thought) at least part of him had believed Kylee's accusation, or part of it. Believed his own family hated him so much they'd ditched him and run away. And they'd died, and that had been horrible, but it still came after they'd already abandoned him.

And now he knew that wasn't what had happened at all.

"Be smart, Dylan," Loch said in a low voice. "If they know you know, they'll kill you. You have to keep on acting normal. You *have* to."

Dylan lowered his hands. His face was blotchy with tears,

but nobody said anything. "Normal!" he said, and began to laugh. It sounded almost like crying. "Normal!" he said again. Before anyone could say anything else, he turned and ran.

"Should—?" Loch asked.

Spirit shook her head mutely.

"If he's going to tell, there's nothing we can do about it," Addie said.

The five of them looked at each other. What now?

"Doctor A—he *lied* to us," Burke said blankly.

An instant later Muirin began to giggle. Addie joined her, hand clapped over her mouth to muffle the sounds. Burke stared at them for an instant and began to laugh—a deep rich belly laugh. Then they were all laughing—his remark had been so ridiculous after everything that had led up to it there wasn't anything else to do. Each time Spirit started to get control of herself, she'd look at one of the others and that would set her off again.

At last, too winded to go on, they wound down. Every few seconds Muirin would make another fizzing sound, like laughter under pressure, and Addie was making chimp-faces to try to keep from grinning.

"I guess in comparison to finding out about this, being outed for being gay doesn't matter that much," Loch said, sitting up and taking a deep breath.

"I guess it doesn't," Burke said easily. "It's not like they really need an excuse for killing you."

"Oh, but there are *telephones*," Addie said. "And— And— And *computers*!"

That set them all off again, until they finally ran down for good. Spirit leaned weakly against Burke's shoulder. "Oh my god . . ." she moaned. Then she tightened her hand on Burke's arm. "Doctor A isn't Merlin. I mean, he *really is* not Merlin. He *was* Kenny, but whatever came out of that oak tree got him, and there's nothing left of Kenny in there. Is there?"

"Yeah, no," Burke said softly. "Don't think so." Then his voice hardened. "Okay. Now we know Doctor Ambrosius is the enemy. He's Mordred. And we know what his plan is. I don't know about you guys, but I'm going to pray," he finished, completely seriously.

"I'm going to write a letter," Muirin said. Spirit stared at her. "Hey, the Bad Guys are even more all over Oakhurst's servers than the teachers were, and that goes double for Radial's Internet node. Most voice and data lines share resources, so you can just bet the phones are being tapped, too."

"Who'd have the time to listen to all those conversations?" Addie asked in disbelief.

"You don't need to," Loch said. "There are keyword-sampling systems like Echelon to do that. They don't even need to build their own if they piggyback onto the Echelon network."

"Right. But dead tree communication is still secure," Muirin said. "And I've got the run of Radial. I figure if I write to the President, the FBI, *The New York Times,* Truthout, BuzzFlash, boingboing, Daily Kos, and *Rolling Stone, one* of them's gonna take notice of a 'terrorist plot' to hack into the missile control software and launch a bunch of nukes."

Spirit shuddered. It seemed more horrible every time she heard about it.

"Maybe," Loch said doubtfully.

"And maybe not," Burke agreed grimly. "But we need to cover every base we can, toss out a lot of stones and hope one hits something. It's a good idea, Murr-cat, and I think you should go for it. But I think we need to do other things, too."

"I can—" Addie began, and stopped. "Now I'm wondering if Oakhurst ever wrote to my trustees at all," she finished in a small confused voice.

"Addie, you asked *Mordred* to send you somewhere safe," Loch said gently. "If they're planning to bomb the world back to the Stone Age somewhere in the next few months, they probably aren't too worried about you or your trustees making trouble for them. And the last thing that Doctor A wants to do is let go of an asset like a Water Witch."

There was a moment of silence. Spirit could see Addie struggling not to cry. She knew how scared Addie was, and she knew Addie had been relying on her trustees being able to protect her. Now that hope had been taken away from her.

"Okay," Addie finally said, her voice a whisper. "And that raises the question: *when* are they going to do this?"

"Beltane," Spirit said suddenly.

"What?" Loch said blankly. "Why Beltane? May First is almost two months from now. Wouldn't he—?"

"He'll want to do it on the anniversary of his original defeat," Spirit said. She didn't know whether it was reading Ms. Groves's book, or just because she'd been thinking about the problem even before she knew how big a problem it was, but she was absolutely certain. "To— To— To *erase* it, right? Okay.

211

To become King, Arthur fought what are called The Twelve Great Battles: the first was at Glein, the second through fifth were at Dublas, the sixth was at Bassas, the seventh at Cat Coit Celidon. The eight was at Guinnion Castle, the ninth at Caer Londinum, the tenth at Tribruit—another river side—the eleventh at Mount Agned, and the twelfth and greatest at Badon Hill. Camlann is the thirteenth, where he dies fighting Mordred. A lot of the old stories say he had to cross the English Channel to come back to England for the Battle of Camlann. You couldn't cross the English Channel with an army in those days except in good sailing weather. The crossing season was mid-March to mid-September, so Arthur must have gotten back to England sometime in April. But nobody—even Mordred—would have fought during Lent, the forty days before Easter—he might not have cared, but his army would. Easter is at the end of April, and the next big holiday—and the next School Dance after this one—is May First. *Beltane*."

"Wow," Loch said quietly.

Spirit blushed. She hadn't meant to geek out on them. It had all just come pouring out.

"And in Celtic folklore, Beltane is one of the important Ancient Holy Days, when the dark half of the year ends and the light half begins," Addie said.

"Only this year, the light half won't begin, if Mordred and Breakthrough get their way," Burke finished grimly. "We have to stop them."

It kept coming back to that, Spirit realized. They had to stop the Shadow Knights. They had to stop *Mordred* and the Shadow

Knights. And she didn't think anybody else had any more idea of how to do that than she did.

"If it's up to us to save the world, the world's in big trouble," Muirin said. "But I think you're missing the small picture here, Burkesy. Forget the apocalypse for a moment—we've got to keep Loch and Spirit alive. And I'm not sure that's going to be easy."

Spirit wanted to say her life wasn't important compared to the lives of everyone else on Earth. And maybe it wasn't. But if they couldn't stop the Shadow Knights from killing the two of them—how were they ever going to stop them from doing everything else?

They talked about it until Muirin (of all people) reminded them of the time. It was almost lights out; they'd all had a lot of practice in sneaking around the school by now, but by unspoken agreement, nobody really wanted to push their luck any farther than they had to.

Not when demerits made you disappear.

All of them hugged each other before they split up. No matter what their past disagreements—and mutual distrust—the things they'd learned in the past two days had united them again. For better or worse, the time of doubting each other and their own motives was at an end.

The stakes were too high.

Muirin gave Spirit and Addie the "all clear" and the three of them entered the Young Ladies' Wing. Spirit whispered a last good night to the other two as they headed to their second-floor rooms.

She knew just how Addie felt. She kept wanting to just pretend none of this had ever happened. She didn't even know how to think about the things she'd learned—and she kept finding herself thinking: *Maybe they really won't start a war. Maybe if they do, nobody will really be hurt.* It was shock, she knew—she'd caught herself thinking the same way in the weeks after the accident: *Maybe my family really isn't dead. Maybe it's all just some kind of really horrible mistake.*

But it hadn't been a mistake. And neither was this.

Mom always said three people can keep a secret if two of them don't know it. And Breakthrough employs hundreds of people. Even if all of them don't know what Mark and Mordred are planning, the ones hacking the missile launch codes have to. Won't they tell? Or sabotage it? Or . . . something?

It wasn't something any of them could count on. It would be too much like hoping. *Maybe QUERCUS will have a suggestion. Him telling me not to trust Doctor Ambrosius makes so much sense now—but how did he know? Why didn't he tell me what he knew? It doesn't matter as much as the fact I can still trust him. . . .*

Then she opened the door to her room.

The door to her fridge hung open. The bed had been torn apart. Books and papers were scattered all over the floor. Someone had searched her room—and they really didn't care whether she noticed or not.

QUERCUS!

She ran to her desk. Both drawers had been yanked out and

they—and their contents—had been tossed on the floor. She knelt in the mess and scrabbled through it with shaking hands. She sobbed with relief when her fingers closed on the Ironkey.

What were they looking for? What—if it wasn't this?

Still kneeling, she picked up her computer. Everything had been swept off the top of her desk. The power cord had come loose and the battery had run down, but when she plugged it in again and rebooted it, her desktop came up as usual. She glanced toward the door to the hall. She'd closed it, but none of the doors in the dormitory wings locked. For a moment she thought about pushing the couch in front of it, but what if one of the Proctors—or the Security staff—tried to open it?

You'll just have to be careful.

She turned the laptop around so she was facing the door over the monitor, and plugged in the Ironkey drive. To her relief, the computer recognized it, just as it always did. It wasn't broken.

But that didn't matter. When she tried to open its browser, nothing happened. The intraweb was down again, and without it, the Ironkey wouldn't operate. *What if it's going to be down forever?* she thought frantically. Then: *No. They wouldn't do that. Having everybody using the chatrooms makes things too easy for them. And the school practically runs on email.*

She had to hope this wasn't just wishful thinking.

But leaving the Ironkey in my room is stupid. I got lucky once. I'm not going to make that mistake twice.

But how could she carry it with her securely? She thought for a moment, then went to her closet. Everything there was a mess, too, but she'd deal with that later. For now, it only took a little digging to find what she was looking for—the sneakers she'd been wearing the day she came to Oakhurst.

She whipped the laces out of them and knotted them firmly together end to end. The Ironkey had a slot on it so you could put it on a key ring or something; she had to poke a little to get the end of the shoelace through it, but once she had, she could wear it as a necklace—or, better, tie the laces around her waist. Somebody might see a necklace, but they'd never see a belt. She'd even be able to wear it in *Systema*.

The thought made her laugh out loud. She'd thought Ovcharenko was the worst thing she had to deal with. But all he could do was beat her to death. *Everything is relative,* she thought, suppressing a despairing giggle.

She tied the Ironkey around her waist now just to be sure. She felt better when she had, and with that taken care of, she could spare the attention to really look at her room.

It was a real wreck.

If the intraweb had been up she might even have risked asking Muirin to come help her clean up the mess. As it was, she'd have to do it all by herself. She walked over to the fridge and shut it carefully. At least none of the bottles of sports drinks had been smashed—or poured on the carpet.

It took her hours to get everything cleaned up and put back in order—clothes hung up, papers reorganized and put away, everything in her bathroom picked up and set to rights. At the beginning she'd been puzzled—what could they possibly have been looking for?—but the closer she got to finishing her cleanup, the more she thought she knew. And she was very much afraid they'd found it, too. After she'd tidied her room completely, she searched it herself—probably more thoroughly than Breakthrough had. At last she had to admit the thing she was looking for wasn't here any longer.

The book of Arthurian myth Ms. Groves had loaned her was gone.

She didn't even bother to try to sleep after that, just sat curled up in a corner of the couch with her laptop, hoping the intraweb would come back up. And thinking—as much as she could anyway. Mostly she just sat and jittered.

Breakthrough was going to bring all of its people—all of its *magicians*—to Radial. And then it was going to launch a bunch of nuclear missiles. At who? It hardly mattered, did it? Once anybody fired off a missile, everybody would start shooting at each other. And then everybody would be dead, or really sick, and nobody would believe a *computer gaming company* had started World War Last.

And that was the same reason telling the FBI—or anyone else—what was going on wouldn't work (unless they came up with a really effective lie, and if anyone could do that it was Muirin). What was going on was *ridiculous*—*she* believed it, and *she* still thought it was ridiculous. So what they needed to do was . . .

But that was where her mind kept stopping, over and over. Because she didn't *know* what they needed to do. All she knew was the end of the world was six weeks away, and there was nothing she could think of to stop it.

Start with the small stuff, Mom would say. Enough ants can move a mountain. She didn't think this situation was what her Mom had in mind, but it was still good advice. The first thing she needed to do was tell Ms. Groves somebody'd stolen her book. Maybe—if Ms. Groves would put up her Warding again—Spirit could tell her the rest of what they'd found out. Even if she didn't have a plan *either,* at least she wasn't a teenager. She could get out of here and figure out something to say that would make people listen, even if it was just that Breakthrough was doing something illegal. Selling drugs, maybe. Something that would get The Fortress searched.

Something.

The intraweb wasn't back up by breakfast time, but at least that meant Spirit wouldn't have to read the Morning Motivational Message today. She'd already showered—just for something to do—and dressed. And today she'd actually have long enough before the start of *Systema* to eat something.

※

She was one of the first people on the serving line. She didn't see any of the others, and she didn't see Dylan either. Because there were so few kids there, she stopped to talk to Maddie Harris after she got her food. Maddie hadn't heard anything about Radial either, and she took the problems with the intraweb as a personal affront.

"How can they expect us to organize the Spring Fling without email, Spirit? It would be bad enough if it was just us, but adding Radial means we have a thousand percent more work to do! This is going to be the worst dance in the history of Oakhurst, and it's my last one, and everyone's going to blame me, and it isn't *fair!*"

Spirit bit her lip. *It's going to be the last* dance *in the history of Oakhurst,* she thought, and barely managed to keep from saying so. But Maddie didn't know that, so Spirit did her best to say sympathetic things until Maddie went to get on the serving line. She couldn't decide whether Maddie's complaints were funny—or made her want to scream. *Probably both,* she decided.

All the books always said that when you were facing the apocalypse you didn't have any appetite, but Spirit was actually hungrier than she could remember being in a long time. She was most of the way through her oatmeal by the time Ms. Corby walked in to the Refectory.

Ms. Corby stood in front of the door holding a clipboard waiting for everyone to quiet down, but it took Dan yelling for them all to shut up for there to be quiet.

"As I'm sure you all know, the school intraweb is down, and there are a number of announcements this morning," Ms. Corby said. Since the first one was apparently the Morning Motivational Message, Spirit mostly tuned her out.

"Oakhurst is saddened to report the loss of one of its most well-loved colleagues. Ms. Lily Groves was the victim of a savage attack by the escaped tiger that has been reported in the area. It is believed that she had gone for a walk when she was taken unawares by the animal."

Spirit set down her spoon and stared at Ms. Corby. *Dead? Ms. Groves is dead?*

"Because the animal is apparently hunting on the school grounds, the previous curfew rules are no longer in force. From now on the doors to the outside will be locked at all times, and anyone needing to leave the building must call for an escort from our Security Department. Failure to abide by these regulations will be punished with severe disciplinary action."

Spirit looked around until she caught Burke's eye. He looked grim. *And you don't even know the half of it. They searched my room. They found the book she loaned me. And that's why they killed her.* Spirit wanted to cry, and knew she didn't dare. She could feel Joe's eyes on her.

"That blows," she forced herself to say, fixing her gaze on her plate. She just hoped the other kids at the table thought she was pissed off by the new rules—and not scared out of her mind.

"Next, starting tomorrow, students will have their Gifts reassessed in order to rank them for advanced placement opportunities. In the event the email system remains down, the schedule for testing will be posted in the Refectory and the Library and copies will be provided to all teachers. Please make a note of the time of your appointment to avoid delays. Last— and I really should not have to remind any of you of this by this point—Oakhurst requires all students to abide by the Dress Code. Since you seem to have some difficulty with understanding precisely what this entails, for the next two months students will be required to adhere to the *strict* Dress Code. Uniform blazers will be worn at all times, trousers are not acceptable for female students at any time, and you will be expected to wear all items of school jewelry in your possession every day. Ms.

Shae, do feel free to return to your room and change before class."

When Muirin got up to change—looking as if she was going to do her best to make trouble for somebody—the first students were already getting up to leave. Spirit got up as well, and hurried to catch up with her—it was hard to feel it mattered now—and she wasn't surprised Addie did too.

"This—this is totally unacceptable!" Muirin sputtered. "Madison isn't going to let them do this to me!" She slanted a sideways glance at Spirit, letting her know what Spirit already knew: this was an act.

I don't think Mark and Madison are going to be in a hurry to argue with "Doctor Ambrosius" after what we heard on the tape, Spirit thought. She only wished she could believe Mordred and his Shadow Knights were going to fight among themselves. It was too convenient.

"It's just the same dress code it's always been," Addie said soothingly. "That part doesn't sound too bad." Her eyes were full of sympathy as she looked at Spirit. Spirit knew it would hurt soon, and terribly, but right now she was just numb. And today she'd walk into her History of Magic class, and Ms. Groves wouldn't be standing at the front of it. . . .

"It means wearing the rings too," she hissed in a low voice. "And they're *magic!*"

She started walking back to the dorm wing—it was where Muirin was supposed to be going right now, anyway.

Addie gave her a "well, duh" look—Muirin was still too furious to do anything but snarl.

"And Doctor Ambrosius is the one who enchanted them!" Spirit added, once they caught up to her.

Now Addie looked horrified. She was wearing her ring, and she slipped it off quickly and dropped it into her pocket.

"We'll need to carry them with us, but we can just put them on when one of the, um—'the Bad Guys'—is looking," Spirit said quietly.

"No, Spirit, nobody's going to let me get away with a thing!" Muirin said, loud enough for anybody who wanted to hear. She stalked off ahead of Addie and Spirit.

"So . . ." Addie asked, "how do we hide from all of Faculty and Admin?"

"We get help," Spirit said. *Muirin and Addie are wrong,* Spirit thought. *There's still one member of the faculty we can trust.*

She thought she knew who "Gawain" was.

†ЕП

Mark was Mark—King Mark of Cornwall. Teddy was Tristan—no wonder Elizabeth had recognized the Breakthrough Shadow Knights: Yseult of Cornwall was part of their story! Ovcharenko was Agravaine. Mordred had mentioned Morgaine, but not as if she knew who she was yet. *But I do . . .* Ovcharenko had called Muirin and Madison Lane-Rider "sisters"—she was willing to bet that made Madison Morgause and Muirin Morgaine. Sisters. *Which makes Morgaine Agravaine's aunt, and could this get any more disgusting?*

"—*Nimue, Morgaine, even Gaheris can be brought to the Shadow*—"

She wished Mordred hadn't said that. She wished she hadn't heard it. *Can be isn't will be,* she told herself. The important thing was what he'd said next.

223

Gawain was one of the Reincarnates Mordred couldn't subvert. Gawain was one of the Grail Knights.

They could trust Gawain—even if he didn't know he was a Reincarnate.

But who was he?

That part was almost easy. Gawain was someone who'd been at Oakhurst before the Shadow Knights arrived, because Mordred said he was specifically collecting Grail Knights as well as, well, everybody with magic.

He was male, because every single Reincarnate they'd heard about so far was the same sex as their original ancestor.

He was somebody Mordred knew—and whether he was Evil Mordred or Dr. Ambrosius, Spirit *still* didn't think he could tell most of the students here apart. Mordred wasn't *quite* sure of Gawain's identity, but he was suspicious—and whoever he was suspicious of, it wasn't somebody he could just make vanish. That meant someone on the Staff, because, face it, the students had been disappearing so fast, the reason Radial had been invited to the Spring Fling was probably just to up the attendance.

The male Oakhurst staff with magic (that she knew *for sure* had magic) who'd been here when she'd arrived and were still here was a short list. A really short list. Like, exactly one person.

She really hoped she was right.

🌟

"I don't usually do therapy in groups, but the way things have been going lately, I think I may have to start," Dr. MacKenzie said. "How are you feeling, Loch?"

Doctor Cooper MacKenzie was the Oakhurst "psychological counselor." He looked like Lenin and spoke with a strong Brooklyn accent. He was the kindest, *nicest* person Spirit had encountered . . . well, since she'd lost her family. When she'd been ordered to go for counseling back in January, she'd figured he was another jerk like the so-called grief counselors who'd made her time in rehab a living hell. But Doc Mac had not only told her it was okay to grieve—and that she'd never really "get over" the loss of her family—he'd also told her she *did* have magic. He hadn't just been blowing smoke at her, either—Doc Mac was a Fire Witch, and he could *see* it.

He'd been the first person she'd told what had *really* happened the night her parents and her sister died. He hadn't said she was crazy. He believed she'd seen what she thought she had—impossible as that might seem. He'd told her that even though it had been a magical attack, it wasn't her fault.

She'd been doing her best to believe him ever since.

She'd trusted him. And she still did.

Spirit and Loch should have been at class, but going to see the school shrink was an automatic "Get Out Of Jail Free" card. She didn't know where Muirin was supposed to be right now, but the same obviously applied to her. It had taken Spirit a lot of fast talking to get Loch and Muirin to agree to come with her to Doc Mac and tell him their story. She would have liked it to be all five of them, but she hadn't been able to catch up to Addie or Burke at lunch to tell them about the appointment.

"Angry someone used me as a tool to kill with," Loch said

tautly. "Because that's what happened, Doctor MacKenzie. That's why we're here."

Spirit glanced at Loch. Was it only Saturday that had happened? It seemed like a thousand years ago now.

"And you—all—feel this is true?" Doc Mac asked delicately.

"Oh hell yeah," Muirin said. "Um, not that I expect you to believe us. I'm just here for my friends."

She smiled brightly at Doc Mac. Spirit had expected Muirin to play fast and loose with the Dress Code, even after Ms. Corby's public call-out, but Muirin was following it down to the letter. Spirit found that particularly disturbing. What did Muirin know to make her buckle under so easily?

"I'll certainly listen to anything any of you wants to say," Doc Mac said. He smiled. "At least you don't have to convince me magic exists. That's a start."

Nobody said anything. "So who wants to go first?" he prompted after a moment.

"I will." It was only when she spoke up Spirit realized she wasn't scared. She was furious. "They said this morning Ms. Groves had an accident. That's a lie. Ms. Groves was murdered. Last week she loaned me one of her books of Arthurian myths and legends. Last night my room was searched. It was the only thing taken."

"And it seems to you there's a direct connection between these two things?" Doc Mac asked gently.

"I know there is. The other week, I was, um, really upset," Spirit said. "She found me crying in the library, and brought me back to her rooms. And . . . she did some kind of spell—a

Warding, I think—and then she told me I was right to distrust the Breakthrough people, and I was in danger. She said there's been a *glamourie* on Oakhurst for a very long time to keep everyone here from noticing all the crazy stuff that happens. She said *I* notice them because I haven't come into my magic yet. And when I point things out, I can break the *glamourie* that keeps people from looking at the weirdnesses. She said she wasn't powerful enough to fight what's organized against us openly, but she's done what she could. Then she gave me the book."

"And last night someone came to your room and took the book, and now she's dead," Doc Mac said neutrally.

"Don't forget that was after I nearly shot Spirit," Loch said vehemently. "And I *did* shoot Mr. Green! I know they say it was a 'tragic accident,' like it was all my fault, but I *hate* guns! I wouldn't play around with one. Ovcharenko called me"—Loch took a deep breath—"he called me a faggot and shoved the shotgun into my hands and forced me to shoot it. But I shot at the *targets*! And then I couldn't drop it, and I couldn't keep it from turning to point at Spirit, either. Yeah, they both know," Loch said, answering Doc Mac's silent question. "I told everybody last night. I told Spirit a couple of weeks ago I'd fallen for Burke."

"Wow," Muirin said. "Sucks to be you, Spears."

"Tell me about it," Loch answered with a crooked smile. "But you see, sir . . . maybe someone, something, wants you—anyone who cares—to think I'd try to kill Spirit out of jealousy and lie to myself about it. But I'm not stupid. Burke and Spirit are both my friends. Burke is straight." Loch shrugged. "And I hate guns."

"And Burke is okay with finding out you're gay?" Doc Mac asked.

"Yeah," Loch said. "I think he really is. But we've got more important problems right now. I had proof—not that I guess it counts for much in a school full of magicians—I'd recorded a conversation between Doctor Ambrosius and Mark Rider. But I can't find my recorder now."

"This office deals more in subjective truths," Doc Mac said. "We'll worry about objective proofs later. Right now, why don't you tell me what the problem is?"

"First could you— Could you do what Ms. Groves did?" Spirit asked hesitantly. "With the—"

"Just a moment." Doc Mac drew the same kind of sigil in the air that Ms. Groves had, and once again Spirit felt the ear-popping sense of *pressure*. "All right. The office is Warded now. I don't normally bother, unless I'm seeing an Air Mage who might lose control of their Gift. Or a Spirit Mage, of course, but there hasn't been one of those here at Oakhurst in a very long time."

"Spirit Mage?" Spirit asked.

"I thought there were only four Schools," Loch said. "Earth, Air, Fire, and Water."

"No, five: Earth, Air, Fire, Water, and Spirit." Doc Mac frowned. "That's odd. They should be teaching all five Schools." He shrugged. "It's not really that important to our discussion. It's just that since the School of Spirit deals primarily with gifts of mental control and influence, an untrained Spirit Mage in crisis could cause a great deal of collateral damage if they weren't properly Warded."

"Yeah, whatever," Muirin said impatiently. "Let's get back to the reincarnation and apocalypse."

Just as they had with Dylan last night, the three of them told the *secret* story of Oakhurst, beginning with Loch and Spirit's arrival—when they'd all become aware of just how *weird* Oakhurst really was—and continuing through the destruction of the Wild Hunt, the terror at New Year's, the arrival of the Shadow Knights—and discovering the Shadow Knights were actually Breakthrough. This time all three of them told the story, interrupting each other, backtracking, reminding each other of details they'd forgotten. As they spoke, Doc Mac looked more and more thoughtful. By the time they got through the second half of their explanation—Reincarnates, Elizabeth Walker, Camelot, haunted oaks, dead bikers, Mordred being imprisoned in the oak instead of Merlin, and Breakthrough intending to start a nuclear war by launching missiles—Doc Mac looked pretty sandbagged. Spirit was glad she hadn't included the part about him maybe being the Reincarnate Gawain. It was a theory she hadn't confided to the others. There hadn't been time and privacy.

"I wasn't aware of any of this," he said, when they finally paused. "Of course I knew we lost a certain number of students each year. But everyone who comes to Oakhurst is traumatically orphaned, and then they have their entire worldview overturned by learning not simply that magic exists, but that they have magic powers. With that much mental trauma, it would be out of the norm for there *not* to be suicides and runaways. That we lost such a small number each year seemed a blessing. I never thought any more about it."

"Some blessing," Muirin muttered.

There was silence for a time. Doc Mac sat and thought; Spirit, Loch, and Muirin just sat. Even if he didn't think they were crazy, it was a lot to take in, Spirit knew. If she'd been told everything she now knew back in September, she would have rejected it utterly.

"If you really believe all you've told me," Doc Mac finally said, "you three took an enormous risk telling me what you have."

"Not really," Loch said, shrugging. "Doctor A—Mordred— wants Spirit and me dead; Mark—King Mark of Cornwall—is insisting it has to look like an accident but he's probably going to cave pretty soon. I don't figure we have a lot to lose at this point. And Spirit says we can trust you—and I trust her."

"And I'm connected," Muirin said, smirking. "Madison Lane-Rider's recruiting me for the Shadow Knights: Join the forces of Evil! Grind your friends under the iron heel of tyranny! And you'd better believe I'm going to go running to her the moment we get out of here to give her a suitably edited version of events." She looked at Spirit and Loch and sighed, apparently realizing they didn't find the situation as funny as she did. "You two wanted to go see the Doc; I tagged along. You guys are all freaked out because you figure you've been marked for death by some kind of Secret Conspiracy you can't get Burke or Addie to believe in. Doc Mac talked you down off the ledge."

"Nice of you to let me know my part ahead of time," Doc Mac said dryly. "I can give you a few more details to make the story convincing, Muirin."

"You believe us?" Spirit said, almost sick with relief.

"Let's say I'm strongly inclined to," Doc Mac says. "I'm not sure about the Arthurian reincarnation aspect of things, but"—he hesitated—"we've lost nearly all the faculty and almost thirty students in a bit over two months. I dislike Mr. Ovcharenko and his private army a great deal, and Lily Groves was a good friend—and not the sort of person either inclined to midnight rambles, or incapable of defending herself if attacked. And the fact I never thought what happened with Loch and Beckett Green was at all odd until you came and talked to me about it is a *big* warning sign to me that I should take everything you've told me very seriously. So—conditionally—I'm in. What do you need from me?"

"What are your conditions?" Spirit asked suspiciously.

"I won't betray a professional confidence—yours or anyone else's. I won't do anything that's both harmful and illegal, so if you're expecting me to *shoot* anyone . . ."

"No!" Loch burst out.

"We need information," Muirin said quickly. "They're going to retest everyone. Why? Who's doing it? And can we get out of it?"

"And if you happen to know anyone in Homeland Security . . ." Loch said.

Doc Mac smiled tightly—that, more than anything else, made Spirit think he believed them. Doc Mac looked *scared*. "Unfortunately, no. But I can find out about the testing. And I can certainly advise that you, Spirit, and you, Loch, be put at the bottom of the list because of your recent trauma."

"Gee, thanks," Muirin muttered.

"You're on your own, kid," Doc Mac said, smiling at her conspiratorially. "I have great faith in your ability to lie like a rug."

Muirin bounded to her feet and bowed, looking pleased.

"Now," Doc Mac said briskly. "You two should exit stage left—"

"—pursued by a bear," Loch added irrepressibly.

"—and complaining you can't decide whether I believed you or not. And Muirin can remain to explain to me all the reasons why I *shouldn't* believe you." He glanced down at his watch and sighed, obviously coming to a decision he didn't like very much. "Loch, I think we'll need to see each other for several counseling sessions in order to work through your conflicts about your sexual identity."

Loch snorted, looking more cheerful than Spirit had seen him in weeks.

"That should also provide something of a safety net if the factionalism you predict comes into play. If the email system is working again, I'll email you. Otherwise, I'll just print out a schedule and have one of the Proctors deliver it. I'm assuming you have ways of communicating with your friends that won't draw unwelcome attention?"

"Aside from the whole 'marked for death' thing, yes," Loch said wryly. "Nobody much notices me."

"I think you underrate yourself," Doc Mac said. "But we'll leave it at that. Okay, kids. Showtime!" He got to his feet, clapping his hands together.

"You're going out there a persecuted lunatic, but you're coming back a paranoid loner!" Muirin said fulsomely.

Spirit laughed. It felt good. For the first time, she felt they were actually doing something that might *help*.

❧

Their visit with Doc Mac had run well into the afternoon. The rest of the day was weirdly tense; Spirit couldn't decide whether she was too scared, or not scared enough. All the equestrian classes had been canceled for the moment—and so had the firearms course, which Spirit didn't think would have happened just because somebody had *died* at the first one—so all the indoor PE classes were being doubled up (even more than before) and so were the History and Language classes. It was almost enough to make it look as if half the student body hadn't vanished in the last six months.

Because of her appointment with Doc Mac, she'd missed her Intermediate Latin Class. Her next class was Jane Smith's Math Class. Ms. Smith wanted them all to talk about their feelings (as usual).

Boy, it's a good thing Breakthrough intends to destroy the world, Spirit thought snarkily. *Because none of us is learning enough academic stuff to get into any college in the universe.*

Jillian Marshall and Claire Grissom both broke down in hysterics, and Ms. Smith (looking pleased) called for a couple of Proctors to escort them to what she called a "quiet room."

Spirit wondered if she'd see Claire and Jillian at dinner tonight.

After Math was her History of Magic Class—Ms. Groves's class. The replacement teacher was Madison Lane-Rider, and if that wasn't bad enough, she said from now on they'd be concentrating on the Arthurian Cycle.

It seemed cruelly, horribly unfair. Ms. Groves had been killed for giving Spirit a book of Arthurian legends. And now Madison Lane-Rider was teaching a class in it. Spirit tried not to wonder if the class itself was some kind of elaborate drawn-out trap. Would students disappear for knowing too much of the course material? Or for not knowing enough?

She was trembling with pent-up nerves and exhaustion by dinnertime. She barely remembered to slip her class ring onto her finger before she walked into the Refectory. The gold felt heavy and somehow greasy against her skin. Moving as if in a trance, she collected her tray and sat down at her assigned table. Joe Rogers was sitting in his usual spot, and Spirit had a flash of happiness at his irritated expression and the gold-and-brown striped tie around his neck. *So you hate the new dress code too? Tough.*

That was until she took a closer look.

The tie tack in the Oakhurst tie was a Gatekeeper emblem.

Joe Rogers had become one of the Shadow Knights.

Spirit didn't bother to look for Addie or Burke after dinner. She hadn't slept since yesterday morning, and the last thirty-six hours had been a series of brutal shocks. Loch and Muirin could fill the other two in on what they'd told Doc Mac; Spirit just wanted to sleep. She'd thought it would be a relief to get back to her room, but the moment she walked in, she realized it wasn't. Having it searched the way it had been had destroyed any sense of safety she felt here.

She wanted to scream, or even cry, but she was too tired for either. She changed for bed, but just as she was about to get into it she glanced at her computer and saw the intraweb icon in the taskbar was lit. The intraweb was back up. She almost ignored it, but . . . what if this was the only chance she got?

She untied the Ironkey from around her waist and sat down in her desk chair. She clutched it in her hand nervously—what would she say? What if QUERCUS wasn't there?—then checked her email instead. She didn't even need to open any of them to know what they were about: at least twenty of them were from Maddie Harris, which meant all of Oakhurst was privy to her hysterics about *prom gowns*.

And today is Tuesday, and tomorrow is Wednesday, and that's the last Dance Committee meeting before the Spring Fling, which is Friday—this Friday. And the Shadow Knights are going to do something *at the Spring Fling—because the Hellmouth opens at every single Oakhurst dance—and last time we had some idea of what it was, and this time I have no clue at all. . . .*

And in six weeks Mordred was going to destroy the world, unless they could stop him. She frowned at the screen, turning the Ironkey over and over in her hands. The five of them needed help, and it sure wasn't going to come from outside. She felt a lot better having Doc Mac on their side, but after what had happened to Ms. Groves, she knew he wouldn't be able to do anything openly. He'd be risking enough just getting them the information Muirin'd asked for.

One person—or even half a dozen . . . The Shadow Knights can just make them go away and nobody will notice. But if a lot of people stood up to them . . .

She knew everybody here wasn't falling for Breakthrough's party line—they couldn't be. The Breakthrough people were glamorous and almost credible, but Spirit bet that about half their current converts would ditch a future as a pawn of evil if they knew those were the actual stakes.

We need to find some way to organize—to get what we know out there and have people believe it. . . .

Yeah, like that's going to happen. Even before Breakthrough showed up, Oakhurst was pitting all of us against each other. Mordred should have just named the school "Thunderdome" in the first place. I know it's what we need to do. I just don't know how to do it.

She realized she was delaying out of sheer funk. Before she could talk herself out of even trying, she plugged the Ironkey into her machine.

Hello, Spirit, QUERCUS typed.

Spirit stared at the words for a very long time without typing anything. What if she'd been wrong from the beginning? What if QUERCUS was a trap? What if— What if— What if—

She had to decide. Friend or foe? Not choosing was as bad as making the wrong choice.

Hello, QUERCUS. Doctor Ambrosius is Mordred.

She counted heartbeats, watching the sentence on the screen. One— Two— Three— Four— Five . . .

I know.

Spirit stared at the words on the screen, too shocked to even know how they made her feel. Questions tumbled through her mind too fast to type: *Who are you? Why didn't you tell me? Do you know what he's planning? How can we stop him?*

You are stronger than you know. The hardest part of your task lies ahead of you. Remain vigilant and in readiness. I will contact you soon.

She wanted to protest, to demand an explanation. But there was no one to hear. QUERCUS had logged off.

I hope I haven't just screwed us all over, she thought bleakly.

When she got into bed, tired as she was, sleep took a long time to come.

❋

On Wednesday morning, the "leaked" memo Loch had warned Spirit about was in her mailbox, along with a follow-up memo from STAFF telling students to delete the first email without reading it. (Maybe some of them even had.) The list of GLBT students was less than a dozen names. (Not surprising, since there were only about sixty students here now.) Spirit wondered if there was any truth to the list. Of the two people at Oakhurst she knew *for sure* were gay, one was on it and one wasn't.

She was so upset by that she almost missed the other memo from STAFF. Today "Doctor Ambrosius's" testing began, and there was a schedule attached. The Proctors would go first, then everybody else. Doctor Ambrosius was doing all of the testing himself.

Spirit wondered how many people he could do in a day.

She wondered what he was looking for.

✦

When Loch walked into the Refectory that morning, several of the boys made kissing noises. Loch's was the only name from the "Platinum Spoon" group on the list. It made him a particular target—as if he "deserved" it more than the others (not that any of them deserved it).

She watched out of the corner of her eye as Loch made his way from the door toward the serving line. At a table Loch passed, Allen Tate swung around and stuck his feet out in Loch's path. Loch leaned over and said something—it was impossible to make out—and Allen scrambled back, tucking his feet under the bench.

Loch caught her eye and smirked, and Spirit suppressed a sigh of relief. It was all relative (she remembered a day, years ago, teasing Phoenix to the point where Fee shrieked at the top of her lungs: "It's all relatives!" and Mom—whose favorite saying was "It's all relative"—had laughed until she had to dry her eyes, and then gave them both Popsicles). You didn't worry about getting beaten up by your classmates when your teachers were trying to kill you. You didn't worry about being outed when the world was going to end.

✦

After spending the morning in *Systema* watching Ovcharenko try to kill Loch and Burke try to kill Ovcharenko (and oh god how she wished she was exaggerating), even lunch came as a relief (even if it put her one hour closer to today's

Dance Committee meeting). Spirit hardly noticed the fights and the quietly vicious arguments all around her. None of the fights were worse than shoving matches, anyway.

Muirin wasn't there (having apparently solved the problem of the dress code by deciding to stop going to classes completely).

At least, Spirit hoped that was why she was missing.

"Hey, where's our warden?" Kristi Fuller asked, setting down her tray and sliding into her seat. She gave Spirit a look of friendly sympathy: Kristi was one of the former Dance Committee members.

"Faculty Lunchroom. Doesn't have to eat with us peasants anymore." Taylor Parker was one of the three kids who'd come to Oakhurst after Spirit and Loch had. (Spirit was secretly amazed he was still here.) "They did Angie and Rick this morning, which is why they aren't here. Zoey Young, too, and what's up with that? I thought they were doing all the Proctors first."

Kristi shrugged. "Maybe somebody bailed."

"What's he doing to them?" Brianna asked. "I know Rick. He's about as sensitive as a brick." She rolled her eyes.

"'Testing,'" Kristi said. "In which we are 'reevaluated' in order to rank us for 'advanced placement.'" The ironic quotes stood out in her tone. She made a face.

"What kind of advanced placement can there be?" Taylor asked in confusion. "It's not like there's another Oakhurst for them to send anyone to."

Spirit had a sudden idea. "I don't know. But . . . I was in Chat last night and somebody said they heard if you don't pass, you get your magic burned out." She kept her voice casual, as if she was just helpfully passing on gossip. Three months ago it wouldn't have worked. Three months ago, there'd been a hundred kids here instead of sixty. Nobody said anything in response, but Spirit was pretty sure the rumor would be all over the school by midafternoon.

In fact, she was betting her life on it.

⁂

"Do you think they'll show up?" Maddie asked, for possibly the tenth time in the last fifteen minutes. "What if they don't show up?"

A table and chairs had been set up in one corner of the gym, and there was a cooler full of sodas and a couple of big plates of cookies. Not much by the standards of the goodie bags Breakthrough had been providing, but lavish in terms of Oakhurst fare. Spirit wasn't even sure why the Dance Committee was meeting here instead of in one of the lounges, or one of the empty classrooms, or the School Library, or even the Teachers' Lounge, but it wasn't like any of them wanted to argue with Admin.

"We cancel the dance and close Oakhurst, what do you think?" Dylan answered.

Spirit had done her best to keep away from Dylan since the night they'd gathered to play back Loch's recorder. She'd been afraid he'd blurt out what he knew. But today it was Zoey who was pinging her radar. Zoey looked *spooked*. More than that, she looked *sick*.

"Should we have gone to the funerals? Would that have

been right? Have they even had them yet?" Zoey asked. "We should have gone. I bet they asked us. Our email's been down, is that why we didn't find out?" Her eyes were fever-bright, and she chattered randomly in a high nervous voice. Nobody'd quite dared to ask her how her retest had gone.

"The funerals were last Friday," Chris said. "It would've been awkward if we'd gone, since two of us were still supposed to be in the hospital."

"I'm a quick healer," Dylan said, and snickered.

"Yeah, well, whatever," Kylee said. "You know they're all going to go back and tell their families they saw all of us here today in the bloom of health."

I wouldn't, Spirit thought. She still had no idea of what she was going to say to the Radial kids, but she knew whatever it was, she didn't want to say it in the Oakhurst gym.

Just when Spirit was starting to wonder if they were coming at all, the doors at the far end of the gym opened and Ms. Corby walked in, followed by the Committee and four Breakthrough security guards. All seven of the Radial teens were wearing black armbands. Their escort stopped at the door and—once the Townies were halfway across the floor—turned and went out again.

Juliette, Brenda, Veronica, and Kennedy—the surviving members of the Radial committee—were there. Juliette had (as usual) brought her twin, Brett, and there were two other new-comers as well: Tom and Adam Phillips. Spirit remembered them from the field trip—Muirin had said once they'd been Seth's partners in his smuggling business. Adam was eighteen and Tom was fourteen and it was obvious neither one gave a damn about the school dance.

I don't know what possible use they can be, Spirit thought in exasperation. *Bodyguards? I could take them both out, and I don't even have magic!*

"Welcome to Oakhurst," Maddie said, standing up and holding out her hand. "I see we have two new recruits."

Tom sniggered and Adam snorted. Neither came forward to shake Maddie's hand.

"Nice place you have here," Tom said, looking around. Spirit suddenly remembered what she'd thought the first time she'd seen the Oakhurst gym. It had looked like something out of a Hollywood fantasy of what an elite private school would be like. And she remembered how—for just a little while, back at the beginning—she'd been dazzled by the luxury Oakhurst had surrounded her with . . .

"If we could just get started?" Maddie said anxiously. "We have a lot of things to cover, and not much time. Now, I know we didn't finalize the colors for the Spring Fling, but we're really out of time, so I thought we could reuse some of the decorations we had here, which would make the dance colors—"

"Is that it?" Brenda said blankly. "Two of my friends are dead, the library's a pile of kindling, and we're just going to talk about the *dance*?"

"Yeah. A dance seems like a really stupid idea in the first place when we just buried Bella and Erika on Friday," Kennedy said.

"Hey if we shut down Oakhurst every time somebody died we'd never have classes at all," Dylan said.

"I just think we should—" Juliette said.

"Finish planning the dance," Kylee said harshly. "That's why you're here, right?"

"We're here because your friends bought the Town Council," Brett said belligerently. "We were going to pull out and not have a dance at all."

"Oh, Brett, you know we all talked about this and we agreed—" Juliette said.

"But didn't Mr. Rider say we had to go through with it?" Veronica said. All the Radial kids glared at her, and she blushed furiously. "I just mean I thought . . ." she mumbled.

"If Breakthrough doesn't see one hundred percent turnout from Radial at the Spring Fling, there's going to be trouble," Brenda said flatly. "But the thing that's really bugging me right now is how none of you guys seemed surprised when those things showed up and tore the library apart."

"We were," Chris protested. "Uh—surprised. But you know everything happened so fast—the noise, the confusion—"

Over Brenda's shoulder, Spirit saw the door leading from the school into the gym silently open. Teddy Rider and Anastus Ovcharenko walked in. The others were so agitated that nobody noticed them but her.

"I didn't even want to come today!" Juliette said. "And Mom said I didn't have to, but she's on the Town Board, so I *know* about Breakthrough, and—is this some kind of cover-up?"

Teddy and Ovcharenko were wandering along the opposite side of the gym, apparently deep in conversation and oblivious to the meeting. Spirit poked Kylee under the table, and jerked her head in their direction. Kylee's eyes went wide, and she turned to whisper into Chris's ear.

"Yeah," Adam said. "Monster robots out of a video game?" He sounded more impressed than worried. Spirit's stomach lurched. He hadn't been there that day—and that meant the secret was out.

"People *died,*" Brenda repeated. "And if you know anything about—"

"If you guys keep running your mouths like this you're going to end up mind-wiped just like everybody else who's ever found out something Oakhurst doesn't want them to know," Dylan snarled.

"Oh come on—" Kennedy said.

"Look, will you guys all just *please* shut up?" Spirit hissed. *"Company."*

The Townies looked around the gym and finally spotted Teddy and Ovcharenko. Suddenly everyone stopped talking. The silence was more suspicious than what they'd been saying. In another moment, the two men would come over, and Teddy would be charming, and ten seconds after that he'd know everything.

Spirit held her breath. *They can't just make the Radial kids vanish,* she told herself desperately. *And it won't help to mind-wipe them, because if Adam knows what happened last Wednesday, everybody in Radial under the age of eighteen must know too. . . .*

But to Spirit's deep mistrust, Teddy simply waved and smiled from across the gym, and he and Ovcharenko walked down to the outside door and went through it.

"Boy, it really must suck to be you guys," Brett said, when the door had crashed shut again.

"You have *no* idea," Chris Terry said feelingly.

"So . . . who wants a Coke?" Maddie asked brightly.

Nobody really wanted to talk about the Spring Fling. Every point Maddie raised—from the Spring Fling colors (silver, pink, and blue) to the song list—was waved aside by Juliette. The Townies resented being forced to attend, and the Oakhurst kids knew there wasn't much point in trying to make decisions about music or anything else: the Spring Fling would be Breakthrough's show from first to last. Tomorrow, Madison Lane-Rider would be bringing several racks of prom gowns to Macalister High; Spirit suspected the Oakhurst girls would just be *assigned* prom gowns.

"I'm not wearing something pink and frilly," Kennedy said through gritted teeth, when Maddie mentioned the gowns.

"Yeah, like anybody's going to care what you show up wearing," Brett said. "But hey, that means there'll be two dresses for Couch, because it'll take two to cover that fat butt."

Veronica hung her head, and pretended she couldn't hear him.

"Hey, do you think you guys could lay off a little?" Kylee snapped.

"Yeah, sure. It's okay for you guys with your trust funds and your fancy school," Tom said. "You don't know what it's like to be pushed around. All anybody hears is 'Breakthrough this' and 'Breakthrough that.' New library, new housing development, skate park—"

"New sewage and water treatment plant," Brenda said softly. "Town's needed one for years."

Spirit wondered why Breakthrough was making all these long-term plans, given Mordred's agenda. The only thing she could think of was maybe Mark Rider was buying Radial's cooperation—but why bother? What did he need from Radial he couldn't just take?

The more the Townies talked about Breakthrough's development plans, the twitchier Spirit got. Dylan knew the truth, and if he came out with it, the news would be all over town by dinnertime.

I should probably be hoping for that, Spirit thought. *Nobody will believe it, but everyone will talk about it. Wouldn't that stop them?*

She didn't know. And what it *would* do would be to lead Breakthrough back to the only possible source of the leak: Muirin.

"But look," Kennedy said urgently. "You gotta tell us. Those . . . things. You told Brenda you'd explain. I saw . . . What I saw . . ."

"Not here," Spirit said quickly. "Not now. I will. I promise."

"But you know, don't you?" Brenda said. "And it's got something to do with why we can't cancel the dance. And why we all have to come."

"You can't!" Zoey spoke while Spirit was still trying to think of an answer. She'd been sitting so quietly for so long the others had almost forgotten she was here. "You can't—that's what they want—that's their plan! But you can't! Stay away! Stay away from Oakhurst—no matter what you have to do—no matter what you're told—tell all your friends—tell everyone! Because if you don't— If you don't—"

"Now, Zoey, we don't want to upset everyone."

It was Mandy Poole, the Breakthrough technician who'd tried to recruit Spirit when Breakthrough had first showed up. She'd showed up at Zoey's side practically out of nowhere—even though Spirit had been watching the doors to see if someone else was going to come in. *Her Gift must be Shadewalking—like Loch's. Or invisibility,* Spirit thought inanely. Mandy took Zoey by the arm and lifted her to her feet.

"She's just tired," Mandy said fixing the others with a professional smile. "Aren't you, Zoey?"

Zoey stared at Mandy, clearly terrified. The Radial kids were looking shocked and confused, obviously without any idea of how to react. The Oakhurst kids were sitting very still, trying not to attract Mandy's attention. Spirit was as frozen as the rest. Her hands were clenched into fists, her nails digging into her palms. She hated herself for not doing something to help Zoey, even as she knew there wasn't anything she could do. She could protest—and be taken to wherever Zoey was being taken.

The place nobody came back from.

"New medication," Mandy said meaninglessly. "Just come along with me. We'll be right back," she added over her shoulder as she led Zoey from the gym.

After that, there was no point in even pretending to have a

meeting. The Radial kids couldn't wait to get out of there. They'd driven up in their own cars, so Chris offered to walk them back to the parking area. Spirit and Kylee went along too, but they didn't get very far. There were two Breakthrough security guards standing right outside the door. Their name tags said LARSEN and MASSEY. Larsen said they'd escort the committee members back to their cars. Chris stepped back.

"See you guys Friday," he said.

The doors shut behind the Townies, and Chris turned away. He looked . . . blank. They'd all known kids were disappearing more and more often now, but this was the first time any of them had seen someone taken away right before their eyes. He walked back to the table; Spirit and Kylee trailed after him. Dylan and Maddie were still sitting there. Chris picked up a can of Coke and rolled it back and forth between his palms.

There was a long frozen silence.

"Guess who isn't coming to dinner," Dylan said at last.

Nobody laughed.

ELEVEN

With the Dance Committee meeting ending so early, none of the Oakhurst kids had any good excuse for not showing up at their afternoon classes. For Spirit, that meant King Arthur 101 with Madison Lane-Rider (Zoey was in the same class, but she wasn't here). There were thick stacks of Xeroxes waiting on everyone's desk—Madison said there hadn't been time to order appropriate textbooks, so they'd have to make do with material from her personal collection. (Madison Lane-Rider was an Arthurian geek. Surprise.) Fortunately this was only the second session and they were still on the introductory material, since Spirit had never felt less like paying attention in her life. At least she could just paste an attentive expression on her face and zone out as Madison lectured—she was showing slides (mostly of Victorian paintings) and the room was dark.

Spirit had figured they'd get to the magic by today, or at least to the "secret history" where Madison talked about how what really happened had been distorted by everyone having to explain away the magic, but (just like last time), all that Madison talked about was the "social purpose" of the "myth cycle." Despite the fact that all of this was new material, it all seemed oddly familiar—and finally Spirit figured out why.

She's doing to King Arthur what Doctor Ambrosius does to religion every Sunday. She's making it seem stupid.

Not all of it, of course. Just the parts about chivalry and honor and "might for right." Madison talked a lot about Art as a tool for social control, and said the Arthurian Cycle was basically State-sponsored propaganda, just like totalitarian regimes used today.

Spirit thought it was the creepiest thing she'd heard lately. Especially since she knew what the totalitarian regime teaching the class was planning. She'd never been so grateful in her entire life to hear the bell ring.

Now she just had to get through dinner without having a nervous breakdown.

But that wasn't easy. If the mood at lunch had been tense, the atmosphere at dinner was worse. Most of the Proctors were missing. Only Joe, Angie, and Mary Morris—Angie and Mary had been in the morning test group; Joe was a Gatekeeper—were there, and all of them (even Joe) looked like they had really bad headaches.

Muirin wasn't at dinner. (Zoey wasn't there either.)

When dinner was over, Spirit waited in the hallway outside

the Refectory to catch up with Addie, Loch, and Burke. There didn't seem to be a lot of point now for them to pretend not to know each other (not with two of them marked for death, Burke going kamikaze, and Muirin playing double agent), and Spirit really wanted to be with her friends tonight. More, she wanted to *warn* them, because she and Loch were at the bottom of the test list, and Muirin might be able to get out of it completely, but that left Burke and Addie.

If anything happens to either of them—to any of us—I don't think I could stand it.

Loch was the first to join her. He looked . . . The only word Spirit could think of was "dangerous," and she knew it wasn't quite the right one. But before they'd found out about Mordred, Loch had been giving up, certain he couldn't escape the fate Oakhurst and Breakthrough had planned for him. And now . . .

Bad as things were, Loch wasn't afraid anymore.

Burke and Addie exited the Refectory together. Burke looked grim, but that wasn't unusual for him these days. It had started when Muirin had revealed that Ovcharenko had murdered his foster parents. In the beginning, Spirit had tried to ignore it, to tell herself Burke was feeling normal grief and anger, but his rage had boiled over the day he'd attacked Ovcharenko, and it had been close to the surface ever since. Once she'd thought Burke didn't have a spark of meanness or anger in him. Now she knew he'd simply kept his temper under rigid control. He wasn't doing that any longer.

And Addie . . .

She'd always been the one saying they should find outside

help, the one who'd refused to believe the truth about Oakhurst, the one who'd been most terrified of it when she could no longer deny what was happening. Now she just looked quietly outraged. As if she'd suddenly discovered she was being patronized and intended to make the people doing it very, very sorry.

Have they really changed, or am I just going crazy? And if they've changed, have I?

"So," Addie said, bright and bitter, "who's up for some mindless vegging in the lounge?"

"Sounds good to me," Loch said. "One of the big ones?" he added, and Addie nodded.

There were six student lounges, three on the first floor (North, South, and East) and three on the second (ditto). They were only open after dinner and until half an hour before room curfew. A lot of the kids used them to study in, because who wanted to spend all their time either in class or alone in their room? Five of the lounges had sixty-inch flatscreen DVD players and microwaves. The sixth lounge was the tiny one behind the School Library—back when they'd hung out together openly, it was the one they usually went to. Tonight they headed for one of the big ones; Oakhurst had a "permitted" list of movies you could run (nothing too sexy, nothing too violent), and they didn't get the new releases until a year later, but a lot of the selections didn't actively suck. Spirit thought she could really go for two hours of watching something where you knew who the bad guys were and the hero was guaranteed to win.

But when they reached First Floor North, they saw several

kids looking at the bulletin board on the wall—the lounge bulletin boards were supposed to be used only for official notices, but everyone used them to leave the kind of messages you couldn't use Chat or email for, like lost and found stuff. Two of them shook their heads, muttering, and walked out.

"Don't even bother," Troy Lang said to Burke as he walked past him. "New rule: the lounges are segregated now. This one's Girls Only."

"What?" Loch said. "All of them? That's going to put a real crimp in Chess Club."

"See for yourself," Josh Quinn said. "East is closed, South is the Boys' Club. Same upstairs." Troy and Josh walked away.

"That's *really* going to put a crimp in Chess Club," Loch observed to nobody in particular. Second Floor East was the little one behind the Library the Chess Club met in.

"I don't believe it," Addie said. She strode into the lounge and read the notice on the board.

"'Failure to observe the new rules will result in the closure of all lounges and demerits for the offending students,'" she quoted when she came back. "This is outrageous—why don't they just send us all to our rooms and seal our doors shut?"

"Don't give them any ideas," Burke said.

"What about the Library?" Spirit said. "We can't watch a movie, but we could still . . ."

"Sounds good to me," Burke said. "Being with you guys is more important anyway."

Addie was still fuming as they entered the Library. Her irritation was all out of proportion to the new rules, especially considering everything else. Maybe that was the point, Spirit thought. This was something small enough it was safe to get mad at it.

When Spirit had arrived at Oakhurst last September, there'd been two librarians who took care of the collection. She wasn't really sure when Mr. Jackson and Ms. Anderson had vanished. It wasn't like they'd been here all the time just to begin with. But she hadn't seen either of them in a couple of weeks, and the books on the shelves were starting to look unloved and faintly unkempt (you didn't have to check books out, since they were all RFID-chipped and the system always knew where they were, but you were supposed to return them to the front desk for reshelving). But tonight Mary Morris was sitting at the check-in counter, looking as if she'd like to be anywhere else.

"No mixed seating in the library," she chanted in a bored voice as they walked through the door.

"Oh come *on!*" Loch said. "What do you think we're going to do in here except study?"

"Not my problem," Mary said. "*You* got a problem, take it up with Doctor A."

Burke snorted. "Come on, guys. We can sit at separate tables and pretend we don't know each other."

Most of the kids who needed to do serious studying just grabbed the books they needed from the Library and did it in their rooms, and the ones who were practicing their magic were either in the practice rooms or (in the case of the Water Witches) the pool. But even though it was a Wednesday night, tonight there were almost twenty kids here—and despite the

"No Talking" rule, the susurrant hum of conversation filled the room.

The four of them sat down, finding seats close to each other, although not at the same table. Spirit leaned over to whisper into Addie's ear. "Dance Committee was fun. I think it was over in about half an hour. Mandy Poole grabbed Zoey."

"Ow," Addie said. She dug in her blazer pocket and withdrew a notepad and a pencil. "Zoey was tested this morning," she whispered back. As she spoke, she was writing on the notepad—if they couldn't talk to Burke and Loch, they'd just have to pass notes. Spirit leaned over to see what she was writing, and grinned despite herself. Only Adelaide Lake would think Latin was a suitable language to write your crib notes in.

In whispers, Spirit filled her in on what she'd found out in the Committee meeting. "Whether the adults know or not, every kid in Radial has all the details about the library attack, and Breakthrough's pressuring Radial to go forward with the joint dance whether the kids want to or not." She described as well as she could Zoey's bizarre behavior before Mandy showed up, but neither of them could really come up with an explanation.

As Spirit spoke, Addie wrote her notes and passed them to Loch. After he'd read them, Loch stuck them in his mouth and chewed them. Even if somebody was paranoid and suspicious enough to want to investigate the lumps of chewed paper (and this was Oakhurst, so just about everyone was), the penciled marks would be gone.

"And Angie and Mary weren't—" *Weren't acting at all the*

way Zoey was, she began to say, but she never finished that sentence.

"Hey! Everybody! Security's searching our rooms!" Troy Lang skidded to a stop in the Library doorway. "Right now!"

✦

By the time Spirit and Addie reached the first floor hallway of the Young Ladies' Wing, there were already a dozen other girls there. A woman in a Breakthrough Security uniform blocked their way, not letting anyone through, and another one stood in front of the door leading to the second floor. In the hall behind the security guard, Spirit could see two more people in uniforms, a man and a woman, going in and out of the rooms. The woman had a big German Shepherd on a leash. The man had a dowsing rod. Doors stood open all down the hall. Ms. Corby stood in the hall with a clipboard, checking off each room as it was cleared.

Spirit turned to Addie, intending to make a joke about double jeopardy—because Breakthrough had already searched her room once—but Addie wasn't standing quietly beside her. She was pushing her way to the front of the crowd.

"Ms. Corby!" Addie's voice rang out sharply over the sounds of everyone else talking at once. "Could you tell us, please, what is going on here?"

Addie's words might have been polite, but her tone certainly wasn't. Spirit winced. *Wasn't getting frozen into the pool and practically drowned enough of a heads-up for you?*

The other girls quieted when Addie spoke. Everyone wanted

to know the answer, but nobody else had quite dared to ask. Spirit saw Kylee, who looked fiercely irritated, and Maddie, whose tear-filled eyes and stricken expression implied she was watching Breakthrough torture kittens.

"Ah, our dear Miss Lake," La Corby said. She smiled; it was an expression of genuine pleasure. "There's no need to be alarmed. Doctor Ambrosius is worried that one of you might have picked up something dangerous—purely by accident. The inspection will be done shortly." Her smile widened further. "Ladies! Ladies! May I have your attention, please?" She raised her voice, and the few girls who'd been whispering to each other stopped. "As an additional security precaution, those of you in first floor rooms will be moved to the second floor. Immediately. Room curfew will be extended by ninety minutes so that Housekeeping can relocate everyone. Please do not attempt to enter your current rooms. Once your personal effects have been removed, all first floor rooms will be locked, sealed, and warded."

Spirit carefully didn't touch the Ironkey at her waist. She suspected—no, she *knew*—it was one of the things Breakthrough was looking for. Whether they knew it or not.

One of the girls timidly raised her hand. "Ms. Corby? Will we be able to choose our new rooms ourselves?" It was Emily Davis; Spirit knew she was School of Air, with a strong Scrying Gift—object-linked clairvoyance and precognition. (Spirit wondered what kind of visions Emily was having these days.)

"I'm afraid not, Emily," Ms. Corby answered. "For your safety, the occupied rooms will all adjoin one another so that

257

we can seal any remaining empty rooms as an additional precaution. Your new rooms will be ready in just a few hours."

"They're probably going to Jaunt all your crap upstairs, Emmie Lou," Kylee muttered, just loudly enough for Emily to hear.

Most of the girls had ground floor rooms, and nobody wanted Breakthrough moving what few personal possessions they'd managed to gather. The noise level rose sharply—for the first time since she could remember, Spirit heard Oakhurst students arguing and complaining about the rules in front of a member of Staff.

"Hey, stranger, what's going on?"

Spirit jumped as Muirin sidled up to her. She was dressed conservatively—for Muirin. Everything was black, but at least she was covered.

"They're moving us upstairs," Spirit said. "I have to talk to Loch," she added in a whisper. "It's urgent."

Muirin nodded, the barest dip of her chin. "Nobody's moving me!" she shouted (even though Muirin already had a second floor room). Everyone turned and stared. "I'm going to go talk to Anastus! He'll fix things!"

She turned around and stomped off, grabbing Spirit's wrist as she did. Spirit followed as Muirin stalked down the hall muttering loudly but unintelligibly. It *sounded* like swearing, but you couldn't make out any of the words.

The chaos was just as bad—and louder—on the Young Gentlemen's Wing. Spirit glanced down that corridor as Muirin dragged her into the Main Hall. She saw a couple of boys shove another one. They'd be fighting in a minute. She was just as glad she was going somewhere else.

Muirin ducked into First Floor North (completely empty) and through the door at the back. Loch had said once that all of the old "Stately Homes" were really two houses: the owner's house, and the servants' areas, interlocking with each other but connected at only a few points. On the other side of the door, the grandeur of Oakhurst became shabby green linoleum and plain white walls. Muirin turned left and hurried down the corridor. It took Spirit a few seconds to orient herself: she was between the Main Hall and the Refectory, so this had to be the kitchen and pantry area.

At the end of the corridor, Muirin turned left again and dragged Spirit through a doorway. From here, Spirit could glimpse the Cold Kitchen—a wall of brushed steel refrigerators and walk-in freezers, with sinks and prep areas lining the other three sides. The room Muirin had brought her to was lined with wooden shelves holding industrial-sized cans and boxes. She could make out a few familiar images in the dimness. *Who knew Crisco came in twenty pound cans?* she thought dazedly.

"This place is like a maze," she said in exasperation.

Muirin shrugged. "They have to store the food somewhere. Now spill it. I know my way around the Young Gentlemen's Wing, but you sneak about as well as an elephant in tap shoes."

For Muirin's benefit, Spirit quickly summarized what she'd already told Addie, then went on. "There have to be other kids here who don't want to grow up to be the minions of a Dark

Lord, Murr," she said. She'd meant to bring this up in the Library, but she hadn't had time. "It's getting really bad really fast—I don't know what Doctor A is testing for, but we have to stop him. We have to find out who's on our side—or who could be—and we don't have much time. The dance is in two days. Loch's seeing Doc Mac tomorrow—he needs to get him to help."

Muirin snorted rudely. "Doc Mac's going to need some time for his head to stop spinning first." She looked at Spirit. "You have *no* idea how much trouble you're really in. I've spent the last two days lying my head off to Anastus, Mark, Teddy, and Madison about how nobody believes your conspiracy theory. That's going to buy you a little time. Not a lot."

"Depends on if they believed *you*," Spirit says. She didn't ask Muirin how Breakthrough had come to believe she *had* a conspiracy theory. They knew she'd asked to see Doc Mac after the not-an-accident on the firing range. And before she'd known how high the stakes were, she probably hadn't been careful enough. (Careful enough would have involved never coming to Oakhurst in the first place.)

"I have years of practice at lying to everybody," Muirin said grandly. "Come on. We better get back out there to complain. And yes, before you remind me, I'll pass your suggestion on to Loch. Although if you're thinking of having the student body rise up *en masse* and declare that it's Spartacus, you're going to have a long time to wait, if you ask me."

Spirit only wished she didn't think Muirin was right.

Despite what Ms. Corby had said about their rooms being ready "in just a few hours," it was almost midnight before Spirit could sit down on her new bed in her new room and look out her new window. Second floor. Not quite in the same place on the wing her old one had been, so there was a nagging feeling of wrongness when she looked out.

She didn't know how the Housekeeping staff had gotten everyone's things moved (*it's easy; all you need is a little magic,* she thought bitterly) but they were here. And neatly arranged— too neatly, as if it had been done by demented mice from the Bizarro Disney universe. Every article of clothing neatly folded, all the bathroom stuff perfectly arranged on the shelves, all the school supplies organized and neatly put away, though not in exactly the places she'd kept them. When she'd opened her closet door and seen every pair of shoes she owned lined up in a neat row, she'd wanted to cry. This was worse than having her room torn apart. This was having it put together the way someone else thought it should be, as if they were trying to erase *Spirit* completely.

She wondered if that was what Mordred really wanted—a bunch of mindless robot zombie minions who would do exactly what he ordered them to and never give him any trouble. (Not like he'd given Arthur. That was for sure.)

She wondered if Mark and Ovcharenko were totally down with that. Not to mention Madison Lane-Rider. A postapocalyptic wilderness didn't seem as if it would involve many fashion opportunities somehow.

She glanced at the clock. *Midnight. The witching hour. (Ha.)*

Forty-eight hours from now the Spring Fling will be over, and if we're lucky . . .

She wasn't sure what outcome she should hope for. She'd told Muirin just a few hours ago that things were getting bad fast. She'd had no clue what "bad" was. Now that they'd all (even Muirin) been moved, there were two Breakthrough Security guards on the floor. She wasn't sure even Muirin could sneak past them, since the guards had probably been chosen on the basis of their Gifts. Muirin had said once that she couldn't be fooled by anyone else's illusions, since that was her own power.

Not that she'd probably have to sneak in and out, even under the new rules, Spirit thought with a sigh. She'd like to wish Muirin would stop playing along with Breakthrough, but dangerous as it was, stopping would probably be even more perilous. And if she hadn't been doing that all along . . .

They wouldn't know the world was going to end.

Yeah, the world's going to end, but morning's still going to come, and god help me if I don't show up for breakfast, she grumbled. She'd never felt less like sleeping in her entire life, but she grudgingly put on her pajamas and got into bed.

The mattress felt different, too.

✦

Guinevere, High Queen, sat like a statue on the bare back of one of the famous white horses that had been her dowry on the day she had wed Arthur. Only the knights of the Table had ever been permitted to ride them, for they were bred to carry kings.

The Table was broken, and the King was dead.

The Dream was dead.

No! *she cried silently.* Arthur's Dream shall be reborn! It lives now in the hearts of men and women of good courage!

And someday it would be reborn in stone and law once again. The shining city on the hill would rise more glorious than before. Camelot would rise from the ash and gall of the Black Serpent's betrayal.

It had been Candlemas when the Black Serpent first revealed his mad ambition, Eastertide when Arthur had returned from Armorica to offer battle, Hallowmas when the evil was run to ground. In her mind, Guinevere gave the Great Feasts their ancient names: Imbolc, Ostara, Samhain. But the Old Ways were fading as the New Religion grew strong. Someday they would be but a dim memory, lost with the magic that was the silver gift of Arianhrodd to all who shared her blood. Guinevere gazed at the rune-scarred trunk of the Dungeon Oak as the wind blew soft and cold over her skin. "Herein lies imprisoned the traitorous son of the Great Bear: Mordred Kinslayer the Accursed . . ."

Imprisoned, but not dead. Trapped, please, Jesus and Epona, until the stars grew dark, but not even The Merlin's great sorcery could slay a necromancer with Death's ichor flowing through his veins. And in his last moments unentombed, Mordred had struck out at the one man with the power to be his jailor for Time and all Eternity. He had cast a spell to bind The Merlin to the body he now wore until the end of time.

All of Arianhrodd's children knew that the mortal flesh was merely a garment to be worn for a span of seasons, while the eternal spirit journeyed forever onward, reborn again and again. To trap someone within the toils of eternal death was a cruel vengeance indeed, but that had only been a part of Mordred's intent. With The Merlin gone, Mordred would have no enemy to thwart him on the evil day he broke free—if that day came.

But he had reckoned without the implacable will of she who was the spirit of the land itself: Guinevere, sorceress and Queen. She had pledged herself and Arthur's knights, pledged all who had loved Camelot, to eternal vigilance.

On the day Mordred broke free, they would be waiting . . .

❋

"Showtime," Loch murmured in Spirit's ear as he passed her in the Refectory at breakfast. She grimaced wryly. She couldn't manage to work up a real smile.

Thursday.

When she'd checked her mailbox this morning, it had contained six separate emails from Maddie about how they should behave on Friday, all with urgent pleas that the Dance Committee set an example and make the Macalister High kids feel welcome—not that an example would really be necessary, since once again Maddie had sent the emails to the entire school, so if anybody didn't know how Maddie thought they should all behave, they had to be illiterate. There'd also been an email from Madison Lane-Rider about the fabulous designer gowns they were all going to be so privileged to wear (and Spirit had been right: they weren't going to get to choose their own—their dresses would be delivered to their rooms this afternoon). After all that, the Morning Motivational Message would have had to be something epic to make an impression. And it was. It had also been about as subtle as an Acme Anvil: all about how weakness, indecision, and cowardice were the enemies of greatness, and the "leaders of tomorrow" rooted out those qualities in themselves and didn't tolerate them in others. An Oakhurst alum led by example and inspired by deeds. Spirit had found herself whistling "Oakhurst We Shall Not Forget Thee" ironically as she'd headed off to shower. Assuming you could whistle ironically, of course.

Her flash of good humor had faded long before she arrived in the Refectory, and while she was waiting on the serving line, she heard half a dozen rumors about the testing, from the one she'd started herself, to one saying everyone got an additional Gift from a School they didn't already have, to the testing gave you a vision of your own death, to one saying nobody remembered what happened during the testing. The last one should have been easy enough to check—at least a dozen kids had already gone through it—but nobody was talking.

By the time she got back to her table, the doors had been barred, and that meant everybody should be here, but the tables were still half empty. At least twenty kids were missing, and a few minutes later Ms. Corby came in and read off a set of names (different than the ones that had been posted) of kids who were supposed to be tested. *And good luck with that,* Spirit thought. She was starting to guess what was going on.

Her first class proved her right. There were supposed to be thirty kids in *Systema* class. There were seventeen. Ovcharenko could count as well as anyone could: he glared at them and stalked out of the gym. About ten minutes later, Mia Singleton showed up to lead the class. She made a point of saying tomorrow's class would be canceled so they could all "rest up" for the Spring Fling.

By lunchtime, it was clear the student body of Oakhurst was in open revolt. Everybody was spooked by the new tests, rumors about what had *really* happened when the library in Radial got trashed had finally made it back to Oakhurst, and having two-thirds of the student body summarily relocated without warning had been the final straw.

Muirin and Loch weren't the only ones who knew all the school hiding places. Anybody who'd ever wanted to make out, grab a smoke, or just get fifteen minutes of *privacy* knew at least three places they could do that. Anybody who didn't want to hide outright found somewhere to be that they weren't supposed to be, even if it was just in the back rows of the wrong classroom. And with their schedules having been changed almost daily over the last three weeks, nobody was really sure who was supposed to be where—even half the teachers.

The security staff roamed the halls all afternoon talking to each other on their radios and wandering in and out of classrooms as they tried to track the missing students down. Add to that the fact that anybody who'd been called for testing that day was either recovering in their room or recovering in the Infirmary (so anybody Security couldn't find might be legitimately sick, hiding, or just in the wrong place), and by the end of the day, the entire staff was looking as if all of them wanted to shoot somebody.

None of the students were particularly sympathetic.

Spirit wanted to think her classmates were preparing to rise up and throw off the chains of their oppressors (or at least stop letting Breakthrough push them around), but she knew better than to really hope. Oakhurst would load them all down with sugar tomorrow night, there'd be a dance, and by Monday they'd probably all go back to being good little sheep. (Most of them, anyway.)

Still, the thought of a rebellion was nice while it lasted.

✦

Spirit stared at her prom dress in disgust. It was gorgeous.

The blue satin was the exact color of her eyes. The boned bodice had a spray of tiny rhinestones swooping across the neckline and then down to her left hip. It fit tightly to the waist, then it ballooned out into a short tulip-shaped skirt over a huge silver crinoline. The dress was strapless, but it came with a short-sleeved shrug in glittery white swansdown. There were even accessories to go with it: a pair of silver sandals, silver pantyhose, and a headband with an enormous blue-and-silver flower at one side.

She'd look like a fairy princess.

She'd feel like a . . .

Spirit shuddered. She'd rather wear the dress Muirin had made for her first dance, even though everyone had already seen it. She'd rather wear a *garbage bag*.

She didn't think that would go over well.

She sighed and hung the dress in her closet, resisting the

urge to just toss it on the floor at the back. And slam the door. And never leave her room again.

It was weird. So many things about Oakhurst Academy should have been, well, *nice*. (In another universe, one where her family wasn't dead.) But everything—the riding lessons, the dances, the laptop and all the fancy toys, the luxurious dorm room—was somehow . . . empty. It had been, even before she'd known the truth about Oakhurst. Everything here was like the Sunday Services: it looked good on the surface, but it just left you feeling empty and dissatisfied.

Goblin Fruit, Spirit thought, thinking about the Rossetti poem Dad had loved to quote. *"Their offers should not charm us, Their evil gifts would harm us." Oakhurst gives us all the things that ought to satisfy us. And they don't, because none of them is really what it looks like. So they want us to want . . . what?*

She didn't want to think about the answer to that question, even though she was pretty sure she knew it. What Oakhurst—what Doctor Ambrosius—what *Mordred*—really wanted was for them to want *other* things. Not friends, but flatterers. Not knowledge, but control. Not wisdom, but supremacy.

And anybody who bought what Oakhurst was selling would find out that all those things left them as empty as the fake "good" things had. And then what was left?

I don't want to be able to think about things like this, she thought despairingly. *I don't want to have to think about things like this.*

She'd wondered how Oakhurst had changed her.

This was how.

She drew a long shuddering breath. There was nothing to

do but go on. "In the midst of life, we have our homework," she said aloud. It was supposed to be a joke, even if a lame one, but her voice was rough and wavery. She closed her eyes tightly for a moment. *They want me to give up. They want me to think there's nothing I can do but give in. So I won't.*

It was cold comfort, but it was all she had.

Aside from—of course—the usual fun-sucking assignment.

Because tomorrow's *Systema* had been canceled (although today they were told it was being replaced with a one-hour Yoga Class, on the theory yoga didn't leave bruises), they'd all gotten extra "homework" today. The new, improved History of Magic Class (which Spirit thought of since Madison Lane-Rider had started teaching it as the "All The History of Magic Breakthrough Wants You To Know Class") had been given an extra research paper to do, on Arthurian survivals in contemporary culture. Madison had urged them to make it a personal document, drawing on their own experience—as if that made an eight page paper due *the day of the dance* any less of a grind. It was just another way for her to try to get into their heads, Spirit guessed. Still, she had to turn in something. Something that didn't talk about Fee, or her family, or her past, because she was damned if she was going to hand over everything she loved to Madison Lane-Rider for her to gloat over.

She sat down at her desk and opened her laptop. She thought longingly of plugging in the Ironkey and pouring her heart out to QUERCUS, but . . . she didn't quite dare. Their secret chatroom and the portal to the real Internet had been safe up until now, but that was before Breakthrough had done all those "upgrades" to the school intraweb. Maybe they'd done it because they suspected someone was getting through the firewall. Maybe they *knew*. Clairvoyance and precognition were Gifts of the School of Air: it only made sense to assume Breakthrough's magicians had any Gift she knew about. *Too bad I don't actually have either of those Gifts, because then I'd know what their limitations are. And I don't know anybody who does, either. Not well enough to ask.*

"Well you're—" *Well you're gloomy tonight,* she'd been about to say, but she stopped short when she heard the shots. Gunfire, somewhere outside—and the only people who were outside at this time of night were the Breakthrough drones.

This wasn't the first time she'd heard shots after dark. The story going around the school was that the security people were still hunting that "escaped tiger"—and maybe they really *were* hunting the Palug Cat. (That was what the thing she'd seen was—it had to have been. Mordred had mentioned it specifically: *"Have not the Palug Cat and the Boar of Triath returned to the world? Did not the Green Knight himself come to our court?"*) Or maybe they were hunting the Boar of Triath, whatever that was. Or maybe they were just practicing for taking over the world.

If they were shooting at anything else, she didn't want to think about it.

❋

✝WELVE

She worked on her History paper until late—it was a lot harder to come up with eight pages of something if you were trying not to give anything personal away—and then logged into Chat. She signed off again a few minutes later—the girls were all going on about their dresses, and it turned out all the boys had gotten custom tuxedos. Nobody was talking about the testing, or about having had all their rooms reshuffled. It would be nice to think everybody'd suddenly developed a sense of caution, but she'd seen too much stupidity in Chat to believe that.

"Bread and circuses." It was Mom's voice in her head (Mom'd had a saying for every occasion), reminding Spirit once again of things she didn't want to know. Reminding her that a lot of people, *most* people, would rather think about bread and circuses (toys and games and music and dancing) than confront a

reality they were afraid they couldn't change (just ignore the fact everyone you know is vanishing one by one).

But we're kids! she cried silently. *This shouldn't be our job! We shouldn't have to face this!*

But it was, because there wasn't anyone else. Mom had loved Westerns. *High Noon* was one of her favorites. Spirit had never understood why—she knew why Gary Cooper faced the bad guys, but she'd never really understood why nobody joined him.

Now she did.

You'd better get some sleep, she told herself. *Everything will look worse in the morning.*

She made herself a cup of chamomile tea, and left it to steep while she went and took a long hot shower. By the time she came out, it was strong enough to have some taste. She squirted a little agave nectar into it and took the cup to bed with her. She curled up against the headboard, and concentrated on the warmth of the cup in her hands.

The bedroom door opened.

Spirit jolted upright with a startled squeak, but before she could do more than that, she recognized Muirin. Muirin closed the door quickly and quietly behind her, and strode across the room.

"You've got mail!" Muirin sang out cheerfully, tossing an envelope down on the bed. "Which is, I have to admit, kind of weird because you're an orphan and who'd know to write you at the drop box in town?"

"How'd you get in here?" Spirit asked, setting aside the mug and picking up the envelope. It was a plain 9x12 envelope, with her name and the P.O. Box typed onto an address label. No return address, and the postmark was too blurry to make out.

"Through the door," Muirin said, smirking. "Funny thing, but your watchdogs have taken a vacation. Somebody spiked the coffee urn in the Faculty Lounge. You know, the one all the security guys hit up all night?" Muirin sat down on the bed, reached for Spirit's mug, sipped, and made a face.

"I hope they *poisoned* it," Spirit said savagely.

Muirin grinned at her. "Better. A big dose of laxative. Nobody's paying a lot of attention to being guards tonight."

Despite herself, Spirit laughed. The despairing anger she'd felt all evening evaporated as if she'd never felt it, and she began working the flap of the envelope open.

"So, since nobody was paying any attention to enforcing curfew, I went down to town to mail my letters," Muirin continued. "I did one to the IRS, too, telling them all about how Mark Rider hasn't been paying his taxes and I hope he's audited until the heat death of the universe—and anyway, while I was there I checked the old drop box, kind of on a whim because hey, it's not like any of the dead kids is going to be writing to their friends at school, and—"

Muirin broke off as Spirit got the envelope open and shook it. There wasn't a letter—just several sheets of MapQuest printouts. And an oak leaf, as fresh and green as if this were June and not March.

Oak leaf. Oak tree. QUERCUS.

"So what's that?" Muirin asked.

"A message," Spirit answered. "A message from a friend. And maybe a place to hide."

Muirin got to her feet. She had that *slanty* look on her face, the one Spirit knew meant Muirin was pretending not to care about being shut out. She turned to go. "Okay. Fine. See you at the dance."

"No—wait." Spirit leaned forward and grabbed Muirin's arm. "I've got something to tell you—about this. It's a long story."

"I guess I've got time," Muirin said neutrally. She sat back down, her face unreadable.

Spirit took a deep breath. She knew Muirin was on their side, not the Shadow Knights', but she was afraid that Muirin wasn't as sneaky as Muirin thought she was. *"Three people can keep a secret if two of them don't know it,"* Mom's voice said in her head. And even one person couldn't keep a secret if somebody was using magic to get at it.

But all along QUERCUS had told her to trust, and he'd always been right. And he'd sent his message by way of Muirin. That had to be a sign.

"Okay. You remember that trip we took to Billings, right? And you had me hold the thumb drives you bought? Well—"

Slowly, skipping back and forth in the story to be sure she was telling Muirin everything, Spirit told her about finding the Ironkey drive, thinking it must be one of Muirin's purchases, tossing it into a drawer and forgetting about it for days, finding it again when she needed a thumb drive to save a class assignment so she could take it to the Media Center and use the printer, plugging it in, and . . . meeting QUERCUS for the first time.

"—and he warned me against going to Doctor Ambrosius for help—back when we thought Doctor Ambrosius was Merlin—but QUERCUS didn't tell me why. And then we found out Doctor Ambrosius *wasn't* Merlin, and that night, when I went back to my room, it'd been ripped apart. They had to have been looking for the Ironkey; that has to be why they searched everybody's room a couple of days later and moved us all around. Anyway, when I could finally get back online, I told QUERCUS what we'd found out, and . . . he wasn't surprised. Like, at all. And he said he'd contact me. And this is it." She waved the sheets of paper.

A map. Directions. To *where*?

"The guy's calling himself 'Oak Tree' and you trust him?" Muirin asked skeptically.

"I know it's freaky," Spirit said. "That's the real reason I didn't tell any of you about him. I mean, you're the first person I've told."

"Really?" Muirin asked. "Not even Burke? I'm the first one?" She seemed to glow, and Spirit realized that Muirin smiled a lot, but she rarely looked really happy. Not the way she looked right now—as if Spirit had given her the most wonderful gift in the world.

"No one else," Spirit confirmed. "And I think . . . I think this map will lead us to a place we can be safe."

"And avert the Apocalypse," Muirin finished. "Cool."

"Muirin, would it be okay if we just don't tell anybody else about QUERCUS?" Spirit said hesitantly. "I'll tell everybody everything as soon as we're out of here."

"Hey, I never want to tell anybody anything," Muirin said happily. "Fine with me." She frowned for a moment, thinking. "We'll need to leave from the Dance."

"What?" Spirit said. She hadn't thought as far as how they'd leave, or when. "But—"

"*But,*" Muirin interrupted ruthlessly, "the Dance is going to be the only time Breakthrough drops its guard and lets everybody get together in a big mob. There'll be a bunch of Townies there, too, so they probably can't do anything majorly magical. I know at least some of the Macalister kids are going to be driving up, so the road between here and Radial will be clear. So here's what we'll do. I'll park my car in with theirs and we'll bail as soon as we can. We'll all be stuck in our Shadow Knight *haute couture*—at least you guys will be; I have no intention of wearing that froofy piece of garbage Madison thinks will look good on me, thank you so much—but I can sneak spare clothes out and hide them in the back. Just leave what you want to wear on your bed; I'll pass the word to the other guys."

"Just as long as I don't have to save the world in high heels," Spirit said shakily. She pushed her hair back out of her face with both hands. Everything was happening so fast: in just a few minutes she'd gone from knowing the five of them finally had somewhere to go, to knowing they were going to leave Oakhurst, to knowing they were going *tomorrow*. "But Muirin—every single dance, you know there's—"

"—been something horrible happening," Muirin finished. "And you think if we stuck around until it happens, we could maybe help. And that's stupid. If we don't get out of here and find your mysterious benefactor, something a lot worse than the Stephen King Memorial Prom is going to happen to millions of people. Besides," Muirin added with an irrepressible grin. "Us bailing might distract them enough so they don't do whatever it is."

"Oh my god I hope," Spirit said feelingly.

"Hey," Muirin said. "We're escaping from the Evil Overlord's stronghold in prom dresses. What can possibly go wrong?"

❧

I s this the *Halloween* dance?" Burke said as he and Spirit stopped outside the door to the gym.

The doors were chocked open; it was the school-side entrance to the gym. The Townies were coming in through the side entrance nearest the parking, so they were coming through the main building as well, but Breakthrough Security staff—wearing dark suits tonight, instead of their black uniforms—were stationed along the route to act as valets and guides. *And make sure nobody goes wandering anywhere they shouldn't,* Spirit thought sourly. Guests had been arriving for the past half hour, and the gym was already crowded—it looked as if most of the Radial kids had arrived, and Burke and Spirit weren't the first of the Oakhurst students to get there—but somehow even with all the noise and people (because of course Breakthrough had provided a professional DJ) the gym still managed to look empty and menacing.

Even though Spirit had known Breakthrough was going to do whatever it wanted, the décor should still have been . . .

spring-like. The Spring Fling theme was "Enchanted Forest," and they had an Enchanted Forest, all right—but an Enchanted Forest right out of the Brothers Grimm. It was breathtaking— the forest was painted onto dozens of transparent scrim panels—and the whole backdrop looked almost alive. But there were shadowy figures lurking among the trees—only paintings, but anything could really be behind those panels, and the longer you stared at them, the more you started to think there might be.

"This isn't even the *theme* we decided on," Spirit said blankly. "It's like they want to scare all of us to death." Those shadowy not-figures painted on the gauze just made her want to keep turning in a circle, trying to keep her eye on all of them. And how could other people *not* be feeling the same way?

"Yeah, well, that's nothing new," Burke said in disgust. "C'mon."

She took his arm and they walked into the gym. The future was terrifying and the present was horrible, but being able to walk into the Spring Fling with Burke was one bright spot in all this, like a window into what she wanted as her real life.

If she lived that long.

Burke led her in the direction of the refreshments table. The Dance Committee hadn't even bothered to plan the refreshments, and of course Breakthrough had taken care of everything. There was a huge ice sculpture of the Breakthrough logo in the middle of the table (*so tacky,* Spirit sniped mentally) with blue lights frozen into the ice. The effect was particularly creepy. In addition to the buckets of soda, and what looked like every snack food in the known universe, there was a huge sheet cake decorated to look like the box for *Final Battle: Rise of the Black Dragon*, and Spirit spotted tables around the edges of the gym holding stacks of the game as well. Despite the fact she saw black armbands on the kids from Radial, everybody seemed to have forgotten about the deaths—or was willing to forget about them for tonight.

She pulled Burke to a halt before they reached the table, and leaned up so she could talk to him without shouting. Shouting right now would be a very bad idea.

"We're leaving Oakhurst tonight. All five of us. I'll explain once we're out of here."

This was the first chance she'd had to talk to any of them privately since the message from QUERCUS had arrived. She had the maps inside her dress—the tight bodice would hold them securely. The Ironkey was tucked into her bra, and tied to one of the straps, just to be safe.

"When?" Burke asked.

He didn't ask anything else. It was almost as if he'd expected this. Maybe he had. Maybe Muirin had warned him. Spirit had wanted to leave telling everyone until the dance itself so they wouldn't give anything away, even accidentally, but . . .

"As soon as we can. I need to tell Loch and Addie. Muirin knows."

Burke looked around the gym, scanning the crowd. "Then I guess I'd better dance with Addie, and you'd better dance with Loch. C'mon. I see them," Burke said.

Navigating across the gym was tricky—it was early, and the

music was hot, and Spirit was jostled several times before Burke had her just follow him. Nobody wanted to get in the way of somebody Burke's size. Finally, through a gap in the dancers, Spirit spotted Loch and Addie standing together in a corner.

Addie was wearing a dress in a dark amber velvet. It was studded with gold brilliants, and every time she moved, she looked like she was on fire. Loch was slouched beside her, leaning against the wall, his hands stuffed into his pockets. Like Burke, he was wearing the outfit Madison had chosen for him. Burke's was a tuxedo, traditional in everything but the color, a very dark brown. The dress shirt with it was a dark cream color. Loch had been put into a dark blue formal suit with satin lapels and cuffs. He was wearing a collarless shirt in pale gray, without a tie.

"—honestly, Loch, all this place needs is some flying monkeys and a haunted castle," Addie was saying when Spirit got close enough to hear.

"Haven't you been paying attention? This place *is* a haunted—"

"Hi!" Burke said loudly, with utterly bogus cheerfulness. "Let's dance!" He took Addie's hand with firm decisiveness, and dragged her out onto the dance floor in the middle of the song.

"You too," Spirit said. Her throat was dry with nervousness.

Loch bowed ironically and offered her his arm. He led her out into the middle of the dancers. This wasn't a slow dance, but Spirit draped herself over Loch anyway.

"I swear, this doesn't look like a dance, it looks like a rollout party," Loch said with disgust. Then, in an undertone fraught with tension, he added, "You don't suppose they've played a diversion on us, and whatever hell is coming is going down somewhere else tonight? Maybe . . . Maybe it's about all the kids that have been getting tested and disappearing?"

"Doesn't matter. I'll explain everything later," Spirit said. "We're leaving tonight—from the dance—as soon as I find Muirin. Burke's telling Addie."

"Spirit—" Suddenly Loch looked more than worried. He looked *stricken*. "They bumped Muirin up in the testing order. Angelina Swanson came and pulled her out of Calculus this afternoon. She probably won't be here at all."

"Oh god," Spirit choked out. Muirin hadn't been at dinner, but that wasn't unusual. If she'd thought about it at all, she'd assumed Muirin was making their last-minute preparations while everybody was safely out of the way. Could they go find her? Where was she? They couldn't go without her. . . .

"Wait!" Loch said.

He was looking toward the school-side entrance. Spirit followed his gaze.

It was Muirin.

She was clinging to Doc Mac's arm. They were both trying to make it look casual, but it was obvious he was the only thing holding her up. She looked greenish-pale, and the dark smudges under her eyes had nothing to do with makeup. Spirit didn't think she was wearing any. The dress she was wearing couldn't be one of Madison's choices—it was black lamé and incredibly too old for her. Spirit saw her lurch and stagger, and only Doc Mac's grip on her arm kept her from falling.

"Muirin!" Spirit cried.

She pushed through the crowd, shoving people out of her way as she headed for Muirin. She was about halfway there when Muirin saw her. She dragged Doc Mac to a stop, hauling on his arm to keep herself upright. Her other hand was clenched into a fist. She brought it up and made a throwing motion. The keys to the Xterra came flying through the air. Spirit snatched them without thought. Her eyes were fixed on Muirin's face. Muirin mouthed one word:

Run.

Loch had seen what Spirit saw. He stuck two fingers into his mouth and whistled shrilly. It was loud enough to cut through the music and elicit a chorus of wolf-whistles and cat-calls from the other kids. Before Spirit could react—or look for Burke and Addie—Loch grabbed her wrist and dragged her toward the doors to the outside. By the time they approached them, Spirit was running ahead. She hit the crash bar and bounced off.

She thought for an instant they were stuck, but as she yanked at the crash bar, the doors rocked inward a little, and she could see they were chained from the outside.

Then Loch grabbed her around the waist and swung her around. Her shoes skidded on the wooden floor, and she flailed for balance. Burke was heading toward the doors at a dead run.

Across the dance floor, Spirit could see Security—at least a dozen people—run into the gym. She heard screams as the dancers saw the guns. She couldn't see Muirin now.

Burke didn't slow down as he reached the doors. He ducked his shoulder—as if he were on the football field—and hit them at full speed. The chain snapped with a ringing sound and the doors crashed open. Burke charged through, with Addie right behind him.

"Muirin!" Spirit screamed, but she ran after the others. She was the only one who knew where they were going. She slipped and skidded on a patch of ice, but the grueling combat courses had been some use after all: she kept her balance. Burke cut sharply left, heading along the side of the gym, then left again at the corner and back toward the front of the mansion, where the guest parking was. As soon as Spirit caught sight of the cars she slowed just enough to wave the chirp-tag on Muirin's keys in front of her, pressing the button over and over until one of the cars lit up and unlocked.

Addie reached the car first; Burke had stopped to watch Spirit and Loch come on. Burke waited until they passed him to turn and follow.

"Where's Muirin? I don't know how to drive!" Spirit screamed as she reached the car. Both doors were open; Loch was climbing into the back seat.

Addie snatched the keys out of her hand. "I do! Get in! We're going back for her!"

Spirit dove into the back seat beside Loch, and Burke flung himself into the front passenger seat. Before he even had the door closed Addie was backing up, swinging the car back around in the direction from which they'd come. In the glare of the headlights, they saw Muirin and Doc Mac running toward them. Muirin's face was distorted with terror. Spirit couldn't begin to imagine what it cost Muirin not just to stand up, but to run.

And behind them came Anastus Ovcharenko.

Then Ovcharenko stopped, and for an instant Spirit thought he was giving up. He was alone. There were no other security people in sight. *Oh it's all right; he told the others to stay behind, and now he's going to let us go, because he really does love Muirin after all*—she told herself giddily.

Then she heard gunshots—loud even inside the car—and Doc Mac pitched forward. He staggered against Muirin as he fell to the ground. She stumbled, staggering sideways for a few steps as she fought to keep from falling—she hadn't been shot, but she could barely keep her feet. Addie cried out in horror and sent the car forward; Spirit saw Burke open his door a crack, preparing to fling it wide and pull Muirin into the car as soon as they reached her.

But Ovcharenko reached her first.

He grabbed Muirin by the back of her dress, yanking her backward and off her feet.

Muirin looked straight into Spirit's eyes. "Go!" she screamed.

And suddenly the night was filled with patterns, colors, flashing light, as Muirin filled the air with dazzling—*blinding*—illusions.

"Floor it!" Burke shouted in Addie's ear. She stomped down on the accelerator—heading straight for Ovcharenko—and Burke yanked the wheel sideways, making the car slew around. Addie was screaming, and Burke was shouting: Spirit couldn't make out any words. She turned in her seat looked back.

No— No—!

There was another shot; it sounded like the crack of lightning, and Spirit's heart seemed to freeze in her chest. Suddenly the illusions stopped. The night went dark again, but now there was a flare of headlights far behind them. Somebody from Security had reached one of the SUVs.

"We have to go back!" Addie cried. The car began to slow as it swept down the driveway. There wasn't any place to turn around here, but she was obviously planning to turn back as soon as she could. They'd reach the road in a few seconds. "We can't leave them!"

Spirit shook her head mutely, her throat tight with tears.

"They're dead," Loch said, his voice harsh and ugly. "They're both dead."

"No," Addie sobbed. "No!"

Ovcharenko stepped over Muirin's body and braced himself, taking aim at their car. In the wash of headlights, Spirit saw Doc Mac drag himself to his knees.

And suddenly, everything behind them that could possibly burn . . .

Burned.

The Xterra began to accelerate again. Spirit gulped back tears. There wasn't time for them now. The trees and bushes in the path of Doc Mac's last spell were burning—and she hoped Ovcharenko was too—but it wouldn't keep the rest of Breakthrough from following them. And she was the only one who knew where they were going—she had to keep her head.

I shouldn't be so calm, she thought. *Muirin's dead. I saw her die. Oh Murr-cat!*

285

"Go through Radial," she said, as they reached the road. "Stay off the highway. Take the farm road."

"One question," Loch asked tensely. "Did Muirin know where you're taking us?"

"How can you think she'd have told!" Spirit demanded furiously. "She died defending us!"

"I don't think she would have if she had a choice," Loch said grimly, and Spirit hiccupped on a sob. *She saved our lives, over and over again, and I was never sure I could trust her, not until the end.* Her eyes stung with tears as she remembered how *happy* Muirin had looked last night when she found out she was the first one Spirit had told about QUERCUS.

"No," she said dully. "She didn't know."

They were still a mile from where they could make the turn into Radial when there was a flare of headlights in the rearview mirror.

"They're after us," Burke said unnecessarily. A moment later someone shone a high-powered spotlight into the Xterra. Addie automatically braked, dazzled by the glare.

"Speed up!" Burke shouted.

"I can't *see!*" Addie snarled, but she accelerated again. The front wheels slipped off the edge of the road and bumped along the shoulder. Addie yanked the wheel back the other way, and the car slewed across the road. She was driving blind. But she didn't slow down.

"Let me drive," Loch said suddenly.

"Are you crazy?" Addie demanded. "I'm doing ninety on ice

and the Legions of Hell are following us! This isn't the time to switch drivers!"

"Maybe not," Loch answered. "But you're the only one here who can take somebody out at a distance, so I think you're going to have to give me the wheel!"

Addie's only response was a wordless wail. Loch began climbing between the two front seats. Addie saw the turnoff into Radial just as she was passing it. She jerked the wheel sharply around. The car fishtailed wildly. Loch was thrown into the front passenger foot well.

"Yeah, that works," he muttered. Addie giggled jaggedly.

Why aren't they shooting at us? Or— Or— Or—something? Spirit huddled down in the corner of the back seat. She should have been terrified, or mourning, but she just felt numb and— weirdly—as if she wanted to yawn. What she wanted most was to close her eyes and just not be here anymore. *Shock,* she told herself distantly. *This is what shock feels like.*

"They want us alive," Burke said grimly. "And they probably think they have a good shot. We're heading right toward The Fortress."

Spirit wrapped her arms tightly around herself. In the front seat, Burke, Addie, and Loch were doing a complicated handoff as Loch slithered into the driver's seat and Burke deadlifted Addie out of the way. The car bumped over the new railroad tracks. They'd reached Radial.

"Where are the lights?" Addie suddenly demanded, her voice high and panicky. "There should be streetlights!"

We have to be in Radial by now, Spirit thought. It might be small, but it had streetlights—and The Fortress was always lit up so brightly every night the glare was visible from Oakhurst. But there was nothing but blackness outside the windows.

"I've got it—I've got it!" Loch said. The car slewed wildly as Burke took his foot off the accelerator, and bumped up over something—curb?—and back down again. The car began to slow. Then Loch floored it, and the car leaped forward. Addie was sitting in Burke's lap now. He wrapped his arms tightly around her waist, holding her steady.

"I was kidnap-proofed when I was fifteen and one of the components of that was an offensive driving course," Loch said. He went on explaining what he'd been taught, his words coming fast and sharp with nerves.

"It's too dark," Addie said, and she sounded terrified.

She's right. Spirit took a deep breath as the realization hit her. Her chest ached as if she'd been holding her breath for far too long. She craned around and looked out the rearview window again.

No lights. No *headlights*. Their pursuers might have shut off their lights—but *their own* headlights weren't showing anything either. Not buildings. Not road. Nothing but darkness—not even fog, because fog should be white, and this wasn't. It was as if the darkness itself was closing in around them. Their headlights were dim and yellowish, as if the car's battery were dying—though it couldn't be with the motor running—and when they faded out entirely the darkness would have them.

"Oh god I can't see the road," Loch whispered suddenly,

breaking off his nervous monologue. He took his foot off the gas.

This isn't fair, Spirit thought. They were going to die—either run into something, or be caught—and Muirin would have died for nothing. She reached over the back of the seat with both hands. Addie clutched her left hand tightly. Burke gently took her right.

"Spirit!" Addie yelped. "Your ring! It's glowing! The stone is *white!*"

For a moment Spirit's only thought—as she tried to tug her hand free of Addie's—was to get the ring *off.* She'd worn it to the dance because they'd all had to wear their class rings to the dance. She could see the light between Addie's fingers, faint but clear, and it seemed to her as if it was the only light in the entire world.

Happy New Year. It was as if someone else was speaking inside her mind, but it was her own voice. Her own thought. The New Year's Dance, and all the lights had gone out, and everyone there had stood frozen and terrified in the darkness, as pure Fear lashed out at them as if it were a living thing. Her ring had glowed then. So had Burke's—Addie's—Loch's.

Muirin's.

And the Fear had come again and again, as if it was hunting for something—for some*one*—but they'd learned to fight back. Staying together. Taking care of each other.

Holding hands.

"Addie! Remember New Year's! Remember what we did! Grab Loch!" Spirit cried. "And Burke too!"

For a moment Spirit thought Addie was too terrified to move. Then she let go of Spirit's hand and gripped Loch's shoulder. Spirit took the hand Addie had released and put it on Loch's other shoulder. Now she could see her ring clearly. The stone glowed as brightly as if it was one of those tiny LED bulbs, and it ought to frighten her—why her? why now? why was it *white*?—but somehow it didn't.

Because they were together. And they wouldn't give up.

Ever.

The fear—the despair—lifted away as if she was waking up from a nightmare. And as if something—something powerful, something *good*—had just been waiting for her to notice it, she felt an uprush of *power*.

Like it was in February, when we faced down the Shadow Knights, all of us together. Like it was at the library—we fought back then, too.

Once again Spirit had a sense of being a conduit for something coming from outside, something using her as a gateway. It should have terrified her, this feeling she was something's tool, but it didn't. It felt *right*. And it was as if this wasn't just power, but illumination, as if something was shining through her, shining through all of them—something *bright*.

The headlights burned white again. The dark fog was gone.

They were in Radial. Its lights weren't out. It looked *normal*. The car was rolling slowly along the road; they were almost at The Fortress, and they were drifting through the gates.

Spirit took a deep breath. "You know, I wasted two days working on that stupid history paper and I didn't even have to," she said loudly.

She felt Loch startle, as if he'd just realized where he was. He hissed something under his breath and jerked the wheel away from the road to The Fortress. The gravel under the tires sprayed as he gunned the engine again.

"There are traps in the road," Loch said, his voice filled with awe. "I can see them. I can drive around them!" He began to slew the car left and right, avoiding traps only he could see.

Spirit looked behind them. The Shadow Knights were at the other end of Main Street—three SUVs. They'd been hanging back—they had to have been, waiting for Loch to just drive right up to The Fortress—but the moment he turned the car away, they accelerated.

Addie saw them too.

"*Water*," she growled, her voice deep and rough with fury. And suddenly, between them and their pursuers, everything containing liquid water in Radial burst open. Jets of water from buried water pipes ripped through earth and blacktop, showering the road around them with debris as the water geysered high into the air. The glass of storefronts sprayed outward, shattered by jets of water striking them with the force of a hail of bullets. The water reared up like a wave, like a living thing, lashing out at the Shadow Knights and turning to ice as it hurtled forward.

"How dare they?" Addie said furiously. "How dare they?"

"On the right," Burke said quietly.

Spirit saw one of the Breakthrough RVs—one of the ones built on a bus chassis—rolling through the gates of The Fortress. It was entering the roadway ahead of the ice-wave that had taken out their other pursuers, and it was gaining on the Xterra, even though the little SUV's engine howled as Loch redlined it. Spirit could see headlights from within The Fortress shining off the side of the bus as it made the turn into the road. There were other chase vehicles following it, but they didn't matter. The bus would reach them first.

"I need more time," Addie said, her voice thin and breathless with strain.

"Oh no hurry. Take all the time you need," Loch said tightly. "Just— This thing won't go any faster."

The bus made the turn onto the road behind them and slowly started closing the distance between them. Spirit could hear the deep roar of its engine over the frantic howl of theirs.

Closer.

The driver of the RV beeped and flashed his headlights at them mockingly. The air horn made Spirit's teeth vibrate; she wanted to cover her ears, but to do that would mean letting go of Loch and Burke.

Closer.

It was less than six feet off their back bumper now, so close the only thing Spirit could see was the dragon-and-tower logo on the front of the bus. In another minute it would hit them. The Xterra was shaking as if it was about to come completely apart.

"Okay—*yeah!*" Addie shrieked.

The ground behind them dissolved. A column of water spurted upward. It couldn't be coming from a water pipe, Spirit thought. There was too much of it—a pillar of water as wide as the front of the bus, white with force as it sprayed out of the ground. It struck the bus just behind the front wheels, lifting it. Flipping it. The bus slid off the column of water, balanced for an instant on its back end, and fell.

The ground shook.

And if that had been all that happened, the four of them would still have been caught, because the nimble pursuit vehicles—two, three, *six* Jeeps and Humvees and one ordinary sedan—swerved around the RV and kept coming, into the spreading lake the jet of water had left behind. They drove right into it, breaking to the left and the right to avoid the crater in the middle.

Drove into the water . . .

. . . and sank.

Spirit saw the headlights slowly dim as the cars drifted into the depths of the sudden Addie-created lake—it *was* a lake, and not just a big puddle with a pothole in the middle. The entire road had to have given way, and the water was still spreading.

One or two of the chase cars hadn't gone in—but they couldn't follow, either. Spirit watched until she saw the Shadow Knights who'd been in the submerged cars reach the surface, then turned away. *I hope you all catch pneumonia,* she thought viciously.

Addie laughed softly. "I apologize to everyone in McBride County for draining the water table dry and causing county-wide drought for the foreseeable future."

"Considering the alternative, they shouldn't mind," Burke said seriously.

I just hope this is *the alternative,* Spirit thought dazedly.

"That's what took so long," Addie continued contritely. "I had to get the water here."

"Okay, where now?" Loch said. He didn't slow down, even though nobody was following them now—that they could see, anyway.

"Just keep going," Spirit said. "We stay on this road for a while." She looked down at her hand. The stone had gone dark again, and the sense of being a pipeline had ebbed, but it was another ten minutes—hurtling through the night with nothing chasing them—before the four of them were willing to let go of each other.

About five minutes after that, Loch let the car slow to the actual speed limit.

"The last thing we need is to get grabbed for speeding," he said ruefully. "Because I don't actually have a license. And, uh, I'm not sure what we're going to do when we run out of gas. The tank's full right now, but—"

"Don't worry," Spirit said, with a calm confidence that surprised her a little, "we have enough to get us where we need to go."

They drove in silence for a few more minutes.

"Uh, where *is* that, exactly?" Burke said slowly, his voice puzzled but not suspicious. "You said you had a place for us to go, and—you know I trust you. I always will, no matter what. But you said you'd explain it to me."

"To us," Addie said softly. Her voice was filled with quiet sorrow. "I just wish—" She stopped. *I just wish Muirin were here to hear it too.* Addie didn't need to say the words for Spirit to hear them.

"So do I," Spirit said, and she heard the others murmur agreement. "Okay. I have a story to tell all of you. It's long. And it's incredible. But it's all true."

She told them the same story she'd told Muirin less than twenty-four hours ago, and maybe someday losing Muirin— losing her *friend*—that way wouldn't hurt so sharply, but for now it did. *I'm so glad I told you,* Spirit thought. *I'm so glad you knew I trusted you. That I believed in you. That's all you ever really wanted. From everyone.*

The other three listened to her story in silence. It wasn't a silence of disbelief, or of doubt. It was just that the night had been so full, and the tale she told was so incredible, that nobody really knew what to say.

A week ago we found out that the reincarnation of Mordred was going to start a nuclear war in a month and a half. Tonight we fought our way out of the school dance—and lost two good friends—and all we know about where we're going is that it's a mark on a map. I don't even know what QUERCUS looks like. Or what we're going to do next. Or how we can possibly win.

"But I believe we can," she said aloud. Addie looked over toward her and smiled. Shakily. Wanly. But as if she believed, too.

🍂

They stopped once, for just long enough to let Addie get into the back seat. Spirit dug the maps out of her dress during the stop—Addie had to unzip her so she could get at them—because it was a long way to their destination, and she'd only memorized the beginning of it.

It was just before dawn when they finally reached the last mark on the map. It was the middle of nowhere, a rutted one-lane back road. Loch had been counting miles since the last turnoff to make sure he didn't overshoot it.

The van parked at the edge of the road was the only thing in sight. In the glare of their headlights they could see it was old and decrepit-looking, its body pitted with rust and painted a patchy primer gray.

"Are you sure . . . ?" Burke said hesitantly, turning to look back at her.

"This is the place marked on the map," Spirit said. "This is where we're supposed to be."

After another moment, Loch turned off the ignition. The silence was broken only by the ticking of cooling metal. He opened the door and stepped out of the car, wincing and stretching. Burke got out as well, and then they pushed the seat backs down so Spirit and Addie could climb out.

The four of them stood in the road for a minute, then Burke walked up to the driver's side of the van. His breath smoked on the freezing air, and Spirit hugged herself, shivering in the cold and staring at nothing. She felt as if she'd been awake for weeks. A moment later Addie took Spirit's hand—her left hand, her ring hand—and held it out. Loch, catching the movement out of the corner of his eye, turned back to regard them in puzzlement.

"I was right," Addie said, still holding Spirit's hand.

Spirit looked down.

When she and Loch had gotten their Oakhurst class rings as one of their Christmas not-really-presents in December, they'd been identical, with stones that were opaque and glittery blue, like artificial opals. They were magic, of course: the stone changed to match the School your Gift was from. The stone in Burke's ring was green for Earth, and Addie's was blue—dark blue—for Water. Loch's stone had turned yellow almost immediately—his Gift was School of Air.

Like Muirin's had been.

The stone in Spirit's ring wasn't pale blue any longer. It was clear and colorless.

"School of Spirit, Spirit," Addie said with a faint smile. "It has to be, right? And you have a Destiny too."

"So anyway, what I know is if a Destiny appears in your ring, it means your future is pretty much set. Fixed. Unchangeable."

Burke had said those words to her on Christmas morning, when Addie had discovered the Destiny in her own stone: the shape of a goblet. Burke had discovered one in his stone soon after, and so had Loch.

Muirin had never let anyone see what hers had been.

Spirit lifted her hand and squinted at the stone in the strengthening light. In its depths was a tiny image, looking as if it had been engraved on the underside of the stone.

A sword.

She slipped off the ring and hefted it in the palm of her hand. It was still as strangely heavy as it had been the first time she'd put it on. On the sides of the band were the broken sword and the inverted cup from the Oakhurst coat of arms. The bezel of the ring said: *absolutum dominium*. Absolute dominion. She bounced it on the palm of her hand a few times.

"I guess I'll keep the Destiny," she said. "But not the dominion."

She turned and threw the ring as far away from her as she could.

"Guess that isn't a bad idea," Burke said, walking back to them. He was holding an oak leaf in one hand and a set of keys in the other. "Keys were in the ignition," he said, looking inquiringly at Spirit. "And the thing is in a lot better shape on the inside than it looks on the outside. There's another set of maps on the dash."

"That's the sign. QUERCUS sent an oak leaf with my first map," she said, taking the leaf. "Who else would leave a car with keys in the ignition out here?"

Burke slipped off his ring and held it up to peer at the stone. "I guess a shield is a good Destiny," he said. When he threw his ring away it glittered as it sailed through the air.

Loch threw his after theirs. "Don't know what a stick means, but I always thought the design was vulgar."

Addie just tossed her ring gently into the weeds at the side of the road. "Can we get in?" she begged. "I'm freezing!"

Muirin packed clothes for us. Before Spirit could swallow the lump in her throat to say so, Burke had unlocked the back of the van.

"Hey," he said appreciatively. "Looks like breakfast—and coats."

He held up the coats to judge sizes, and then passed them around before shrugging into his own. Down parkas, and the moment Spirit put hers on, she felt warmth enveloping her. In the back of the van she could see a gallon thermos and a cooler—and a pile of blankets.

"You guys ride in the back," Burke said to Loch and Addie. "I'll drive for a while."

"Why am I the only one who doesn't know how to drive?" Spirit grumbled, just for something to say.

"I'll teach you," Burke offered, smiling at her.

Addie and Loch climbed into the back of the van. Loch handed Addie a blanket. Burke slammed the doors shut and rattled the handle to be sure they'd caught. Then he put his arm around Spirit's waist and walked her around to the passenger side of the van. He opened the door.

"I guess if we're going off to save the world, I get to kiss my girl first," he said, looking down at her. Spirit reached up and put her arms around his neck, and Burke held her tightly.

It was only the second time he'd ever kissed her really-for-real, and for a wild moment she didn't want him to stop, didn't want to go on and do the next thing, didn't want this moment to ever end.

But it did, of course. And Burke smiled at her, and put his hands on her waist, and lifted her up into the passenger seat as if she didn't weigh anything at all. Then he closed the door very gently.

A moment later, he climbed into the driver's seat and slammed the door. The engine roared to life the moment he turned the key. Although Spirit didn't know much about cars, the engine sounded smooth and very powerful. "Ready?" Burke asked.

"No," Spirit said. "But let's go anyway."

Burke's grin got wider. "Hey. We're together. We lived. We've already beaten the odds. Now let's try pounding the odds into mush." He reached across the dashboard and scooped up a thin sheaf of papers and handed them to her, then put the van into gear. "For Muirin."

"For Muirin," Spirit said, swallowing hard.

They drove off, leaving Muirin's car behind them looking lost and lonely.

ABOUT THE AUTHORS

MERCEDES LACKEY is the author of the Valdemar novels. She has collaborated with Andre Norton on the Halfblood Chronicles and with James Mallory on the bestselling Obsidian Mountain Trilogy and Enduring Flame Trilogy. She lives with her husband in Oklahoma.

ROSEMARY EDGHILL writes under her own name and various pseudonyms. She lives in Maryland.

Read the entire collection from the *USA Today* and *New York Times* bestselling team

Mercedes Lackey and James Mallory

The Outstretched Shadow
Book One of The Obsidian Trilogy

"In this captivating world conjured by veteran Lackey and classical scholar Mallory, there are three types of magic, each of which has its own rules, limits, and variables. The narrative speeds to the end, leaving the reader satisfied and wanting to know more." —*Publishers Weekly*

To Light a Candle
Book Two of The Obsidian Trilogy

"Lackey and Mallory combine their talents for storytelling and world crafting into a panoramic effort."
—*Library Journal*

Read the entire collection from the *USA Today*
and *New York Times* bestselling team

**Mercedes Lackey
and James Mallory**

❧❧

When Darkness Falls
Book Three of The Obsidian Trilogy

"Highly readable . . . High-fantasy
fans should appreciate the intelligent
storytelling with an unmistakable
flavor of Andre Norton at her best."
—*Publishers Weekly*

❧❧

The Phoenix Unchained
Book One of The Enduring Flame

"Sets a lavishly detailed stage peopled
with intriguing and well-developed
characters whose futures hold both
promise and peril. A good addition to
most fantasy collections."
—*Library Journal*